Nothing Tastes as Good

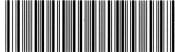

Nothing Tastes as Good

CLAIRE HENNESSY

HOT
KEY
BOOKS

First published in Great Britain in 2016 by
HOT KEY BOOKS
80–81 Wimpole St, London W1G 9RE
www.hotkeybooks.com

A CIP catalogue record for this book is available from the British Library.

ISBN: 978-1-4714-0574-7
also available as an ebook
3
This book is typeset in 10.5 Berling LT Std using Atomik ePublisher

Printed and bound by Clays Ltd, St Ives Plc

Hot Key Books is an imprint of Bonnier Publishing Fiction,
a Bonnier Publishing company
www.bonnierpublishing.co.uk

SEPTEMBER

Chapter One

Don't call me a guardian angel. No wings, no heavenly music, no fluffy white clouds here – just me and the Boss (not God, don't go getting any ideas there) and an assignment. My first. Hopefully my only.

'We've got a soul in need of help,' she says to me, or rather thinks at me, 'cause, let me tell you, speaking is tricky when you're lacking a body.

'What kind of help, exactly?' I want to know. I'm anticipating something big, the kind of stuff that fills misery memoirs and cheap magazines.

'Her name's Julia,' the Boss says. Which, you'll note, is not actually the information I was looking for.

'Right, okay, what's wrong with her?' Do I get a file, is what I really want to know, some list of perceived issues put together by a team of medical professionals so smug you'd want to punch them in the face?

'There's nothing wrong with needing help, Annabel.' Now she's sounding shrink-like, which is the last thing I need. If my eyeballs weren't six feet under I'd be rolling them right about now.

'Yeah, okay, except most people who need help don't get it from –' I stop. I don't even know what to call it, what I am now.

'Spirit guides?' the Boss suggests, which has me missing my eyeballs all over again.

'From *me*. What am I supposed to do to help her? What's her story?'

'You need to discover that for yourself.'

'You're not going to tell me anything?'

'Spend some time observing first. Get to know her. You'll be able to tell what she's thinking, and the longer you're with her the more you'll be able to sense what others –'

'How much time are we talking about here?' This sounds like a suspiciously long-term assignment. 'Isn't there someone else I could talk off a bridge or something?'

If the Boss could smirk, she'd be doing it right now. 'This is the one for you.'

'You sure there's no one else?'

'This is the one –'

'There's got to be someone else you need fixed.'

'That *I* need fixed?' There's this flash, where I can almost see what she might have been like when she was alive, like she's peering at me over the top of spectacles. 'You're not doing this for me, Annabel.' Classic shrink move: repeat the name of the person you're talking to, so it seems like you care. Spare me. 'You're helping her for yourself.'

That's true, though. Complete the assignment and I get what I want. I'm not just doing this out of the goodness of my heart.

My heart, my heart, my pathetic little heart.

It's been three weeks since that heart gave up on me.

Chapter Two

I hate to disillusion you but I don't fly or float my way down to Julia's bedroom, feeling *at one with the universe* or whatever. I'm just *there*, as soon as the Boss confirms that this girl is officially my assignment, and all I can think is that this is not a room where bad things happen.

Appearances can be deceiving and all that but this is a room where there are bookshelves filled with non-frivolous things – with newspapers and magazines and hardbacks about things like politics in the Middle East and the history of women's education. This is a room with a tidy desk, a laptop opened to Microsoft Word, a swivel chair with a woolly cardigan draped across the back of it. I imagine its warmth.

This is not a girl whose parents neglect her or who might drop out of school or who's likely to have a drug problem. I can tell all this already and I'm starting to feel like this is just a waste of time, just some stupid test for me – and then in she walks.

Two things hit me right in the gut, or would if I still had one. One: I know this girl. Two: she's fat.

If I'm supposed to save her from obesity, this is really not funny.

The girl. Her name's Julia Jacobs and if you're thinking that's a good name for a writer, so is she. Right at this moment, this moment in late September, just as the mild summer weather is evaporating, her head is full of school stuff: homework and teachers and exams at the end of the year, but mostly what's going on with the school newspaper. Julia's the deputy editor, I suddenly know, and her editor and sort-of friend, Lorraine, is in big trouble with the school for printing an article about suicide.

Tell me I don't have to talk this girl out of killing herself because I really honest-to-God (except I'm pretty sure he doesn't exist, because it's been three weeks and you'd think even with everyone dying he'd pop in for a chat or something) don't have the energy for this.

I push at her a little bit, reach out, and there I am further inside her head, caught up in this inner monologue about Lorraine and the piece and wanting it to be sorted out and freedom of the press. *Freedom of the press.* Is she for real?

Anyway. I know her. Or knew her, once upon a time. We were in school together, back when I went to school. My fifth or maybe sixth. My last. What I remember from the Julia of a year or two ago: she used to put up her hand in class a lot. And she wasn't fat, not like she is now. She wasn't super-thin, no gaps between the thighs for her, but slim. Slender. Those fake-nice words people use when someone's not fat but not thin.

There's a crying noise, one of those screechy demanding wails, from the room next door. Julia shrugs her schoolbag off her right shoulder and goes out again, and I can follow her now. It's a baby.

Something like a fizz goes through me. This is it. This is the why. It's her kid. She's your classic high-achiever who never thought it would happen to her; decided to keep the baby but it's so difficult, she's about to snap . . .

It'd explain so much – the fat she's carrying, the way she has a mystical girl helper assigned to her by some high-up power. But she takes the kid into her arms and I can tell, just tell, that it's her sister. Grace.

It turns out even when you're weightless, disappointment is a heavy thing.

'Shhh, Gracie,' Julia says, and I feel it – she's kind of pissed off because she has homework to do and, well, crying babies are annoying, but she loves her. She's cute and all that. Not old enough yet to have borrowed her clothes or asked her questions about boys or told tales.

I could maybe, maybe understand if we were somehow matched up because of sisters, and how they can hurt you, but there's nothing like that coming from Julia. Already I want to get out of here. I hate being around people like her, spilling out of their clothes, so out of control.

I look at the brightly coloured posters on the wall of the kid's room, and it's like certain letters light up just that little bit more, so that I can spell out the message. *Watch*. Yeah. Thanks, Boss.

Chapter Three

Things observed, since I am all about the observing:

1. After Julia settles Grace down, she goes back to her room and sits in front of the computer, clicking through different news sites the way other people look at porn or thinspo, eyes glued to it. The waistband of her skirt – school uniform, grey – is digging into her tummy, and I know without seeing it that she's going to have a red mark there. I'm guessing she has a lot of those around her body. Disgusting.

2. All the while, there are thoughts about homework and the newspaper floating around, and there's editor-girl Lorraine and some guy named Gavin and then this sense of unfairness or something before it swoops back around to homework again. For a while I hope that maybe the pressure of being in her final year of school, of having life-determining exams approaching, is what's getting to her, what

might drive her over the edge, but no luck. Not a single suicidal thought in her heavily insulated bones.

3. Julia gets a message from her BFF (that's what normal teenage girls call it, right?), Deb, about a party that weekend, which is when I think to consider the day. Friday, apparently. *Heya, said 8 to people so if you wanna get here for 7 maybe and we can do pre-drinks? Bad news on the grown-up front though (AAAAGH), Mum says she definitely won't be able to get back in time but 'luckily' Dad and The Slut are going to be around so will be 'supervising' (is The Slut even old enough to be in a position of responsibility, like???). Apparently turning 18 means the world treats you like an adult but your parents still treat you like a fucking CHILD.*

4. And then another message, sent two minutes later. *Sorry for ranting, just RAGING here. Dxxx*

5. The messages feel like they have thorns. I can't tell if that's because I have some vague memory of Deb not being someone I especially liked (I can't quite picture her yet), or because Julia takes her time replying. There's something shaky going on inside her, like it takes effort for her to type the very short: *7 is cool. That does sound annoying but we're still going to have a brilliant time, okay? See you then!* ☺

6. After Julia types this, still shaky, she goes downstairs to the kitchen and puts the kettle on. While she waits, she has a packet of crisps. Cheese and onion. Lethal things. And then another. Makes a mug of hot chocolate, reaches into the cupboard yet again and takes out another packet of crisps, and then a second, and goes back up to her room.

7. By the time she goes to bed – flesh wobbling as she undresses, to be thankfully covered up with a baggy nightdress – there are six empty crisp packets in the bin. This on top of dinner, on top of biscuits with a cup of tea in the evening: Julia's parents, somewhat sickeningly, take it in turns to make a pot of tea for the family each night.

Things concluded:

1. She's fat. She's fat because she eats too much, and she has no control, and it's disgusting.

2. I really want another assignment.

Chapter Four

'You want to give up?' the Boss says. Doesn't exactly say. Thinks, but thinks in a more precise way than real thoughts, which float a bit more, don't always coalesce into sentences. Already I'm learning that from Julia – how scattered it can be inside someone else's brain.

'Not completely. Just with her.'

This is a place – is it even a place? – of impressions. I can't see the Boss, but I know she's there. I have a sense of others, voices, but all at a low murmur, like we've got a table tucked away in the corner of a cafe.

We're not floating but we're not grounded either. And 'where' feels like the wrong question to ask, like it's a different language.

'This is your assignment, Annabel. She's what we've got for you.'

'She's not in need of help! A diet plan, maybe, but not this. All she needs to do is stop stuffing her face, for God's sake.'

She lets the God thing go, which I'm thinking is a sign that even in this place it's just an expression. Instead she goes, 'You know it's not that simple.'

I don't like her tone. 'Why, how do I know? Why me?' If I had hands they'd be on my hips right now.

'You know why. There's always more to it than what we can see.'

Here we go. It's what's on the inside that counts, don't judge a book by its cover, blah blah blah. I wonder how long the Boss has been away from the real world, where that's all anyone does. It's how things work.

In the world, when someone looks at a person like Julia they think *weak*. They think *lazy*. They see the fat and they know exactly how she got that way. Even the most politically correct individual knows it deep down but bites their tongue in public. We all know what it means, to be fat, to fail.

'So you're not going to let me transfer to another assignment?' Because there must be something. There's the entire planet to choose from, billions of souls in need of help, and I just want to get this over with and get what I need out of it.

'I'm afraid that's not an option.'

'Why not?'

For a second I think I might actually get a non-bullshit answer out of her, but instead it's, 'This is what you're meant to do.'

Like hell it is.

'So you can stick with her. Learn about her. Get her to listen.' There's an 'or' coming, I know, I can feel it. 'Or . . . you could opt out.' And she has me there.

'I'll stick with her,' I say.

For a moment I think she'll do something really patronising – tell me I'm a good girl, say she's proud of me for accepting the challenge or something like that. Like this is *a very special breakthrough* we've just had.

Instead there's a flicker, and I can't see but I know that she's gone, that we're finished here. Until our next meeting, because apparently even the adults in the afterworld think it's a good idea to *check in regularly*. Like they all have the same manual to try to make our lives – and deaths – fit into their warped ideas of how we should be improving. Progressing. *Recovering*. Not that there's much chance of that last one any more.

Chapter Five

Julia's getting ready for Deb's birthday party. Trying on outfits in front of her mirror. So far today she's already gone way over even that lie of a 'recommended for women' number of calories those little panels on packaging say, so it shouldn't be a surprise to her when she stares at her reflection, in between outfits, and sees herself.

Fat. Fat. Fat.

She stands there in her underwear, plain white bra and pants. Slightly off-white from being in the wash with other things, not clean and pure. She's been wearing jeans all day so the imprint of the waistband is still there – little pink stripes going all the way around – and the belt buckle, too, at her belly button.

Her belly kicks off from just under her bra. Where there should be ribs protruding, gorgeous bone, there is fat. It bulges out all the way down; a different kind of bump to the kind you'd get if you were pregnant but just as gross. If I could throw up I would. This is wobble-when-you-walk fat. Blubber.

Her pink fleshy thighs rub together, all cellulite and flab. Her calves are like jelly. Jiggle, jiggle. How can she live like this?

The realisation of the fatness takes her by surprise, like she hasn't quite noticed this before. She's been maybe aware that she eats more junk food than is good for her, that's not a surprise, and maybe that she's put on a bit of weight, but she didn't realise it was like this. So visible.

I actually feel a little sorry for her now. A little.

And then I wonder: is this me? *Get her to listen.* Is this me getting through to her already?

She tries on something else. Jeans, a different pair from today's, nicer, and a top, this red gypsy-style thing that floats rather than clings, which is kind of what she needs even though I don't think she's fooling anyone. You can't tell how fat she is, but you still know she's fat. And the jeans are too tight – she tries sucking in her belly and holding her breath but they still won't button shut. She strains, gets the button half in before it slips through her fingers.

'Crap,' she says. She hasn't worn this pair of jeans in a while. They've shrunk in the wash, she thinks. Denial is a powerful thing. I try to *tap tap tap* away at her skull, to see if I can get the message across. *They didn't shrink. You grew.*

I can't tell if she's listening. I try louder. I want to help. She needs to know. Needs to see it.

She lets out a sigh, and hop-struggles her way out of the jeans. She'll wear today's pair, because at least they fit. Red-lined skin is what counts as 'fitting' in Julia's world, apparently. They're not dressy but they'll do.

She looks in the mirror again. 'You'll have to do,' she says, putting on a brave face. A smile. I can't tell if she's deluded enough to believe it.

Chapter Six

The friend whose party it is, Deb, is Deborah Keenan. As Julia gets closer to the house, I remember. Every break time, Deb would have a chocolate mousse, one of the Cadbury's ones. You could smell it, wafting across the classroom. Slim but no discipline.

When Julia arrives, Deb opens the door and says, 'He-ey! Come on in.' Like you need to specify this to someone who's here for a party you've invited them to. And there's a flicker of something else I can't quite put my incorporeal finger on.

They hug and then Julia enters, nervous – stomach churning, palms sweaty. The sweat might be to do with being fat, though. 'Anyone else here?' she asks.

'Not yet. Lorraine's on her way.' Deb glances around like she's checking for an audience, even though they're obviously the only ones here, and then leans in. 'Wait till I tell you. They broke up.'

'What?' Julia's heard it, she just isn't processing it. Like learning the sky's actually made out of marshmallows.

'Yep.' Deb nods, revelling in being the one who knows, the one who gets to tell the story. 'Gavin and Lorraine are officially over. For good.'

'They'll get back together. They always do.' Julia quenches something with this. For her own sake.

Deb shakes her head. 'Nope. This is it. I was talking to Lorraine today and she said they actually broke up a week ago – you know how he was all quiet at the newspaper meeting on Monday?'

Julia remembers, but she'd chalked it up to his unease at Lorraine's enthusiasm over writing about suicide. A quick flash here: Julia glancing around the rest of the newspaper crew, hoping desperately none of them had ever lost someone to suicide and were finding Lorraine's relish at exploring all the gory details insensitive. 'Yeah,' she says weakly.

'So they broke up but decided they weren't going to tell anyone, in case they got back together.'

This has happened before, apparently. Julia remembers past arguments, strained moments in school or at gatherings, occasional fractures before rapid mending. Her memories merge with mine for a moment and I remember now – Gavin and Lorraine have been together since they were fourteen, making them the teenage equivalent of an old married couple. Over the last few months, though, they've been fighting more; Julia's seen glimpses and worries each time, for both of them, but also talks herself out of the little flicker of hope that appears.

So she likes this guy. I never paid much attention to the boys but Julia's thoughts open up just a crack further now and I understand: she finds him attractive and adorable and all those other good things, and has done for a while.

It's pitiful. She doesn't stand a chance.

'But if it's only been a week . . .' Julia says, trying to convince herself. 'They still might sort things out.'

'No, Lorraine said this was *definitely* it.'

'Did she break up with him?' Julia wants it to be Gavin's decision, not that she's quite letting herself articulate that hope. Like she knows that she can't let herself dream about anything happening. Smart girl.

'Mutual, apparently.' Deb rolls her eyes. She knows there's no such thing as a truly mutual break-up. She's Julia's best friend, allegedly: can I slide inside her brain for a moment or two? I can't tell if what I discover is because of the connection to Julia or because it's so close to the surface anyway, but here it is: Deb Keenan, the relationship expert, has had all of two boyfriends, but then there's her parents' divorce to help that knowing cynicism along.

The sitting room is all set up for a party – a table laden with food. Nuts and crisps drenched in salt and soaked in fat. Gooey chocolate brownies (normal, non-stoner ones; these guys are too wholesome and well behaved for illegal substances, ignoring how dangerous the legal ones are). Fizzy jelly snakes that demand you eat more and regret it later, alongside some dolly mixtures; I can't tell if this is childhood nostalgia or Deb being *ironic* but neither of the options make me any fonder of her.

Neither Julia nor Deb worries about this temptation, this danger lurking in their midst. Julia tries to think of a way to keep talking about Gavin and Lorraine without making it obvious that that's what she's doing. 'And is Lorraine upset?' she finally asks.

Deb considers the question as she leans over to the table and gathers up a handful of salted peanuts. 'Hard to say. She only sent me a message about it this morning, and then I rang her, and, like, she didn't burst into tears or anything but . . .'

'Of course she's going to be upset,' Julia says. She's thinking about Lorraine her friend, Lorraine her fellow journalist, now. She tells herself: the poor girl.

There is a voice she's not letting herself hear, faint but real. The voice that says: Lorraine takes him for granted, she doesn't deserve him, you do, you do, you do.

I disagree, Julia. But I don't think she can hear me just yet. Maybe earlier was a glitch. Maybe I'll spend the rest of her life struggling to be heard.

'Yeah,' Deb says. 'I think it's, you know, one of those things where she knows it's for the best long-term but it still hurts.' She shrugs. 'That's how it goes, right?'

Julia nods like she knows what Deb is talking about. She doesn't, though. She's never known one of those moments. There's something sharp here that she swallows down. Something she can't think about. I wonder, is this all it is? Just a bad break-up, just some stupid girl wallowing in empty calories? What an utter waste of time.

'Oh!' Deb says. 'Do you know who's going out with Maria now?'

Julia has to shake herself back to this conversation. 'Maria who?'

'New girl Maria,' Deb says. Which unsettles me, though I don't know why.

'Oh yeah, of course,' Julia says. There's a flicker of something positive here – friendliness. *Maria'd probably be a better friend for you than Deb, Julia.*

19

'So, she's going out with Patrick,' Deb says. 'Good luck to her, like.'

Deb's thoughts are right on the surface again. Patrick's her ex-boyfriend, and their break-up was not quite mutual, but – I can deduce from what she's saying rather than anything she's admitting to herself – the injury seems to be more to Deb's pride than her heart. She keeps talking at Julia, relating how she found out, what Patrick's friends said, how people stupidly even thought she might be upset, how Patrick is okay but not really the most amazing guy in the world . . .

Deb, I discover as she yammers on and bits of the conversation bring different thoughts to the surface, also writes for the newspaper: an advice column. One of those things where it's supposed to be a secret but everyone knows it's her, especially because there's an edge to it that makes it a funny read but also not the most sympathetic if you were really upset over something. Julia's sort of interested in what Deb's saying, but her brain keeps going back to Lorraine. Then Gavin. Then Lorraine.

Julia reaches over and takes a handful of those jelly snakes. She bites the heads off first, then the bodies. She sucks off the sour-sugary coating first, then starts chewing. The first one is green and orange, tastes like a generic fruit-flavoured sweet, which is to say, not that much like actual fruit at all. Chew, chew, swallow, down it goes, down into her stomach.

I try to block it out, and tune back into what Deb's yapping about instead. This new girl, Maria. 'Maybe I should talk to her? I mean, she doesn't know all the history, and we've all known each other for ages . . . someone should talk to her.'

They've all known each other for ages. That's it, the unease. New girls are a rarity in the Richmond School. It's small. It hangs onto its students and keeps them close – there was only a space for me after someone else moved to a different country.

Which means there is only a space for Maria now because someone else didn't come back. Because someone was out of school for so long and then finally – well, you know. All those euphemisms. Shuffled off their mortal coil. Went to a better place.

I have to get out of here.

Chapter Seven

'So tell me something,' I think-hiss. 'Is this the big plan? I'm supposed to help this girl make friends with someone who's stolen my life?'

There's no answer from the Boss, and I realise all of our meetings have been on her schedule, not mine. Wherever I am, she isn't there – and after a few moments I no longer am either. I'm – outside the front door of my house.

We moved house after I started at the Richmond School, but were still close enough to it if I was able to attend – even though by then I was mostly in and out of hospitals, near and far, wherever they thought would *cure* me. Just what I didn't need. The house is in the middle of nowhere, gorgeous countryside and not much else – in this darkness the mountains feel closer than they are and you can't see the green of the fields. Never impressed me much anyway. My parents loved it. Nature. Always struck me as the sort of thing only adults were impressed with.

I can't stare but the house seems to be staring at me. The cream paint is starting to show wear and tear, peeling off around the windowsills, and there are scuffs – that scrape where Imogen dragged her bike along trying to get it through the narrow gap between the house and our dad's parked car. He's inside, and so's Mum, and Imogen, and maybe I can get inside. Maybe I've done it already, completed my stupid mission without even realising it, saved Julia from herself.

I try to move, but nothing. There's nothing. I push, but I've nothing to push with, no arms or legs, just me, and it doesn't work. Like I'm suddenly paralysed. But when I turn and move away – well, that's all cool, apparently. It's like the house floats away from me, but when I rush towards it again it's like hitting a brick wall.

Why can't I go inside? I ask the silence, seeing as the Boss doesn't appear to be around.

I push and push and then I edge away again. No use. I turn left and right towards the other houses, where neighbours I never spoke to still live. I'm sure I could appear inside those if I wanted to, but I don't. The house at the end, the one with the big garden and bikes resting up against the wall, has music thump-thumping out of the slightly ajar front door. Everyone's got a party to go to.

Two words that speak to me, from the thumping song. *Too. Soon. Too. Soon.* There are other lyrics but those have an extra charge. Message received. Fuck you, universe, but message received.

Chapter Eight

Back at Deb's party, where I finally return after further useless attempts to get through that door, Deb's father is surveying the now-lively scene. He's in his early forties, thinks he's still cool, and his new wife Sylvia agrees with him. His name's Dermot Keenan and he's a journalist, which maybe explains why editor-girl Lorraine has him cornered. He's loving the attention.

Lorraine is thin. And tiny, like a bird, which makes me wish this skill I have feels like flying instead of just *being*. She's going on about the piece she ran about suicide in the school paper, the thing Julia's been thinking about.

'Basically,' she says, 'none of them have actually read the whole thing. They're taking quotes completely out of context.' She shakes her head like she's his age, world-weary. I creep inside her head for a moment to see what I can find out about this piece: lots of detail in there, which seems to be the problem. The teachers think it'll give people ideas, as though that's all it takes.

On the other side of the room, Julia's half-listening to the conversation. Mr Keenan – no, 'call me Dermot', he says to

Lorraine – says something about freedom of the press and launches into an anecdote of his own, about some feature for the *Irish News* back in the day, and Julia almost, almost smiles when she realises it's a familiar story. Dermot versus The Mighty Editor, taking a principled stand and ultimately making everyone see sense. This guy clearly likes to talk about himself a lot. He'd do well in therapy. I tune out and instead tune into the conversation Julia's actually having, which is with new girl Maria.

Maria looks nothing like me – or, at least, how I used to look – which is reassuring in a strange way. Freckles and strawberry-blonde curls. 'Obviously acting's really tough,' she says. 'But I *know* that, and I think if you're aware of it going in, it lets you build up your resilience, you know?'

Julia nods automatically, privately – not-so-privately, as I'm eavesdropping – thinking that Maria's a little naive. Acting professionally is almost impossible. Then, much too soon for my liking, she chastises herself. Why not Maria? Who's to say that she doesn't have the talent and the perseverance? Somebody's got to do it, after all.

'That makes a lot of sense,' she says, genuinely now, thinking of how hard it is to be a journalist these days. *These days* carries with it a flavour of someone else, like call-me-Dermot has delivered another anecdote about that. He must love having a receptive audience among so many of his daughter's friends. And then Julia's thinking about the internet and blogging; how everyone with a keyboard thinks they can just bang out articles no problem, never mind research or quality control. 'Yeah. It totally does.'

Maria smiles. 'Now I just need to convince my parents of that.'

'Do you really want it?' Julia knows it's a weird question to ask. Wanting anything – really longing for it – can be dangerous to admit.

'I –' Maria's about to say yes, of course she does, she's wanted this for years, but then she takes a moment to think about it. 'I don't think I'd give up *everything* for it, or . . . whatever, sleep with someone to get ahead . . . but I'd give up a lot, you know?'

'I know what you mean,' Julia says. She's still eating those jelly snakes, sugary slimy beasts. Maybe she'll throw them up later. There's still hope.

Maria smiles, and there's something behind it – a sag of relief. She is a girl in a new school worried about whether or not people will take her seriously, a pretty little thing wanting what seems like an impossible fairytale of a career, and clicking with Julia Jacobs – smart, confident, kind – reassures her. (Fat, Maria. Fat. But as far as I can tell it's only my assignment girl who'll ever be able to hear me.)

Oh. There's a change in the air, a tension. Lorraine notices him first, with a jolt of both irritation and sadness; why did he have to come? Julia's conscious of him a split second later. Hello, Gavin.

The main thing I notice is that he's neat and tidy, but Julia, who's been nurturing an obsession for months, goes straight to the feelings – nervous and excited and just plain happy to see him, all at once.

He catches her eye and nods in acknowledgement, smiles at her, but doesn't come over. Instead he approaches Deb. 'Happy birthday,' he says, kissing her on the cheek. It's a grown-up affectation that he can only just about pull off. Barely. He hands over a shiny silver gift bag. Inside: champagne (well, prosecco; he wanted to get champagne and his mother said to get prosecco because it's far cheaper and just as nice and also she was fairly sure that good champagne would be wasted on this crowd) and a box of chocolates. Very generic, but Deb is touched. The girls have been better with the gift-giving than the boys, who have mostly brought six-packs of lager for themselves.

'Thanks, Gav,' Deb says, leaning in for the hug. 'How are you doing?'

'Yeah, cool.' He shrugs.

'Really?' she says. In a meaningful way.

'Lorraine told you?' He allows himself a rueful grin.

'Yeah, just today.' Deb attempts to look as sympathetic as possible. 'Are you okay with her being here?' Not that she's going to do much about it if he isn't, but she feeds on this kind of drama.

'Ah, no, it's cool.' Gavin is an agreeable sort. Gets along with lots of people. Will get into arguments about politics but not about social etiquette. Right now he's thinking: wish I'd stayed at home. But also: ah, but I couldn't miss Deb's eighteenth, she's a nice girl.

'You sure?' She's ready to pull him aside and be so supportive and listen to his woes, and then report back to Lorraine.

'Yeah.' He is tempted to reach into his pocket and check his phone, do something that isn't having this conversation. Instead he smiles. 'Did you get something nice from your parents?'

'Cash,' she says, and laughs. 'I didn't really know what I wanted, there's nothing I'm dying for at the moment, you know?'

Funny how people use that phrase so often. Dying for.

She relates some of the gifts from her friends: Julia got her a box set of some TV series she's been meaning to watch for ages, Carolyn bestowed upon her a mysterious plain box, which she's been told she needs to open while alone, away from parental eyes.

'So, a dildo,' he says.

'Or a vibrator,' Deb says.

Gavin is unsure of the difference, exactly, but doesn't question.

Deb offers him a drink, and he indicates the plastic bag swinging from his arm. Gavin is already eighteen, and past the age where purchasing alcohol is a minor drama. These cans of cider were stored in the fridge at home, instead of being hidden somewhere; they're cold and ready to go.

He cracks a can and someone else from their class arrives that Deb must go to greet, and he realises suddenly that this is the first party since, well, so far back he can't even remember, where he hasn't had a girlfriend.

Chapter Nine

Things observed at Deb's eighteenth birthday party:

1. Sylvia approaches Dermot and Lorraine after they've been talking for a while, grabs Dermot's arm and hisses in his ear: 'Leave the poor girl alone, for God's sake.' Either Sylvia is not quite as vapid as she seems or she's starting to get insecure about their relationship already. She's younger than Dermot by ten years and he left his wife for her. Understandable why Deb hates her.

2. Maria and Patrick – Deb's ex, the one she's *really fine* with going off with the new girl ('Are you sure?' Julia asks, only to get a half-impatient 'Of course, oh my God, I just hope she doesn't have high hopes for him' in reply) – slink outside for a cigarette and end up staying there for most of the evening, lost in each other's eyes. Maria imagines what it'd be like if it were a movie, what songs would play over the two of them having these moments. Young love, blah

blah blah. But it is strangely reassuring that Maria's so unlike me, rather than being a better version of my living self. And anyway, I was thinner.

3. Carolyn of the mysterious and possibly sex-related gift knocks back several alcopops (Deb keeps calling them 'wine coolers' in an attempt to sound either sophisticated or American) and tries to get a game of Spin the Bottle started. 'Ah, go on,' a newspaper type named Frank says hopefully, but it never quite gets off the ground. 'We're a little past that, don't you think?' Lorraine says, sounding like she's talking to children, and everyone agrees, even though the general aura is one of disappointment and not of maturity.

4. Deb sneaks up to her room to open Carolyn's present, and doesn't come downstairs for a while.

5. Everyone's eating and drinking like there's no tomorrow. The table, with its elegant little bowls of dangerous snacks, is almost bare, reduced to crumbs and traces of sugar. You can imagine, almost, licking your finger and pressing it against it to pick up those remaining traces. If you were disgusting.

6. On her way back from the bathroom, Julia finds Gavin sitting on the stairs, and sits down next to him.

Chapter Ten

'Hey,' she says as she sits. She takes the step beneath his, rather than trying to squeeze herself in next to him.

He does that nod of acknowledgement again. His shoulders untense just a fraction. 'Having a good night?'

'Yeah. You?' She's not really sure if she is or she isn't. She'd prefer it if Deb's plan – a supervision-free house, with her mum away for work – had worked out. But she's glad Carolyn's attempts at getting them all playing Spin the Bottle didn't come to anything. And now she's sitting next to Gavin, so that's a plus. I want to shake her. For him this is his friend coming to hang out with him for a bit, keep him company, not some magical moonlit moment. *Don't read too much into the warmth, Julia.*

'Yeah, it's cool.' Gavin is a man of a limited vocabulary, apparently.

'So why are you sitting out here all by yourself, then?' Julia smiles a little, to show she's not criticising, that she's sympathetic. But there's also something a little flirtatious in it, too. Some edge.

He smiles right back at her. 'I needed a break.'

Even though he's looking at her like she's beautiful, which means maybe he's had too many of those cans of cider, she gets nervous. There's a panic in her chest. 'Do you want me to leave you alone?'

Immediately he shakes his head. 'No, I didn't mean that at all. Stay.' He means it, but he's also horrified that he might have come across as rude.

'Okay,' she says.

She wants to ask about Lorraine. Except that there's another part of her that's quite happy leaving Lorraine out of this.

They look at each other. He gives her a little sheepish smile. 'Don't ask me about it,' he says.

'About what?' Julia plays innocent.

'You know what.' Gavin sounds weary, but when he looks at her there's another of those smiles. I edge my way closer to his thoughts again.

'Has everyone been asking?'

He shrugs. It's more the looks – the sympathy. No, pity. Everyone knows what's happened. There are few secrets in a school this small.

'Ah, Gav, I'm sorry.'

'It's okay,' he says automatically, and then his good-boy politeness kicks in. 'Thank you.'

'Plenty more fish in the sea,' Julia says, suddenly nervous. Heart pounding. Slight dizziness. She's sitting next to Gavin at a party and he's single and it's actually really happening.

He makes a noise that is somewhere between a grunt and a laugh.

'Seriously,' Julia says. 'I mean, when you're ready. You're probably still getting over –' Her voice falters. She doesn't want to say Lorraine's name. Not here, not now. And Gavin doesn't want to hear it. 'It takes a long time to get over someone,' she amends.

'Yeah,' Gavin says half-heartedly; the idea of getting over Lorraine is too huge and too big and not what he wants to be thinking about. Not tonight. He shifts on the step slightly, leans his head against the wall.

Julia's hand reaches up to pat his head, like a small child, and then it's stroking his hair of its own accord. She's about to stop when she realises, about to pull away and apologise (but it's so easy to touch him, so natural) when he looks at her. Eyes on eyes. They both know, both get that flicker, before it actually happens; his face tilts towards her and he kisses her. The angle is slightly awkward, but neither of them seems to mind.

Gavin cups her face, properly going for it now, throwing himself into it, and she thinks, is this actually seriously happening? It's the dream scenario suddenly brought to life, and it's amazing and too much at the same time. She can't do this.

They break for air, and he looks at her, all goofy, and she says, 'Gav, come on, we shouldn't.'

He blinks. 'Why not?' He sighs. 'I'm not with Lorraine any more, it's cool.'

'You've been broken up for what, a week? You were together for years. Come on.'

He runs his hands through his hair, making it even less neat and tidy after Julia's mussing. 'If you don't want to, that's fine.'

Julia can feel a stinging at the back of her eyes. 'It's not that.' She doesn't want to be his rebound girl, is what she's thinking. What she actually says is: 'I don't want to be your sorbet girl, okay?'

Chapter Eleven

Some things I know about sorbet:

1. It's sugar and water and flavouring, frozen. It's supposed to be light and airy and all that jazz.

2. Typical flavourings include lemon, strawberry, and other fruits, but you can also have alcohol in there. The alcohol messes about with the freezing temperature so that it's likely to be softer than your regular fruit variety.

3. You can get brain freeze from it.

4. Your standard restaurant serving is likely to be at least 150 calories. It's got about half the calorific content of ice cream, on average. It is better than ice cream but not actually good for you. It feels more virtuous than it is.

5. You're likely to find it on the dessert part of a menu,

but it can also be used, especially at fancy things like weddings, as a palate cleanser between courses. Sets you up for lots more stuffing your face than you might otherwise manage. In this scenario it's not a main course, just something to get the taste and weight of whatever you had before out of your mouth, before you move on.

6. This one is new. When Julia says 'sorbet girl', it comes – not to sound too shrink-like – with baggage. She's imagined saying this before, maybe even to Gavin, maybe even in a scenario like this. But when she played it out in her head it was breezy and light, not something almost choked out, like it was painful.

Chapter Twelve

Gavin, of course, is baffled. 'What?'

Julia's face heats up. 'Look, let's just leave it,' she says. She knows she has to get out of this. Right now. 'Sorry.' She won't even look at him. Just gets up and thunders down the rest of the stairs and tries the door of the bathroom, which is locked, so she hurries outside instead before she sees anyone else.

It's dark out, and Deb's back garden is mostly deserted, apart from Maria and Patrick who are so caught up in one another that they don't notice anyone else. Julia can hear the slurping kissing sounds from where she is, several feet away; she leans against the wall of the house as though she's trying to make herself invisible. Not a chance, Julia, even in these shadows.

The kissing sounds, being so close to other people being intimate, makes her weepy. She wants it, wants to be wanted like that, but she's also scared of what might happen. She's not a sorbet girl, not something light and easy to pave the way for the next girl.

An echo of something here: for a second we're back in Julia's bedroom, but she's slimmer now, and her computer's a different model, and this is before, before whatever it was, and all Julia can think is, *he loves her more, he loves her more*, and it's strangling her. Gavin and Lorraine? Or someone else? I can't tell.

Then we're back, and she can't quite believe she actually said the phrase 'sorbet girl' aloud to Gavin. He must think she's crazy. I imagine he does. I can't quite focus on what he's doing right now; I'm here with her, and I can't tell what's going on inside the house apart from general impressions (drinking, laughing, flirting, bitching). Out here, though, I can tell that Maria and Patrick are really into each other, at least for the moment, but that's not exactly a secret. Slurp. Slurp.

Basically, in my professional opinion, if you can count this as a job, this is a classic case of fat-girl insecurities and rightly so. If she's worried about Gavin using her as his palate cleanser, well, what else does she think she's good for? Boys don't go for fat girls. They talk about wanting 'real women', but what they mean is big tits. Not thighs, not bellies, not fat bums. They want skin and bone.

Let me be clear on this: I don't think you should shape yourself for a boy, or anyone else. I didn't. You need to know deep down, in your own truest self, that you are more powerful when you're not lugging around all that flab. You are in control. You are strong. You are glorious.

Julia slumps down to the ground, pulling her knees close. She thinks about moments with Gavin over the past year or so. That time he touched her arm and asked her if she was okay when she was upset over an essay her English teacher had demolished with red pen. Working with him on the newspaper and proofreading his pieces, and the way he laughed when she suggested he needed an intervention for his addiction to comma splices (I don't know either). A sigh escapes.

She wants him, and I almost do feel bad for her. You'd be so much happier if you were thin, I tell her.

She doesn't listen. She's trying to talk herself into taking a chance here, telling herself that maybe it's time to get over it. It is how she thinks about whatever it is. Being fat? A bad break-up?

And then she's striding back inside to the party, filled with hope and purpose.

No good can come of this, Julia. And I realise, suddenly, I really do want to save her. I want to make her shrink. I want to make her strong.

Chapter Thirteen

And there he is, still on the stairs. Gavin. His hands entangled in some girl's hair. Their faces are pressed together. It's the same smooching sound Julia heard outside from Maria and Patrick, something between eating and vacuuming. It takes her a moment to identify the dark curls as Carolyn's.

I was right, she wants to say, with a shaky sort of triumphalism. Maybe even wants to raise her fist in the air and be smug – she was right, he's already moved on to some other girl. Already. She's not special. Just in the right place at the right time. And Carolyn is the fun sort of girl who doesn't overanalyse what it might *mean*. The word 'slut' comes to Julia's mind and even though she hates the word, the concept, she wants to say it. But she can't say anything, just watches the two of them kissing, and then forces herself to turn around and power-walk away. The intention is to head straight back to the party, but she actually smashes right into Dermot Keenan.

'Sorry, sorry, sorry,' she says to his feet. This is a terrible party, she thinks. *Right there with you, Julia*. And then, slightly hysterical, asks herself: is this actually happening?

'It's okay,' he says, half laughing. 'You're a woman on a mission, I see.' She looks up, not quite meeting his eyes, and he sees that she's been crying, understands that she's about to start again. His hand goes to her arm. 'Julia, what's wrong?'

'Nothing.' She is, of course, lying; she just wants to get out of there as quickly as possible. The warmth of that hand – the *concern* – stabs her in the gut.

'Did something happen?' He looks over her shoulder; he can't see the stairs from here, can't see Carolyn and Gavin going at it, but he's thinking about upstairs and bedrooms. Thinking about himself in noble terms, maybe storming up there to deliver a stern lecture to or even throw a few punches at some lecherous teenage boy.

Julia finally meets his gaze. And she is smart, I realise, not just book-clever but shrewd, because she knows it's exactly what he's thinking. 'No,' she says, 'everything's fine.' A shrug, and the hand moves away. She doesn't need reassuring, or so she thinks; whatever higher-up power has assigned me here would disagree.

'Are you –' he begins, but she interrupts politely.

'Thanks for having us all here,' she says, even though it's an odd thing to say. He's sort of the host but sort of not. He doesn't live here any more, and near where they're standing now there used to be a framed photograph of him and Deb's mum, Tracy, hanging on the wall; the absence of it still strikes Julia every time she comes over.

'Julia,' he says, but she's already opening the door back into the sitting room. I wonder if she hates Dermot on Deb's behalf, for being the father who left; if this is what normal best friends (BFFs!) do. For a moment I think about Helen, and then make myself forget.

Inside the sitting room, Lorraine and Deb are huddled together. Julia decides not to tell them about what Lorraine's ex-boyfriend is doing. Between Deb's nose for gossip and Carolyn's chattiness, it'll probably be common knowledge by the end of the night anyway.

'Hey,' she says, 'I'm going to head off now.'

This prompts dismayed expressions, which seem to be genuine. 'Aw, no, don't go yet,' Deb says.

'Yeah, stay, come on,' Lorraine adds. 'It's not even that late.'

There's a tightening in Julia's chest. She needs to get out of there, that's all she knows. 'No, really, I'm going to go.'

Once she's made her first socially mandated request for Julia to stay, Lorraine considers herself off the hook; Deb continues pleading for a while ('Come on, stay for a bit, it's my *birthday*') until Julia invents a paracetamol-resistant headache that's been plaguing her all day. So there are hugs and farewells and then she gets her coat and shuts the door quietly behind her. Outside it's getting chilly: definitely autumn. But it's not raining, so that's a plus. She puts on some music – no, a podcast, that's what she's got zapping through those wires into her ears – and sticks her hands in her pockets and walks home. Leisurely, nothing fast-paced or aerobic about it. Try running, Julia. Try feeling the adrenaline pushing through you until you think for a moment you might be lighter than air, just try it. She doesn't.

At the next corner there's a guy heading in the opposite direction, and she puts the podcast on pause. 'Hey,' he says, 'are you going home already?'

41

'Yeah,' she says, putting on a bright smile. There's some context here – she knows him from the newspaper, though they're not that close – but there's something familiar about him that feels like it's mine, not hers. He has the collar of his jacket turned up, a hat pulled down over his forehead, and it's dark, but –

'Is the party still going on?' He's more concerned about that than why she might be leaving. Will. That's his name. That's who he is.

Their voices fade out. We are on a bed together, me and Will. A year ago, maybe more. 'You're gorgeous,' he says, running his hands along my body. I am not. I know this to be true. I am not thin enough. Not yet. He doesn't understand this.

'You know you don't need to keep up that stupid diet, right?' he says. 'I like you just the way you are.'

Something stings behind my eyes. It's not about you, I want to say, but I have no voice. I pull him towards me. Kiss him. It stops him from talking. He will never say the right things.

I reach over and switch off his bedside lamp. Darkness. He wants sex. He always wants sex. He can have it as long as he doesn't look at me. I am not tiny enough yet. I am not good enough yet.

I don't know why I'm in bed with him, except that he wants this and it is something I can do.

When I tune in to the present again, Will has arrived at the party, and Julia's at home, raiding the kitchen for snacks.

42

Chapter Fourteen

Will was not the love of my life, if you believe in such things. I don't.

'Love is for other people,' Helen used to say in the hospital, on those nights when we'd sneak out of bed to power-walk the corridors. Ordinary people. Weak people. We were different.

Dr Fields asked about Will. About boys in general. I think it was her default theory. Helen revelled in never telling her about her stepfather. We liked leading Dr Fields up dead ends. I devoted a whole session to Will, making up the bits I couldn't remember or had never known. I still can't recall his last name. Then the casual reveal: it was all too recent to be the great cause she was looking for, the ultimate explanation. I think she hated us, despite the concerned looks and earnest note-taking. She must be relieved I'm not her problem any more.

I miss Helen. When Julia wakes up on Sunday morning there's a big fry-up waiting for her in the kitchen. Bacon and sausages and black pudding, all sizzling and oozing fat. It's too much, and I need my old life, or what's left of it. I need her.

Apparently it's not *too soon* to visit Helen. I arrive at what I'm guessing is her house, so she's out of the hospital now.

There she is at the breakfast table with her mother and the stepfather and her half-brother, eating toast.

It's hard for her, to be doing this. It's dry toast, though, which is something, untainted by butter or Nutella or anything else the rest of the family are smearing and slathering on their bread.

Helen, don't do this. Why are you doing this to yourself? I have to try, even though she's not my assignment, even though I don't think she'll ever be able to hear me. Because I know Helen would listen. *I know you. I know this is not the real you. I know you want to stop now, after two mouthfuls. Two mouthfuls is enough. Remember what we used to say? Every time you say 'no, thank you' to food, you say 'yes, please' to skinny. Remember how powerful that 'no' is, how you feel it all the way through, like electricity in your veins?*

She chews and chews and chews and then finally swallows. Her mother is watching her with concern, and Helen scowls. 'Stop it, Mother.' Used to be Mum or Mummy, before the stepfather.

Her mother tenses up. 'I'm just so happy to see you eating,' she says. Without even really meaning to I'm edging closer to her thoughts, because what do mothers really mean, what do they *really* think when they say these things? Helen's mother wonders why her daughter doesn't understand how much she cares, how much – no, screw this. I push away from her brain, and wish I could squeeze Helen's hand.

'Well, you don't have to watch.'

'Don't be like that, Helen,' the stepfather says.

'Like what?' she hisses. Her eyes are dark, angry.

44

'Neil, stop it. She's sick.'

'Sick,' he repeats, mocking.

'Stop it,' the mother snaps.

Helen takes another bite. She tries to block him out. Block all of this out. She doesn't want to engage with any of this. She doesn't even really want to eat. Except she knows she has to. Deep down inside, this is her new certainty: she has to eat.

I want to step in here, tug Helen away. It's wrong. What happened to her? This is too much.

What *happened*?

And that question takes me to another room. Another girl. As soon as I recognise her I long for my eye-rolling abilities, my capacity to make faces. Of course Susan's out of hospital. She was always more of a tourist than anything else.

Her bedroom walls prominently feature several collages of inspiring women authors and poets and singer-songwriters. Collaging. It's creative, therapeutic, blah blah blah, spare me. They love recommending it because it works even if you're completely shit at art. Even if you can't manage a pair of scissors, the rough edges of your glossy magazine photo will look deliberate.

She is writing in a brown-and-gold leaf-patterned notebook, looking earnest. This page begins, *Last night I dreamt about Sylvia Plath again.*

It's like inspecting a car crash. I can't help myself. The next thing I see is, *I wanted to float away from the earth, not be tethered to this mortal coil.*

Past tense, you'll notice. Total tourist. Red lines peeping out from underneath her sleeves, but never going deep enough.

45

Never had the guts. Just enough blood to make people worry about her, to land her in with the rest of us.

But now I've seen you up close, Grim Reaper
Now I see your ugliness, truly revealed.
I don't want that for myself any more.
Not after seeing her there, the empty shell.
She could have been anything.
A pilot. A teacher. A doctor. A zoo-keeper.
A mother. A CEO. An archaeologist.
A painter. An actress. An accountant.
Instead she chose to be thin.
Instead she chose death.
Now I choose life.
I choose life.
I choose life.

Tedious repetition there, Susan. We get it. I look at the top of the page. Oh, she hasn't. She wouldn't.

The poem's title is 'Floating', and underneath that, the little bitch has put in her stupidly curly girlish handwriting, *In memory of Annabel.*

Chapter Fifteen

I arrive back at Julia's house in a fury. There should be rules for appropriating your memory of someone else and using it in crappy poetry. Some kind of etiquette about it. Susan wasn't even a real friend. We were stuck there together, and she never understood how we were at war the whole time. *I can't eat everything on my plate. That scale's wrong, I've actually gained weight, don't put that sugar water inside my veins don't you dare this is inhumane this is barbaric.*

I want to punch something. I remember back in school, maybe my third, being taught the right way to angle your fist to protect your wrist. The solidity of the bag, the way it thudded back each time. I want that.

What I have is Julia. Julia who is eating. Julia who is thinking about Gavin and how she's better off as she didn't get a chance for a second kiss, a future, and the funny thing is, she seems to mean it. She's pulling an invisible blanket around herself, becoming a girl that walks away instead of being left.

Carolyn's thinner than you, I say to her.

There's a tiny flicker and I realise the thought's made its way into her head. She doesn't know where it's coming from.

She doesn't recognise it as foreign. It's just there now. She thinks about how she looks a little like Carolyn, same dark curly hair, same pale skin, except how there's so much more Julia. More flesh, more bulk.

She shrugs it off.

No, Julia, no. You need to understand. Just because Helen's been corrupted, just because Susan's added me to her moronic collection of sad dead girls doesn't mean I was wrong. Do you know how strong you'll feel?

Everyone has cracks in their skin. I push and push as she reads the Sunday newspapers, as she spends more time than she usually would looking at style sections. Yes, she knows the models are airbrushed. No one could really be that thin, she tells herself. She's wrong.

There is something about the visual, though. She feels it and I know it. This is why we look at pictures, to inspire us. To help us see what we can be, to remind us that we can be better.

The next time she's in front of the mirror, in a baggy nightdress before bed, I tell her, *Julia, you need to stop eating.*

I need to stop eating so much, she thinks.

Not quite there. But it thrills me: it's a start.

OCTOBER

Chapter Sixteen

The Monday morning after the party, Julia is online before school begins, occasionally clicking away from articles about the housing crisis or funding cuts to the health service to consult websites that reassure her the carrot sticks in her bag are the key to losing weight. It's a start, I keep reminding myself.

In the tiny sixth-year kitchen, she puts the kettle on and keeps scrolling through the morning news on her phone. Lorraine, tiny bird-like Lorraine, stalks in just as the water's boiled, and Julia's immediate instinct is to apologise for kissing Gavin at the party.

'I've got to go meet Mrs Kearney this morning,' Lorraine announces.

Julia's relieved, then not. Mrs Kearney is the deputy principal. This is about the newspaper. The suicide story. 'What time?'

'First class.' Lorraine pours the steaming water onto three spoons of cheap instant coffee. 'I'm pretty sure she's going to fire me.'

I'm not convinced it counts as being fired if it's a school paper and no one's getting paid, but they both seem to take it seriously. This is their thing, I realise; the mutual respect of two girls intense about this newspaper. 'She mightn't,' Julia says. 'Maybe she'll just want a retraction.'

'Well, she can forget that.' Lorraine crosses her arms.

Something sparks in Julia's mind. 'Or a follow-up piece. You wouldn't have to apologise for any of it, just clarify. Maybe even ask some of the teachers for their responses to the original piece, make everyone feel like you're taking their concerns seriously?' She's getting going now. 'And it'd mean we'd have a piece that's not just about raising awareness of suicide, but talking about censorship, about the role of the media –'

Lorraine lets out a heavy sigh. 'It's not going to work.' She's made up her mind already.

Julia feels it like a slap. She busies herself with her own coffee. No sugar today. Good girl. 'I really hope it goes okay,' is what she eventually says. But there are worries swirling around her – about the paper, about Lorraine and about herself.

Among the many things I don't understand about this girl is this: she wanted to be editor. She was disappointed when Lorraine got it, but not entirely surprised; everyone seemed to like her better. ('Everyone' in her thinking features Gavin quite heavily.) And now it's within her grasp, if Lorraine really does get 'fired', but there's a thud-thud-thud of not-good-enough in her head.

They finish their coffee in silence, and the bell – first one of the morning, indicating five minutes to class – prompts Julia to wish Lorraine good luck and Lorraine to grimace.

Not good enough, not good enough. I wriggle away from Julia and follow Lorraine up to the office, where she's left waiting for a few minutes – one of those obvious feel-inferior tactics so beloved by authority figures – before being asked to come in.

Mrs Kearney is plump, which is one of those words (along with curvy, voluptuous, zaftig) that basically means fat but tries to cushion (no pun intended) the blow. She's wearing a wool dress that clings where it should fall gracefully, and she doesn't seem to mind; she sits back in her chair without a care for how she's arranging herself. 'Now, Lorraine,' she says, 'why do you think I've asked you in here today?'

I hate her already.

Lorraine raises an eyebrow. 'I imagine it's to do with the suicide story.' No feigned innocence here. 'Have you actually read it? The whole thing?'

Mrs Kearney doesn't like this. 'Yes,' she says sharply. 'It's incredibly irresponsible. It goes into an inappropriate amount of detail, it glamorises –' She's ticking these off on her fingers in a way I remember from school assemblies.

I read the piece over her shoulder, skim through the discussion of a recent report published about youth mental health in Ireland and the statistics about suicide, until I come to the paragraph that Mrs Kearney's clearly more bothered about than all the rest, where a pen's been pressed down so hard there are tiny blue holes in the page. *The shocking lack of support in schools cannot be glossed over or excused*, it begins, but then a phrase from earlier in the piece jabs at me. *Heart failure*. It sends me right back over to the other side of the desk again.

'It does not glamorise suicide,' Lorraine says firmly. 'The entire thing is about making it unglamorous.'

53

Mrs Kearney glares. She's having no nonsense. 'Really.'

'Again, I have to ask, did you actually read the whole thing? Because I don't think talking about bowels giving way after you're dead or the risk of liver damage or renal failure from overdoses or anything that was in there is actually glamorous.' Lorraine crosses her arms. Glares right back.

I'm not sure I like Lorraine, exactly, but she's right. Glamour stays far away from real death. Nothing Hollywood about it.

Mrs Kearney opens up a desk drawer and takes out a plastic file. Inside: a document, several pages long, titled 'Richmond School Mental Health Guidelines'. She ostentatiously flips through it until she gets to the bit about discussing suicide, and then hands it over to Lorraine.

Lorraine is a quick reader. Used to skimming things for the key information, too. 'This refers to teachers discussing the subject,' she says. 'Also, I think shutting down discussions in the way that's suggested here is actually potentially more dangerous. Someone who's really interested will just look on the internet. It's like porn. The stuff you stumble across is much worse.'

Mrs Kearney bristles at the mention of pornography. In her head Lorraine is basically a child. She tries another tactic. 'Lorraine, that article is being read by all our students. Including our first years. You're telling twelve-year-olds about things that are seriously psychologically damaging for them. They can't possibly understand the consequences –'

'You're worried about a suicide epidemic?' Lorraine says, incredulously.

'Well, yes, ultimately, that is what we might –'

'Because actually you're supposed to avoid using that term.' Lorraine taps the document with one finger. Another eyebrow raise. I wonder if she practises this in the mirror. I bet she does.

Mrs Kearney is sort of wishing they were allowed to hit the students, although she'd only ever admit this out loud after a bottle of white wine. She's just about old enough to remember being a kid in the days when you genuinely feared teachers (except she thinks of it as *respecting authority*). 'Don't try my patience, Lorraine.' Sharper than before.

I want Lorraine to say something marvellously bitchy here, like *You're trying mine*, but she seems to slip into student mode now. Powerless. She sits back in her chair, and waits.

'Regardless of whatever good intentions you might have had in publishing this piece, it's just not acceptable. I think you know that.' Now Mrs Kearney is taking on a reasonable-sounding voice, although it's with great effort. 'Certainly not for a school newspaper. It's not appropriate content.'

Idiot. Dying is an ugly, ugly business. Shed a little light on it and maybe you'll stop people from overdosing or hanging themselves.

I suddenly hear Dr Fields in my head: *Annabel, do you want to live?*

Different situation, though. Completely different. If I'd wanted to kill myself I'd have gone for razor blades or pills. I'd have *done* it.

'So you're firing me,' Lorraine says.

Mrs Kearney has a *well, what did you expect* face on her. 'It's a school newspaper, Lorraine. We need to be able to stand behind it . . .'

55

On and on she goes about parents, about the board of management, about the very fine reputation that the school has. Lorraine makes a show of taking her keys out of her pocket and sliding one off the ring – the one that opens the door to the photocopying room, which doubles up as the newspaper office.

'Now, if you'd like to still submit an article or two for the paper I'm sure we can discuss that,' Mrs Kearney says as Lorraine drops the key on her desk. 'Maybe after Christmas when you've had time to think about –'

Lorraine laughs, a bark at odds with her tininess. 'Right.' No way she's hanging around doing the same old stuff she's done for years after being kicked off as editor. 'I don't think so.'

She slams things – locker doors, her hand against the wall – on her way back to class, and it's funny how her brain and body lie to each other. She doesn't know that she likes this distraction from the Gavin break-up, this righteous fury; her body fizzes with it. While she throws herself back into her seat next to Deb, who is all sympathy and concern and passing notes as their business teacher talks exam strategy, Mrs Kearney pops into the staffroom. Mr Briscoe, Julia's red-pen-addicted English teacher, looks up. 'Did you talk to her?'

Mrs Kearney nods, mouth pursed. 'She has some cheek, that one. Do you have the sixth years today?'

Mr Briscoe nods. 'Next class, actually.'

'So you can let Julia know.'

'She'll be good.' He looks thoughtful. 'I just don't want to see it taking up too much of her time; she needs to make sure she's getting a bit of exercise as well.'

Mrs Kearney agrees that Julia's 'got a bit heavy lately', and then they get yammering about recent research into childhood obesity and parenting today – very self-congratulatory for people with their waistlines, if you ask me. I'm just about to drift away when she asks how the new sixth-year girl's getting on.

'Maria? Grand. Seems to be settling in nicely. Getting involved.'

'That's what we like to hear,' Mrs Kearney says with a smile, seeming to really mean it.

I wait for something more here. Something more about the girl who should have had that place, who should have been back this year, but was too sick, and then too dead. Do they know? How much did my parents tell them? I imagine the phone ringing, wondering if Annabel McCormack will be back in school this year. Imogen would answer, maybe, and it'd be, 'Can I speak to your mummy or daddy, please?' in that way that makes her roll her eyes, and then she'd put on her best grown-up voice and say, 'And whoooom shall I say is calling?'

And then – would it be Mum? Dad? Which of them would pick up the phone and say it?

Maybe it was an email. Maybe they just typed 'no' and that was it.

The teachers don't say. They move on, with their petty self-righteous concerns about the students, and I zip back to where I belong.

57

Chapter Seventeen

Of all the things to imagine after learning that she's the new editor, Julia spends the class after English visualising a Careers Day somewhere in the future, being invited back to her *alma mater* as a success story. 'Well,' she's saying to some aspiring young thing who reminds her of herself when she was that age, 'I started writing for the school paper back in first year, and I think it's a good idea to start as soon as you know you're interested. You build up that experience and a body of work, which is important.'

She tells the interviewer about starting to send pieces and pitches out to local papers, her work experience with *Dublin Daily* in fourth year and then with the *Irish News* in fifth year. 'It actually,' she says, one elegant hand moving in front of her as she speaks, a single slim gold bracelet on her wrist, 'wasn't that helpful. You're not really doing anything apart from making coffee and photocopying things for people.'

'And was there anyone there who might have offered you any good advice, or anything like that?' the interviewer asks, wanting there to be a mentor who guided her, who saw her potential and opened up the world for her.

Julia pretends to consider the question. 'Not really. I think there were people who maybe *thought* they were doling out wise words . . .' And she smiles, with just a hint of an edge, encouraging everyone else to do the same.

'Julia?' It's not the interviewer this time, it's her maths teacher. Julia reddens, hoping she wasn't actually smiling in real life. She flips open her A4 pad at the right page for last night's homework.

A few desks behind, Lorraine scratches her pen deep into her own notepad. Julia agreed it was an important issue to write about, she thinks, and offered to take a look over it before it all went to print. She should have let her; Julia's got a good eye – but Lorraine liked it as it was, raw and honest. The kind of thing that gets you noticed, wins prizes, gets into the real papers. Fucking school. She glares at the back of Julia's head, even though she knows deep down it's not her fault. But it's easier to be angry than sad, to feel the loss – Gavin, the newspaper. And then there are exams looming at the end of the year, ready to determine her future, and it's easier to be angry about the system that assesses them on a handful of days instead of their overall capabilities.

The exam worry and rage hovers over most of the students in the room. There's not-the-love-of-my-life Will, more recognisable now in his school uniform, but still a stranger in so many ways, thinking about whether maths will ever click for him. There's Maria, debating whether or not to take the lower-level paper, which feels like an easy escape, an admission that future drama students are too fluffy and ditzy to handle things like calculus, even though she has not only exams to think about but auditions. And there it is in Julia's mind, too, along with doing a good job as editor, along with not letting her parents down, along with something else she won't even let herself think about. But she has the job, she has what she wants, so I'm finished now, aren't I?

Chapter Eighteen

'Annabel,' the Boss says in a way that lets me know I am trying her patience. 'What do you think?'

'I think she's got something she really wanted, so . . .'

'You're not finished.'

I know. I know. Wishful thinking.

'It must be hard for you,' she adds. 'Being back there, seeing the life you should have had.'

I stifle a laugh. As though they're happy. As though I envy them. I never fitted in there, and I wouldn't now. It's like Mrs Kearney said – they like the students who get involved, who care about things like school newspapers and student council and environmental committees. I can almost hear Helen's voice in my head: 'Can you imagine anything more boring?'

'Maybe not,' the Boss amends.

'Can't you just tell me what you need me to do?'

'Help her.'

'She doesn't need help!' A diet, maybe.

'You wouldn't be able to reach her if she didn't need you.'

Need me. Funny how no one needed me when I was alive.

'Do you really think that's true?' she asks, and I realise I've been thinking too loudly.

'Yeah. It is.'

'You don't think your parents needed you? Or your sister?'

I want to laugh. If Imogen had needed me, she wouldn't have betrayed me. She wouldn't have told tales. I wouldn't have been in the hospital. I'd have been left to my own devices. My own life.

I disappear from the meeting without saying goodbye to her. I'll go help Julia. Whatever it takes.

It's the only way I know, the only way the Boss knows, to earn the right to get one last message through to my family. And I need that. I need that more than anything.

Chapter Nineteen

Lunchtime: Julia texts her parents about the news. No reply from her dad, who's probably not able to check his phone right now. Both her parents are police officers, used to long shifts and strange hours, but her mum, back at a desk job since Grace was born, replies within a few minutes: *Thats great! Can u pick up G @ 4.30?*

OK, Julia texts back. Deflated. Not just because her mum left out an apostrophe.

'I'm starving,' Deb announces. 'Will you come to the chipper?'

Julia contemplates the remaining carrot sticks in her lunchbox, thinks about brown paper bags stained with vinegar and bursting with chips. 'Yeah,' she says almost instantly, and I despair.

After school, she sneaks into the newspaper office. It's not really sneaking – she has a key, courtesy of Mr Briscoe – but it still feels as though she's out of bounds. She's never been in this room, with its two mostly functional computers and printers and heavy-duty photocopier, on her own before. Only with Lorraine, or at the weekly meetings.

She lets out a genuine squeal. Then she remembers there are almost certainly other people still in the building, and arranges her face in a dignified expression. But the grin keeps bursting through. She perches on one of the desks and swings her legs.

Her phone beeps. Reminder to herself: *pick up Grace from the minder's*. Right. She gets up, locks the door behind her, and then she hears footsteps and voices. 'You going to the gym?' That's Will.

'Yeah, that's the plan.' This voice she knows very well. Gavin.

There's a number of the sixth-year boys who take advantage of the gym across the road from the school; they offer a special discount to staff and students. For a moment, guilty with the memory of her fast-food lunch, Julia considers getting a membership. She's never been inside a gym, but she pieces together a composite from TV. Lots of sweaty (and very good-looking) guys in tight shorts lifting weights and grunting, lots of absurdly beautiful and skinny women in tight, tight Lycra, cycling like crazy.

The footsteps get closer, and she moves towards the stairs, trying to look purposeful instead of panicked, like she hasn't been hanging out grinning in the office like an idiot.

'Julia?'

She turns back. 'Hey, guys.' Offers up a small smile.

'You all moved in?' Gavin asks.

Julia stares blankly at him for a moment.

'The office.' And then adds, 'Madam Editor. Nice one.' He means it, too; there's no dark undercurrent of jealousy here.

'Oh. Yeah. Yeah, it's –' She sighs. 'I wish they'd let Lorraine stay on.' She sort-of does, but is also conscious of not looking like a bitch, revelling in Gavin's ex-girlfriend's defeat.

Gavin shrugs. 'It's a shame, but, look, she knew what she was doing with that piece. Anyway, congratulations, you'll be great.'

Will says nothing. Both boys are on the newspaper, and Will's not even that bothered about it most of the time, but he feels like maybe he should have been asked to replace Lorraine. Two female editors in one year – isn't it a bit much?

Julia blushes. 'Thanks, Gav. I really appreciate it.' Warm smile, a genuinely warm one – he's the first one to properly congratulate her about this – and then she remembers, as their eyes meet, and it hangs there. Carolyn. The stairs. The kiss. 'Anyway. Have to go – see you guys tomorrow!'

She's out of school by the time it occurs to her she should have reminded them that she's sent everyone on the newspaper a message saying there's a meeting tomorrow lunchtime – usually it's a Monday, for the paper to come out on the Friday, but with all the Lorraine fuss it was up in the air. It's easier to berate herself for forgetting this than for not being cooler with Gavin. She doesn't want to be cold – that'd suggest she's still thinking about their kiss – but too nice implies she's fawning over him, being the sad fat girl foolishly lusting after the guy everyone else wants.

You need to eat less, I tell her. *You need to shrink. You need to be thin.*

She doesn't know it's me, but she hears me. She hears me and she's full of hope. Things are going to change. One success already. Next step: lose weight. Become lighter. Better.

Chapter Twenty

Imogen McCormack, aged eleven and ten months, is probably not asleep. It's a cold, windy night and every other light in the house has been switched off, except for hers, a tiny square of light in the dark.

She has nightmares. Wakes up crying in the middle of the night, like she did when she was a baby, tiny and perfect. Annabel, meet your baby sister. She was so small. I worried she'd break, but they let me hold her. I never dropped her. I could stare at her for hours.

Some nights she'd knock on my door and ask if she could crawl into bed with me and I never had the heart to say no.

Lie. I did. I started to. It was hard enough to sleep on that mattress, my knobbled spine and aching hip bones too heavy, too there, without having a bratty little sister squirming and asking for a story. I learned to say 'Go away', and then 'Fuck off', and when she told our parents all my secrets I knew it was revenge for that.

'I don't want you to die!' she screamed at me once. Maybe a few weeks before I did. A few months? I can't remember. But I knew why she'd really told. She wanted to hurt me. She knew just how to do it.

I look up at her window and stay there for maybe minutes, maybe hours. Until the light goes off. Until she's safe from the monsters under the bed.

Chapter Twenty-One

Newspaper meeting, Tuesday lunchtime. 'Guys,' Julia says over the chatter, and then again, louder, 'guys!'

The room isn't full, but it is noisy. Julia tries thwacking her A4 pad against the side of the photocopier in an attempt to create a loud bang, but it just looks like she's furious with it. Then she opens the door and slams it. Silence. 'Now that I've got your attention,' she says, trying to be smiley, 'let's get started.'

She wants to be confident. She wants to be a good female leader and role model – there are books on her shelves about this very issue. But in practice it's harder when the newspaper crowd – most of them, anyway – are all staring at her. When the first thing her dad said when he came home last night was, 'How was today?' instead of 'Congratulations', until she reminded him.

'So, let's talk through what we've got lined up for this week,' she says.

A flutter runs through the room. 'What, this week?' the third-year representative says. Looks around, panicked.

'Next week,' Will corrects.

Julia blinks. 'Yes, this week,' she says to the third year.

'We're not doing one this week,' Will says, as though he's kindly reminding her.

'Says who?' She thinks: did Mr Briscoe announce this and forget to mention it to her?

'Oh, come on. We don't have time this week, it's already Tuesday.' *Will always knows best. You don't need to diet. I like you just the way you are.* The surge of irritation towards him that wells up in Julia now isn't entirely her own.

Others nod, fully in agreement with Will. Thinking of homework, of TV to catch up on, of the relief at having a week off from the paper. Deb is among them, and Julia feels the tiniest slice of betrayal.

'Guys,' she starts to say, but then the door pushes open with a late arrival. Gavin. He does his nod-smile thing at everyone in the room.

'Guys,' she says again quickly, before there's a chance for chatting to start up again, 'the whole point of this meeting is to sort out the next issue. What did you think I meant when I sent the message?'

'*Next* week,' a fifth-year girl says. She's starting to regret coming today; she could be out the back sharing cigarettes with her best friend.

Julia just stares at her.

'Wait, what's going on?' Gavin asks.

Julia wants to sound calm. In control. But then he looks straight at her, hazel eyes concerned – those eyes her eyes met before that kiss, that stupid kiss – and what comes out is less measured than she'd like. 'Apparently people have decided that we're not doing an issue this week, even though that's what this meeting is about.'

'We don't have the time,' Will says.

Gavin sees the way Julia's biting her lip. 'Come on,' he says to everyone. 'When have we ever had anything substantial done by this stage in the week? We've plenty of time.'

I can sense that this is true, that they know this. But they are also conscious that it's October now, that the teachers are already talking about Christmas tests and mock exams. The new shine the newspaper had at the start of the school year has worn off.

'Look,' the third year says, 'everyone in our year has a lot of homework this week –' Which turns into a competition about which year is hardest hit by workload, until Julia slams the door again.

'All right,' she says, 'we all have a lot of work –'

'So let's just leave it for this week,' the fifth-year girl says, like it's so obvious and can't they just go have their lunch now?

Julia opens her mouth.

'We can't just leave it whenever we feel like it,' Gavin says. 'It's a weekly publication. We all knew that when we committed to it. I don't know about the rest of you' – his eyes sweep the room at this point – 'but if this is just some half-arsed thing we do whenever we feel like it, I don't want to be involved. I want it to be something we can be proud of.'

Oh for God's (just an expression) sake. But it works. The sheepish nodding starts, goes around the room like a Mexican wave.

'Okay,' Julia says, trying so very hard to sound bright and cheerful, 'so what do we have?' She assigns stories and confirms regular columns – Gavin's sports section, Deb's advice column, Will's satire pieces – all without making eye contact with anyone. 'And, as ever, if you've any particular photos you want to use, send them on to Frank first.' She nods towards their photo guy, a shy boy in her year who has spent most of the meeting sufficiently distracted by his lack of success with girls to care much about whether they put an issue out this week or not. 'That's it. See you all next week.'

Gavin shoots her a grin as he leaves, a sort of conspiratorial thing, and she stares right through him. Don't take it personally, she's distracted, he thinks, as he heads off to get his books for the class after lunch.

She's not. She closes the door once everyone's left and locks it from the inside, then leans against it. Don't cry, she tells herself. Don't cry. Gavin's little speech replays in her mind – so moving, so inspirational, so very much exactly what she should have said if she'd been able to pull it off.

Charmer. Fucking charmer, she thinks. Stepping into the breach and not giving her a chance to turn things around herself. Of course he doesn't take her seriously, of course he's one of those guys, one of those men who might seem to respect her and think she's clever but really – really –

Why do they all end up treating you like a silly little girl in the end? she wants to scream.

She thinks of pasta in a creamy sauce, of warm mashed potato with butter. Comfort food. Like a duvet being wrapped around her. Like a hug. And she knows that's what will fix this.

Julia, no. Be strong. Remember those celery sticks in your lunchbox today – remember those? But she's refusing to listen, the stupid girl, no matter how much I scream. There is a louder voice in her head, and it wants to cram carbohydrates down her throat until she's ready to explode.

Julia, have you considered that you might have a bit of a problem with food?

Chapter Twenty-Two

My mother said, once upon a time, 'Annabel, have you considered . . .'

She struggled with it, with the exact way to phrase it. I see that now. Then, I only knew that it was coming and that it had to be deflected immediately.

'No,' I said, before she could finish.

'Have – you – considered,' she said again, shaky, her eyelids fluttering shut, 'that you might have a bit of a problem with food?'

I remember now, when it was. We'd just moved house again. I was about to turn fifteen. I could tell you how much I weighed, but it wasn't good enough.

'Mum,' I said firmly, 'I'm just watching my weight.'

Acceptable terminology. Every few weeks there was another story in the newspapers about how obesity was a huge health crisis. I was being healthy.

'Sweetheart, you don't need to watch your weight, you're fine. You're beautiful.'

You're my mother, I thought. You have to say that.

And then with tears threatening to spill: why don't you understand?

I looked at her. She was about to start crying, too.

'Imagine if Imogen was doing this to herself,' she said. 'Do you want her to grow up and think like this –'

'Stop making this about Imogen,' I said, barely able to get the words out. It was nothing to do with her. It was nothing to do with my mother, either. Why couldn't she just leave me alone?

I couldn't be there. I got up and left, even though it was my bedroom. By rights she should have got out, but that's not how mothers operate, or sisters, either. Get out, get out, get out, and they come back with false concern. Jealousy, maybe. She is not thin, my mother. Her belly bulges out over jeans, over the waistband of her skirt. Cellulite on her thighs. Her breasts drooping. Sometimes when she looked at me I wondered if she felt like the wicked queen in *Snow White*.

I left the house, slamming the door behind me, and ran until my lungs ached. By the time I came back the dinner she'd left in the kitchen for me was cold, and easier to say no to, easier to scrape away into the bin.

Years later, in the hospital, Helen said solemnly, 'Have you ever considered that we might have a bit of a problem with food?' Right after we'd been warned about eating everything on our plates, reminded of IVs and feeding tubes. Stern, pretend-concerned faces.

Right then it was the funniest thing in the world.

Chapter Twenty-Three

Hi everyone,
    Just a reminder that it's Thursday and that the deadline was 5 p.m. today (i.e., an hour ago). In case you are incapable of reading your watch or have trouble understanding what day of the week it is or have suffered some newspaper-specific amnesia since the meeting where you all said you'd GET YOUR WORK IN ON TIME.

Julia stops typing and exhales sharply, then hits the delete button.

Hi everyone,
    Deadline was 5 p.m. – know it's been a crazy week but we can't wait much longer if we want to get this issue out tomorrow.

She uses 'we' deliberately. We. A team. A bunch of people, all of whom signed up for this.

If you can get your work to me by 7 p.m. on the dot that'd be great. After this, don't bother.

She examines the screen and then deletes the last sentence.

After this, anything that comes in will be disregarded, or held until next week's issue if it's still relevant.

She likes the sound of that. 'Disregarded' is a good word, she thinks.

Best wishes,
Julia

Should she put down 'Editor' after it, like people do with business emails, or is that too much? She stares at the screen and sighs. Is it too passive-aggressive to add something about whether people want to still be involved with the paper? Too needy?

And the ultimate question: what would Lorraine do? Except Julia knows already: Lorraine wouldn't be in this situation.

She thinks about *Macbeth*. She thinks about usurpers. (Seriously. She uses that word. In her own head and not just for an English essay.) Paranoia flickers through her: everyone knows. They know she kissed Gavin. They know she doesn't deserve him, which somehow in Julia's head morphs into not deserving anything Lorraine has ever had, including the respect and deadline-observance of the rest of the newspaper team.

When I tap away at the logical side of her brain I learn that Julia does know people often get stuff in late, that she's used to sitting down with Lorraine on Friday mornings before school starts for last-minute proofreading sessions. But even that knowledge doesn't soothe her; this feels so much worse. What if there isn't enough for a paper at all? What if it's incredibly obvious to everyone that she can't be taken seriously? And then the memory of Gavin rallying the troops hits her again, and she desperately, desperately wants to cram food down her throat until she forgets.

You have to respect your writers, but you can't let them take the piss, either, a voice from long ago whispers in her head. Not mine. This is career advice, an area I'll never be qualified in, unless 'invisible spiritual advisor' starts coming with a salary.

She types: *P.S. Those of you that haven't yet got in touch to explain the delay* – this is ignoring the fact that none of the late people have contacted her yet – *please do so and advise whether you're still interested in contributing to the paper this year. Thank you.*

And send.

Nothing yet from Deb – her advice column and horoscope section are often late, but Julia's taking it personally anyway. Julia scrutinises Gavin's opinion piece about a recent rugby match and its coverage in comparison to women's sports for something she can find fault with, and when she can't she sighs and refreshes her email, checks every single messaging service on her phone, resists the urge to scream.

She cares. She cares so much. It pulses through her, this feeling of frustration at not having the others get it: this is one of the few ways they can actually make their voices heard, to engage with the world, to express their own thoughts instead of regurgitate whatever the right exam answer is.

Dr Fields in my head: *What do you want to be when you grow up, Annabel? What matters to you? What do you care about?*

I only had one answer for her, and not the one she wanted.

Julia's phone beeps. Gavin, asking if she's still in school. *Do you want some help? Or need me to go beat up anyone for you?* ☺

She glares at the winky-face. No, she does not need any help. She is not a damsel in distress waiting for some knight on horseback, and anyway decent knights don't make out with two girls (at least, she thinks suddenly. What if there was someone else after Carolyn, or someone before her – what if he was just at it all night long?) at the same party.

Julia gets to work, proofreading and then slotting in the pieces she does have into the template for the paper. The photos have come in from Frank, and she picks out more than she needs, to try to make up for the lack of text content. She's mid-click, trying to adjust the size of a picture from this week's hockey match, when the screen freezes.

'No. No, no, no,' she says to the computer. 'You're not going to freeze up on me. NO.'

Clicking, frantic, she can feel her head ready to explode. 'Work!' she yells, and that's the moment when the door swings open and Gavin sticks his head in.

Chapter Twenty-Four

'How's it going?' Gavin asks.

Julia indicates the frozen screen. 'How do you think it's going?'

He steps inside and leans over her, pressing keys.

'Don't,' Julia says, grabbing his wrists. Warm hands. Oh. 'Give it another minute.'

'I'm just going to –'

'No,' she says, looking up at him, twisting around in her chair. 'I know how to press Control-Alt-Delete, Gav, thanks very much.'

'Then do it,' he says, exasperated. His brain: there is an obvious solution here. Let us jump on the fix-it wagon.

'I want to give it a minute.'

'It's not going to restart the computer,' he explains. 'It'll get this thing called the Task Manager up –'

'Oh good grief, Gavin!' Julia's voice is shrill. Her brain: she's not an idiot. Her nose: he smells delicious, soapy and clean, not too overpowering. Her brain again: she can't let him know she's smelling him, for God's sake. 'I understand how computers work. I understand how *this* computer works, and if you get the Task Manager up then you'll just end up having to close the program, which means losing all the changes you've made to a document, which means' – she jerks her hands, still clutching his wrists, for emphasis here – 'I am going to *give it a minute* and see if it gets going again.'

Her face is flushed now, and he is both frustrated with her and also kind of turned on. She's still holding onto him, fingers warm, and their faces are very close, and if this were a romantic comedy she'd drop his hands and they'd lunge at each other like crazy people. Cue the music.

He grins at her, a little sheepish, and is about to maybe make a move when she scowls at him. The deviation from the rom-com scenario jolts his system. 'Calm down,' he says, finally, the smile fading.

She realises with horror that she's still holding onto him. The fingers release. 'Sorry,' she mutters, about the physical contact rather than the rant. Her cheeks are hot.

'It's okay,' he says, misinterpreting what she's apologising for. 'It gets pretty stressful this time of the week.'

'Especially this week,' she says heavily. 'So many people just –' She tries to think of the precise word, and finally settles on 'suck'.

He grins, but also makes a gesture to the door. Oh. Julia's not turning yet, but I see her: the fifth-year girl – Sally, her name is – is waiting impatiently for Gavin. (And also: she's very glad that she went to the library after school instead of racing home, as that's where they ran into each other. And got kicked out of, after the librarian found them kissing behind the new books display.)

Gavin, you are such a man-whore. Seriously.

'Seriously,' Julia continues, 'I'm still missing loads, nothing from the fifth years at all. Sally hasn't even bothered coming up with an excuse –'

Sally clears her throat, as Gavin repeats his too-subtle indicating. Julia spins around. It takes her about two seconds to piece it all together.

Julia turns around and looks straight at the screen. 'So are you going to get your piece in or not?' she asks. Hoping her voice doesn't sound shaky. If she has to look at Sally she's going to cry.

'Yeah, totally, sorry, I just need a bit more time,' Sally says. Automatic response and actually a blatant lie. She has no regrets that her evening's been diverted by Gavin. Her immediate plan is not to sit down and get working, but to get him away from their new way-too-intense editor and get her tongue down his throat again.

'You have until seven,' Julia says mechanically.

'Okay,' Sally says. Whatever gets her out of here.

Julia clicks again, and it's still frozen. Damn it. She hits the magic combination of keys, which doesn't have an immediate effect. She wants to cry, but knows it is very important that she keeps it all in until Sally gets out of here.

Gavin peers over her shoulder. She can't look at him. 'Do you want me to stay and help?'

She shakes her head. Doesn't trust herself to speak. She can still smell him, and for the first time I think I understand perfectly how she feels. It's your favourite dessert set out in front of you, and you breathe it in, but you know how dangerous

81

it would be to let yourself taste even the tiniest bite, how much safer it is to step away.

'Come on, we'll get it done quicker if it's the two of us.'

'No,' Julia says, and the force of it almost but not quite breaks her. The tears are on their way. Another girl. Another one. She can't look at him. Why won't they just *go*, leave her alone, go back to their fun make-out session and let her get on with it?

Gavin senses she might be upset. 'Julia, come on, just let me –'

She spins around from the computer. 'I don't need your help. Go. Enjoy the rest of your evening.' She gives Sally a little tight smile, indicating she knows damn well that Sally doesn't have a hope in hell of getting her article in within the next half an hour.

Gavin hovers for a moment, and then Sally says, 'Come on, Gav, let's leave Julia alone.'

If this were a movie, 'alone' would echo over and over as they disappear down the corridor and down the stairs to the exit, as the school's extra-curricular enthusiasts slowly filter out, leaving Julia the last one in the building until the caretaker knocks on the door to remind her he's closing up now, that she's the last one left. But it's not, and I can't do sound effects, so I just watch and float around and note the way that the school's anti-bullying posters have certain letters lit up more for me. *Help her.*

But Julia doesn't seem to want anyone's help, and even though she clearly needs it, I understand that steel inside her that won't let her accept it. Maybe she knows, like I do, how harmful help can be, how sometimes the people who claim to care about you can hurt you the most.

Annabel, it's for your own good. We just want to help you.

I follow Julia home and tell her, *It's okay. I'm not going to be like they were. I'm going to help you be as strong as you can on your own – that's what you want, isn't it? To not need anyone? I know how to make you strong.*

She's not listening.

No, I think, because I am *au fait* with that therapist bullshit of putting a positive spin on things and I finally get it. She's not listening yet. But she will.

Chapter Twenty-Five

Some observations on the first issue of *The Richmond Report* to be edited by Julia Jacobs:

1. It's down to the wire, and slightly slimmer than it usually is, but it is ready for distribution by Friday lunchtime just as it always is.

2. After Gavin picks up a copy, he looks around for Julia to tell her, hey, fair play for getting it done, but she's not in the canteen, and when they have a class together that afternoon she's busy scribbling away and doesn't look over in his direction once, so he gives up.

3. There are two typos – one misspelling of 'principal' as 'principle', and one instance of both a semi-colon and comma being used. Julia notices this immediately after it's gone to print, and spends the rest of the day distressed about it. When Gavin notices her scribbling, it has nothing to do with

what their teacher's talking about and everything to do with trying to keep herself distracted. She's making lists of future story ideas for the paper and trying to figure out who she might be able to ask to contribute in the future.

4. No one else notices the typos, except Will, but mainly he's irritated by the fact that Julia's cut some lines out of his satirical piece about public sector workers. He sends a snarky message to her after school, even though he's in that same class with her, and she composes various drafts of a response (ranging from a calm, reasonable defence of public sector workers, thinking of her parents and also the teachers at their school, to a definition of 'satire' copy-and-pasted from Wikipedia) before saying politely that she of course understands how frustrating it is to have a piece edited without getting to discuss it first, but that there simply wasn't time in this instance to do so.

5. Deb says, 'Wow, I can't believe you actually got it done,' not managing to actually utter the word 'congratulations'.

6. Lorraine has been deliberately not paying attention to any newspaper-related talk this week, and spends lunchtime in the library (fortunately, Gavin and Sally are not there) catching up on homework, so doesn't

even realise there's a new issue until later in the day. She feels too self-conscious to pick up a copy. It'd be pathetic, she thinks. She doesn't want to look like she misses it.

7. Julia wants to feel proud, but instead she's just exhausted.

Chapter Twenty-Six

Julia. Julia. You need to lose weight. You need to be thin. Come on. Listen to me.

There is a word the shrinks love using. It is 'resilient'. The idea seems to be that some people, better people, have thick outer shells and don't let things bother them. Don't let the voices in.

Except it's a lie, because what they want is for you to let their voices in, to overpower your own.

I'm not a shrink, I'm on your side.

But even though she hears me, she's distracted, she's busy: she's working on the third issue of the newspaper, and it's almost the mid-term break, and she has homework to do and reading to catch up on and a college open day to decide whether or not to attend and all of these things swirl around in her head.

Tired, too, though. So I'm waiting. The moment is so close I can almost taste it.

Friday evening. Julia has a week off school ahead of her, all her homework done, a new issue of *The Richmond Report* on the kitchen table at home. Most of her friends will be at Gavin's house tonight for drinks before heading out to a club, but she's staying in.

Sure you're not gonna come tonight?? Deb messages.

Yeah, wrecked! Sorry.

Nothing about Sally. She hasn't wanted to ask. Deb would know if they're still together, or if it was just a fling, but Julia's afraid to know the answer. Is it better if they are, if Sally's the new Lorraine? Or if Gavin's just running around with every girl in sight?

It's easier to focus on the words on the page than the stories in her own life.

A key turns in the door. Her mum's footsteps; she'd know them anyway, even if her dad wasn't on another late shift. 'Hey, pet,' she says when she comes into the kitchen.

They are not a terribly touchy-feely family, but her mum smiles at her. (When was the last time my mother smiled at me?) 'Good day?'

Julia shrugs. 'Yeah, it was fine.' Without being asked, she pours a cup of tea for her mum.

'You're a star. Is Grace upstairs?'

'Yeah, she's asleep. How was your day?'

Her mum sighs heavily.

I don't know what normal mother-daughter conversations sound like. For obvious reasons. But when Julia's mum talks about her day, and the stresses of her job, and how tired she is, it doesn't sound like she's talking to her child. 'And then he turns around and starts lecturing me on his rights under the law,' she says, eyes to heaven – if it existed.

'Nice that he's educating you,' Julia says, grinning. She's used to these stories: the petty criminals who think they know the law better than the people upholding it. Sometimes she even sees their side, though she'd never admit this to her parents.

'Some people! Jesus Christ.' A yawn, a stretch.

'Did you have dinner?' Now Julia sounds like my mother. I hate her a little bit for that.

Her mum shakes her head. 'I'll put something on in a second.'

'I'll do it, it's fine. Go have a little nap.'

'If I start napping I'll never wake up,' her mum says, but follows instructions: heads up to the master bedroom, removes shoes and half her uniform, falls onto the bed.

Downstairs, Julia looks at the copy of the newspaper left out on the table and wonders if either of her parents will ever read it. Read any of them.

Logic-brain: they're busy, they've demanding jobs, they've a fifteen-month-old in their late forties, when they thought they were almost finished raising kids.

Heart, heart, heart: sometimes she just wants her mum to be *her mum*.

This is the moment I think I have her, as she's heating up a lasagne for her mother. This is when she will look at the cheesy, meaty carbohydrate mess that her mum wants and will feel superior, because she'll know that she is better than that.

She's better than all of this.

I'm naive, because even as she heats up another portion for herself, I don't really think she's going to eat it – *not another dinner, Julia, for fuck's sake* – until she does, too fast, too tasteless, and follows it with a raid of the stacks of chocolate in her bedside locker.

Julia. Julia. What are you doing to me?

89

And then. And then. The wave of revulsion hits, so strong I can't tell if it's her or me: fat. Fat. Fat, ugly, useless, weak, disgusting. This needs to stop. This needs to stop, she thinks, she *knows*, and there's a panic in her chest pounding away, and oh God (metaphorically), it's beautiful, it's beautiful, it's beautiful.

Chapter Twenty-Seven

Recent search history from Julia's browser:

'minister for education reform'

'minister for education speech October 21'

'education funding cuts'

'ba journalism dcu'

'best journalism courses ireland'

'best journalism colleges uk'

'ba journalism + new media'

'dermot keenan irish news'

'summer journalism internship dublin'

'summer journalism internship london'

'guardian work experience'

'bmi calculator women'

'women in leadership how to take charge'

'women leading meetings'

'how accurate is bmi scale'

NOVEMBER

Chapter Twenty-Eight

Five weeks into Project Julia. 'I think it's going well,' I tell the Boss cautiously. I don't want her to be proud of me or anything. But it feels like Julia's finally listening. Nothing too drastic yet: she went out jogging with her mum a couple of times over the mid-term break, stupidly proud of being able to keep up; she's replaced crisps with celery sticks and a low-fat spread (a start, a start: she doesn't understand yet that it doesn't matter how awful celery tastes, that nothing will ever taste as good as skinny feels).

'That's good to hear,' the Boss says. 'Well done, Annabel.'

I swallow the tiny burst of pride. It's been so long since anyone said that to me. (Helen was the last, maybe, except then it was always: 'I'm so jealous.' But I knew what she meant.)

Her school skirt is still too tight on her, imprinting in red around her waist. If you can even call it that. But on this Friday, after another issue of the paper is ready and out in the world, she is determined.

Fridays are the safest. Gavin and Will and the others go to the gym during the week, or sometimes at weekends. Friday evenings, though, are for getting ready to go out. Deb and

Lorraine and some of the others are going to see some local band made up of earnest bearded young men ('Come on, come,' Deb implores; Julia claims she needs to babysit her sister). Maria, who complimented Julia on one of her articles at lunchtime, will be over at Patrick's house, pretending to care about some new game he's obsessed with. Sally is dropping hints to Gavin about doing something over the weekend, but Gavin, either being terribly crafty or just clueless, responds generically: he has homework, he might go out with the lads tonight, not sure yet.

Julia is only tangentially aware of everyone else's plans. She has her school PE tracksuit in her bag, and as soon as the day's over she changes into it and forces herself not to immediately take it off again. Like many of the sixth-year girls, she avoids PE whenever she can: even the thin girls don't like communal changing rooms.

(There will always be someone better. You employ more gymnastics to get in and out of your clothes without anyone seeing your body than you do in an entire PE class.)

Julia has a printout of the gym membership in her bag. Since the age of fifteen she's been allowed to use her parents' credit cards for anything she needs, so long as she pays them back: no questions asked. (Why would you question a daughter who mostly uses it to buy online subscriptions to the *New York Times* and hard-to-find books on Amazon? Suspicion is reserved only for girls who borrow their dad's credit cards to order weight-loss meds – girls who were never trusted to begin with.)

'This is your first time here, is it?' the pretty blonde at the reception desk says when she hands over the form.

Julia nods.

The blonde girl is in a tight purple T-shirt and leggings. Taut abs. 'Would you like to arrange your assessment now?'

'No, it's okay.'

There is something about Julia's voice here. It's quieter. This is not a space where she belongs. She knows it.

'Are you sure? They'll weigh you, show you how to use the machines, help you come up with a personalised –'

Julia's made up her mind as soon as the words 'weigh you' are mentioned. 'It's okay. Really.'

As soon as she swipes her new membership card and crosses the threshold, she wishes she'd taken the offer. She finds the lockers first and deposits her schoolbag there, then it's onto the machines.

She doesn't know what the etiquette is, but then, like a beacon, there's one that's free. She strides past a bunch of men and women in various stages of red-faced sweatiness, each on their own bit of equipment, and launches herself onto the cross-trainer.

This is Julia's first time in a gym. A treadmill would have been a better place to start. But this is the machine that's available. She puts her feet in but it starts to move and she slips, then clutches at the upper part for support. She is half-on, half-off, and in the scramble to right herself she feels like the stupidest person in the world.

'Do you need some help?' There is a not-terribly-cute man in his twenties watching her. Kind eyes.

'It's fine,' Julia says.

She is editor of her school paper. She is on track to get all As in her exams. She is going to go to college and kick ass. She cannot be defeated by the gym. She willpowers her way into the right position, and pumps arms and legs, staring straight ahead.

Don't look at anyone else. Don't cry.

It feels like she's been there for hours. *No pain, no gain, Julia.*

Her arms get tired first. She's not used to swinging them this way, putting any sort of demands on them. And then her legs start burning, her calves insisting: stop. Stop. Enough.

Never enough. Never enough.

She steps off the cross-trainer. Checks the clock. It's only been a few minutes.

She doesn't trust herself with anything too complicated, with anything that involves weights. The treadmills are all taken.

It's too much, this place of sweat and pushing through the pain. She can't do it. She crosses her arms over her belly and goes to collect her stuff.

Chapter Twenty-Nine

A memory. Not mine. Julia's. It slides into her head after the next newspaper meeting, the Monday after her failed gym workout. She watches Sally slide into a seat next to Gavin, full of hope and promise, and she tries not to snap out something like, 'This is a newspaper, not a dating service.' She has not eaten lunch yet. She will skip lunch if she is working through it, she's decided, instead of cramming a sandwich down her throat in the last five minutes of the break.

This memory is a few months old. Last spring. A long weekend, and Deb's over at Julia's house ranting about men. It's after her boyfriend, Patrick – now Maria's Patrick – has cheated on her but is insisting he still loves her. After call-me-Dermot has left Deb and her mum to go be with Sylvia, whom Deb will only refer to as The Slut. She turns to Julia and declares, dramatically, 'There are no good men left in the world.'

'There are some,' Julia says, slightly uncertainly. On principle she feels such statements are sexist, contributing to an ongoing sense of distrust of the opposite sex; it's like saying all women are evil/slutty/crazy. Not helpful, not feminist, not okay. On the other hand, good friend that she is, she's upset about the situation, too; she thinks it's completely shit.

'Name three,' Deb challenges.

'Uh – Gandhi.'

'Name three who are alive and in close proximity,' Deb amends, rolling her eyes.

'Fintan O'Toole,' Julia chances. She's just finished reading that day's *Irish Times* and he has a column in there that she nodded along to emphatically.

'Who? The journalist guy? No. Journalists are evil.' Call-me-Dermot floats in the air between them. 'And anyway, isn't he ancient?'

'He has a certain refined . . . stately look about him.' Julia's only half-kidding. She has a weakness for eloquent men, smart men. A good turn of phrase carries a lot of weight with her. There's a silvery politician in his fifties that she'll watch with fascination if he's on the news or some current events show; she doesn't agree with all his ideas, but he can make her laugh while making a point. (*Julia, Julia, do you have a totally dysfunctional relationship with your father or something?* I tap into her memories a little more, but it's all pats on the back and being proud of her doing well in exams. Like her mum, he doesn't worry about her: Julia's a good kid.)

'Stop it, I'll puke.' Deb scowls. 'Come on. Nice guys. Good guys. Ones we actually know.'

'Nice or good?' Julia asks.

'Both. They're the same thing.'

Julia can't look straight at her. There's something heavy in her chest. 'I think people can be very nice and charming without being decent human beings,' she says, addressing the wall.

Deb considers this, mentally making notes for a future advice column. 'Yeah, I suppose. Okay, good guys. Can you think of one, even?'

Maybe all the good guys are already taken. Snapped up by savvy girls. And then she has it. 'Gavin,' she says triumphantly.

Gavin.

Oh God, *Gavin*.

This is where it begins. Deb rolls her eyes and agrees, but insists that Gavin's the exception to the rule and the rest of them are monsters. Julia listens but the door's already opened, just enough to let something grow inside her. That night she begins cataloguing his positive qualities: eloquent, particularly when doing public speaking. Handsome, but not overly aware of it (minimal use of hair gel, etc.). Well informed about current events. Opinionated, but still polite. Loyal (to Lorraine, and to his friends) – this last one is both the clincher and the reason it can never happen.

There is a moment between them, a month or two later. Gavin is a friend; they hang out in the same group. The newspaper crowd, the student council crowd, the good-kid crowd (not that there's much of a bad-kid crowd in the Richmond School). They're at someone's house, someone on the paper in the year ahead of them at school, now off in college, and Julia's been watching Gavin all night, the way he drapes an arm around Lorraine's waist, or presses a kiss against her cheek. In quiet moments she allows herself to imagine Gavin being like that with her, and the yearning is delicious.

She indulges in it the way she indulges in junk food at home; it's never quite enough, but she wants it anyway.

In the sitting room, someone's discovered a DVD box set of some Scandinavian crime series, which half of them are paying attention to and the other half are chatting through. Julia focuses on the screen, and next to her Deb looks up from her phone. 'My dad's picking me up at half-eleven, do you want a lift?'

'No, thanks. It's out of his way,' Julia says.

Deb sighs. 'Yeah. But he won't say no, and it'll piss him off.'

'Oh, Deb.' She is torn between sympathy and saying, grow up, you're acting like a kid.

'I can't believe I have to spend the weekend with the two of them,' Deb continues. 'It's fucking ridiculous. And that bitch trying to be *nice* to me . . .'

'Nightmare,' Julia says, but her brain's not fully engaged; Gavin and Lorraine have just left the room looking serious, or rather, with him looking serious and her looking furious.

'I need another drink,' Deb decides, because unlike good-girl Julia and her fizzy orange, she has a glass that is more vodka than anything else. Julia accompanies her to the kitchen, and the tension is immediately palpable: Gavin with his hands in his pockets, earnest yet frustrated, and Lorraine with hands on hips and chin jutting out. As soon as she's aware of the girls, she storms off into the hallway. Deb chases after her.

'Are you all right?' Julia asks Gavin, all gentleness.

He shrugs, gives her a little, tight smile, and then she catches just the faintest glint of a shine in his eyes, and she's hugging him before she realises quite what she's doing.

'It's going to be okay,' she says. Not that she believes this, but she wants it to be true. So does Gavin.

She can't tell, but I can, now, what it does to him to have someone reassuring him like this. Alongside the tears he's blinking back, embarrassed, there's a wave of pure fondness rushing over him, affection that has nothing to do with Julia as a girl and everything to do with her as a friend. The boys are useless at these moments, offering up vagueness and beer and claps on the back.

They talk, post-hug, leaning against the kitchen counter. Lorraine wants to go, Gavin wants to stay; Gavin is happy to stay at the gathering solo, Lorraine insists they leave together. 'She just wants to spend time with you,' Julia says, deciphering the code.

Gavin sighs. 'Yeah. I kind of get that, but she – it's like I can't say anything right.'

Julia's heart breaks a little for him. 'Hey,' she says. 'You're a good guy. Remember that.'

Gavin looks at her. The possibility of a kiss dances around them, and they both know it, but Lorraine's presence hangs there, too, a non-negotiable barrier.

'Go talk to her,' Julia says, nudging him in the arm, hoping that Deb's conversation with Lorraine has been about talking her down and not riling her up. She watches him leave, and lets the almost-ness of the moment sink in.

She adores Gavin. Fantasises about him. But this is the right thing to do. Send him back to his girlfriend. This is the right thing to do. The safe thing to do.

Chapter Thirty

Coffee. Coffee is her friend. Julia's thinking about coffee and the newspaper and not her growling belly, because she is too fat and she deserves to feel hungry, when Mr Briscoe calls her up to his desk at the end of their English class on Wednesday.

'Julia. How's it going?'

She feels a flutter of panic as the rest of the class filter out to their break. Does he hear the rumblings? Or is this about the just-short-of-an-A-grade essay she got back yesterday?

'Fine,' she says.

'I'm sorry, I've been meaning to talk to you about this for a while . . . we need to get you a deputy.'

Not what she was expecting, but it comes as a slap. There isn't always a deputy editor. When she was given the job back in June, just before the summer holidays, it felt like a consolation prize for not being editor.

'Okay,' she says. 'Do you have someone in mind?' Not Deb, not Deb, not Deb.

'I wanted to discuss it with yourself,' he says, leaning back in his chair. 'I have one of the fifth years in my class, Sally . . .'

'No.'

Mr Briscoe raises an eyebrow, gestures for her to continue.

'She's not committed enough,' Julia says. 'She's a good writer, but I think she's better off just focusing on that rather than taking on a leadership role.' This sounds so terribly mature and reasoned that Mr Briscoe would be surprised to hear inside her head, which is full of not-Sally and there's-a-special-circle-of-hell-for-women-who-don't-support-other-women and it-can't-be-Sally-it-just-can't.

'That makes sense,' Mr Briscoe nods thoughtfully, and then suddenly I see what he's done. Sally is his token female suggestion. His actual shortlist: Frank, Will, Gavin. 'Is there someone else you think would be particularly good?'

Julia runs through everyone in her head several times before daring to say it aloud. Half hating herself for it. 'Gavin might be good, I suppose.'

'Grand.' That's another thing ticked off Mr Briscoe's list. 'Will I let him know, or do you want to?'

'Oh. You. You do it.' It comes out in a rush. 'I mean, I think it'd just feel more official if it comes from you.' She's flushing now. Doesn't want Gavin to know she suggested him. Doesn't want to have to approach him with good news and then wonder if the first person he tells will be Sally. Or Lorraine. Maybe they're still talking, secretly.

Her head is in a swirl of hypotheticals about Gavin's love life when she runs into him in the corridor. 'Just who I was looking for,' he says with a smile.

Does he know already?

'Do you remember what our economics homework was?'

Oh.

105

She reads out the information from her trusty notebook and watches him jot it down. His hair – she remembers what it's like to touch it. His mouth, his mouth – she looks at the curve of his lips, caught in neutral as he writes, and still so kissable.

'Thanks,' he says, looking up: catches her.

Eyes. He remembers.

'See you later,' she says. Escaping.

Too embarrassing is what this is. To think Mr Briscoe will tell him, oh, Gavin, you're the new deputy editor, Julia really wanted you, and he'll think, oh, God, this is awkward, she fancies me, the fat girl fancies me, how do I get out of this while still being a nice guy?

So don't be fat, Julia. It's the only thing I can tell her that might work.

Chapter Thirty-One

It is the tiniest thing, but it makes me proud: when Julia puts on her smart black skirt one Saturday morning, she doesn't need to hold her breath and suck in to fasten it shut. True, it is still tighter than it might be, and in a size large enough to terrify me, but it is progress. Slow and steady.

She's persuaded the school to cover her entrance fee to a Women in Leadership conference this weekend. The whole thing sounds disgustingly inspirational: there are women from all different fields talking about their careers and strategies and blah blah blah. Julia's going to write about it for the paper, but has also pitched it to her local newspaper: a teen take on leadership advice today. (The local newspaper consists mostly of regurgitated press releases and local-interest pieces, but never mind that.) Advice from once upon a time: *if you have a story, try to get at least three articles out of it.* It was a revelation, and seemed almost like cheating, until she saw how to change the slant, make it fit for different publications.

Today she feels like a real journalist. She has an old-style dictaphone in her handbag, even though her phone's recording app works just as well. When she walks into the conference centre, swarming with women from twenty-something up to sixty-something, in everything from tailored dresses and sleek suits to jeans, she breathes it all in.

Nervous. But the good kind. She gets her lanyard from the check-in desk and picks up a coffee before going into the first talk. Everyone's still milling around. Julia spots a woman, maybe her mum's age, already sitting down. Breathe in. Breathe out. 'Hi,' she says. 'I'm writing an article about the conference, would you mind if I asked you a few questions?'

Once she's done it once, it's easy. Interviewing skills. The thing is to let people talk. For a piece like this, you don't need to have an agenda just yet. You'll get the material and then analyse. Julia's predisposed to be in favour of these kinds of things – but she's prepared to listen.

She scribbles furiously during each talk, each panel; interviews women of different ages from different backgrounds during each coffee break. The last panel of the day is about women in engineering, and there's a drinks reception afterwards. She might go, she thinks. She was planning to go home, then go for a run (it is dark out so no one will see her), but she's eased into this. It's a collection of tantalising glimpses into possible futures. Julia imagines being confident in meetings where she presents her findings to a board mostly full of men; imagines calmly telling a colleague that she doesn't appreciate him commenting on her outfit; imagines being one of the speakers at one of these conferences down the line, editor of something important – the *Guardian*, maybe. Or *The Irish Times* if she stays in the country. Or maybe one of those super-smart edgy American magazines . . .

'Julia? I thought it was you.'

She jumps. She's just about to help herself to a glass of water – good girl, avoid the free wine – and there's Tracy Keenan. Deb's mother.

'Hi!' Julia's suddenly a little girl again.

'What are you doing here?' Tracy asks. Kindly, but it still makes Julia feel about eight years old.

'I'm, uh, writing an article about it.'

'Oh, for the paper? That's great.' Tracy has no plans to avoid the free wine; she has a half-empty plastic glass in hand. 'I hope it wasn't too boring. My work sent me.'

'I thought it was interesting.'

'They're all a bit intense, though, aren't they? Jesus, your one going on about the guy who was just trying to be nice . . . you need to learn to take a compliment, you know?'

That was one of Julia's favourite speakers. But she nods, frozen to the spot. 'Yeah.'

'I mean,' Tracy continues, reaching for another glass, and it occurs to Julia there was complimentary wine at lunch, too, 'at the end of the day you need to have a life, too, and most of us meet people in work. Especially at my age.' Conspiratorial, now. 'If I didn't dress up for work I'd be living like a nun these days.' She laughs, clutches at Julia's arm.

Julia smiles politely.

The problem, actually, is that she always liked Tracy. It'd be easier for her now to go along with all of this silly tipsy chat, but she feels too young and too old all at once.

'Go on, what's the scandal these days?' Tracy says. 'Deborah tells me nothing. Are you seeing anyone? God, do they still even call it that?'

'Sometimes,' Julia says, offering up another polite smile. 'I suppose everyone has their own phrase for it.'

'When I was your age,' Tracy begins, and Julia steels herself for the condescension, 'I hardly ever saw boys my own age. Convent school. Jesus. Terrible idea. You need to go out and enjoy yourself, Julia. Have fun. Don't be afraid of it.'

Maybe you should have *enjoyed yourself* more with your ex-husband, Julia thinks. Says nothing. Smiles. Makes excuses. Slips away, feeling the goodness of the day fade.

I know what's coming and I hate it. By the time she arrives home her handbag is stuffed with chocolate, crisps, popcorn, sugary treats. By the time she goes to bed, it's empty, and I have failed, failed, failed.

Chapter Thirty-Two

Julia sees it just before the meeting. She is reading the online edition of the *Irish News*, where she did her work experience, where Dermot's columns still appear every so often, and when she clicks on an article about youth mental health, she knows, even before she sees the by-line. Lorraine. Lorraine's controversial suicide piece, amended slightly, but there, picked up by a national newspaper.

She can imagine it: Dermot at Deb's birthday party handing over his business card, telling Lorraine to let him know how it all turns out with the story. Maybe even saying straight out, 'I'll pass it on to a few contacts of mine, see if we can get it a wider audience. Don't worry about the school. That's kids' stuff. You're better than that.' Maybe taking her for a celebratory glass of champagne once it got accepted . . .

'Important to get a real teen voice on this!' says one of the comments below the article, and even though Julia knows it is madness to read the comments, she can't help herself. Aside from a few nutters and some ranting about 'middle-class privileged brats' the vibe is generally positive, a collective *well done, Lorraine*.

It haunts her throughout the newspaper meeting, not helped by the dwindling attendance. Gavin's there, of course, her optimistic deputy, and Frank and Will and Deb have all made it, but Sally's sent a message saying she can't make it, and a few of the students in the lower years just aren't turning up. 'And, guys,' Julia says as she finishes up assigning the week's stories, 'do make sure you get everything in on time. If you can't, let me know. In advance.'

Deb tries not to roll her eyes at how seriously Julia takes all this. 'We're just doing one more before the Christmas holidays, right?'

It's the end of November. Julia frowns. 'We've three and a bit more weeks in school.'

'Yeah, but, come on,' Deb says.

'What?'

'Everyone has Christmas tests.'

'We don't, the third years don't – we'll manage,' Julia says, having already anticipated this. Exam years are spared Christmas tests and have their mock exams in February, I remember. 'And there's so much stuff to cover – Mrs Kearney's still arguing with the music teacher about what kind of songs the choir can do at the Christmas service, which is going to be a great jumping-off point to talk about . . .' Julia trails off, looking around the room. She has notes made for three issues before the Christmas break. She has a plan. But everyone's wearing expressions ranging from *are you kidding me?* (Will) to *sympathetic but really, come on, Julia, it's not happening* (Deb, Gavin).

Lorraine has a piece in the *Irish News* and Julia's contact at the local paper still hasn't got back to her to thank her for sending on the piece about the Women in Leadership thing and suddenly this all feels too much like kids' stuff. She's too tired to fight for it, and when her eyes meet Gavin's, she knows he's urging her to just go with the rest of them.

(But when she hesitates, he wonders should he say something, stand up for her, support his editor . . . support Julia? The way her face lit up when she talked about that choir story . . .)

Julia breaks eye contact. She doesn't need him stepping in here. 'Oh, you know what, it's crazy, you're right,' she says, trying to sound breezy. 'Sorry, guys, of course, one more issue, no one will be reading it after that. We'll put a note in next week's one saying we're back in January.'

The right decision to make, Will thinks, and I remember suddenly the tiniest of moments, saying I'd liked the movie we'd been watching, and him explaining to me why it was crap. It feels sharper now, weirdly, like it's only just happened. I don't think it upset me at the time. Easier not to argue. Easier not to care.

'That's everything, guys. See you later.' Julia busies herself with her notebook, scratching lines through plans for the issues that won't happen. She senses someone hovering even after everyone else has filtered out, and looks up eventually. There's a jolt of disappointment, shot through with relief, when she sees it's Deb.

'So that's good news, right?' Deb says. 'We can take it easy for most of next month.'

'Yeah.' Like that's what Julia wants.

'You should come over to mine next weekend. It's been ages, like, and I need to give you the latest news about The Slut.'

Something slams in Julia's chest. 'Yeah, maybe. I might have to mind Grace. I'll see.'

'Cool. Let me know. It's been ages since we had a good rant session. And trust me, this latest thing is ridiculous.' Deb's dying to – her thoughts, not mine – tell her.

'Can she even get more ridiculous?' Julia says lightly.

'She's pregnant. Can you believe it?'

Julia shakes her head. She can't.

Deb continues on about how insane it is that she's going to have a baby sister who's going to be nearly twenty years younger than she is, how her dad's way too old to have another kid (I bet call-me-Dermot would love to hear that), on and on and ignoring the fact that Julia doesn't want to hear this. She's trying not to listen. She wants to walk away, and is held in place only by social niceties.

I suddenly understand that this is how it works for them. Julia listens to Deb and lets her rant. Deb doesn't return the favour. Deb offers advice to the entire school in her little column, but never to Julia. Is it because she knows Julia refuses help or because she thinks Julia doesn't need it?

Julia really needs help. I see this, now, because no one else does. She gets a geography essay back with an A at the end; she sees Mr Briscoe after school, who tells her she's doing a great job. She gets an email from the local newspaper confirming the article will be in next week's edition. She goes home and helps her dad get the Christmas tree and decorations down from the attic.

And then she dives into junk food, a newly purchased stash. A whole bag of delicious treats she can't resist, her eyes blind to the calorie count – the girl who can't resist the printed word suddenly ignoring the information on the packaging – and all before dinner. Even without my body, I feel sick watching it.

I think of that line the adults always pull out when they want to really get to you. *Julia*, I think, *I'm not angry, just disappointed.*

Chapter Thirty-Three

You know how people say, you'll have plenty of time for sleep when you're dead? It's not true. You don't sleep. I don't, anyway. Maybe there's some space beyond – fluffy clouds, flowing white dresses, all that jazz – where you can close your eyes and snooze.

But here and now, there's just being awake. Not quite like the buzzing in your head that keeps you up all night – *must be better must be better must be lighter* – but not like being bright and sparkly and ready to leap out of bed before the alarm even goes off, either. Not that I was ever much of a morning person.

So we have our catch-up meeting, the Boss and I, late at night when Julia's asleep, her belly stretched with late-night snacks. And I get asked the question I don't want to answer. 'How's it going?'

I send something that feels like a sigh in her direction. 'I thought I was getting through to her but . . . it's not working.'

The Boss throws out thoughtful vibes. 'Are you sure you're trying as hard as you can?'

'I'm trying,' I snap. 'I'm doing the best I can.' I used to be good at doing my best. Best at not eating. Best at hiding it.

Best at getting so thin that it killed me. Beat that.

Is it my fault Julia's fallen off the food-wagon?

'Okay. Do you think it's a lost cause, then? If you're doing your best and it's not working?' She pauses, for effect. 'Do you want to give up?'

'That means I don't get my message through,' I say. Almost sulkily. I know how it works. But one final from-beyond-the-grave message to my family doesn't feel like that much to ask. It doesn't feel like I should have to work this hard for it.

'Annabel. You have to earn the connection, you know that.'

Suddenly I miss being able to cry. What a strange thing to miss. 'Isn't there anything else I could do?'

'Not right now.'

'Come on. There's got to be lots of other sad fat girls out there *in need of help*.'

There is almost a frown. 'There are plenty of souls in need of help –'

A flutter of relief. 'So give me one of them.'

'But Julia's the only one right now who can earn you your connection. She's yours, Annabel.'

I don't want her. I seize on the glimmer of escape. 'The only one right now?'

A pause. 'Maybe in a few years, there might be someone else who's a match for you – or a few decades. We can't say.'

I can't wait that long. I hate her. I hate this.

'I'll try harder,' I say, longing to grit my teeth. 'I'll get through to her.'

'Good. I'm glad to hear that.' She pauses. 'I know it's hard, but it'll be worth it when you get to pass on your message.'

And then she's gone.
Have to do better. Have to try harder.
I wish so much I could just sleep.

Chapter Thirty-Four

Wednesday afternoon, on her way to the newspaper office, Julia runs into Lorraine in the corridor, tiny Lorraine with her gym bag setting off for a session on all those complicated machines Julia doesn't want to think about.

'Hey,' Julia says awkwardly, not having spoken to her much over the past few weeks, not one-on-one. She notes the gym bag, immediately feels self-conscious.

'Hey.' Lorraine nods in the direction of the office. 'Staying late?'

'Yeah.' Julia pauses. 'Congrats on the *Irish News* piece, that's brilliant.'

Lorraine glows with a satisfaction that goes beyond pride. 'Aw, I can't believe you saw it.'

Like Julia doesn't read at least five newspapers a day. 'It's great,' she says. 'Did, um, Mr Keenan put in a good word for you?'

'He just sent it on to the editor.' Lorraine is breezy. No. Outwardly breezy. Inwardly smug. She's *delighted* with herself. Who cares about the stupid school paper when she has work appearing in the real world? 'And she said she'd be interested in seeing more of my stuff.'

Julia swallows back the jealousy. She swallows the words 'I kissed Gavin', even though she wants to fling them at Lorraine now. Her brain knows it's just a petty, pointless attempt to even the playing field. Lorraine is winning. Girls like Lorraine will always win. 'That's amazing,' she says. She tries to smile. It's a valiant attempt.

Lorraine accepts the compliment. She sails off in a cloud of satisfaction. Let Julia be editor. Fine. Let her work alongside Gavin and the rest of them. Lorraine couldn't care less.

It is, I have to admit, interesting to see how talented people are at convincing themselves the lies they whisper in their heads are true.

Chapter Thirty-Five

'Ugh, I can't believe Mrs Bennett gave us so much to do.' Deb scowls at her mid-morning snack. She's moved away from her daily chocolate mousse, but hasn't strayed too far; Julia can smell the brownie with its similarly intoxicating scent. The kind that makes your mouth water.

If I had a body I'd nearly be hungry myself . . . but you can't let yourself obsess over what other people are eating. You're better than them, stronger than them. I tell Julia not to notice, but she's already working hard to snap herself out of it. Good girl. There might be hope for her yet.

'Just because she's done this all before doesn't mean we have,' Deb continues through a mouthful of brownie. She's careless with her bites, no precision whatsoever. 'That essay's going to take ages.'

Julia sits there, saying nothing. Deliberately. It's Thursday break time. She's waiting.

Deb looks at her. 'What? It's ridiculous, we've ten million things to do at the moment.'

Julia shoots her what she hopes is a pointed look – a slight raise of her eyebrows, the corner of her mouth tightening.

'Shit. It's Thursday.'

Well done, Deb.

Julia feels the urge to cry suddenly. She wants to be cold and disapproving and instead her tear ducts are threatening to revolt, turn her into a weeping mess. 'Yeah,' is what she says.

'How desperately do you actually need the piece?' Deb says, with a little wince.

Julia cannot believe this. She can't believe Deb's actually trying to wriggle out of it. Her mouth opens slightly, and she's waiting or hoping for some kind of epiphany on Deb's part, but all she's getting is that same trying-to-be-let-off-the-hook face. 'You said you'd do it.' The words don't shake on their way out. She's proud of her control. If only she could reclaim some of this for her eating.

'I know, but this week . . . it's mental,' Deb says.

Julia glares. 'All the weeks are, aren't they? That's why we're only doing one more issue before Christmas.'

Deb's jaw drops. 'Oh my God, are you seriously pissed off with me about that?'

Julia says nothing. Already feels she's revealed too much.

'Come on. It's just the school paper, don't stress yourself out about it.'

Julia just nods. 'Okay. I'll see you later.' Gets up.

'Aw, Julia, come on, don't go off in a huff.'

Julia turns to ice. 'I'm not *going off in a huff*. I'm going to the office because I need to write up something to replace the piece you were supposed to send me.'

'It's just this week . . . it's crazy for everyone.'

'It's always crazy for everyone, apparently.'

122

'Well, you know what? Some of us have more going on in our lives than the paper.' Deb regrets it as soon as the words are out of her mouth.

'Right,' Julia says tightly.

'Come on, I didn't mean it like that. You just take this so seriously. I know Lorraine used to get stressed about it, but . . .'

The mention of Lorraine is like a punch. Lorraine, who had Julia there to help proofread and make decisions when she was editor, instead of Gavin trying to keep everyone happy. Lorraine, who has articles appearing in real newspapers. Lorraine, who is tiny and skinny and successful and everything that Julia is not.

'See you later,' Julia repeats in a monotone. She grabs her bottle of water, and leaves. Only six minutes left of their break; she knows as soon as she's left the room that it's a waste of time, but she can't go back in there.

The sense of betrayal is overwhelming, a pounding in her chest. When she gets to the newspaper office, she wants to do something dramatic – fling herself onto the ground, maybe – so the presence of teachers is an unwelcome intrusion.

'Julia,' Mrs Kearney says.

Mr Briscoe turns around. 'Hi.' He nods towards the copier. 'The other one's out of service, so we're using this one today.'

Julia nods wordlessly. She knows this is always an option, but the breaking of the unwritten rule that the teachers leave this machine to the sixth years for newspaper stuff, for student council business, for anything else they need, makes her feel like the bigger kids have come along to the playground and commandeered the swings.

'You seem to be getting on well in your new role, Julia,' Mrs Kearney says.

Julia remembers her good-student face and smiles. 'Thank you.'

'You're not finding it too much?'

Julia feels it like a slap, regardless of the intent. 'No, it's fine.'

'I know it's an exam year, and you need to make sure you're getting some kind of balance . . .'

Julia nods along. Meanwhile Mr Briscoe observes her, thinks that she looks like she's lost a bit of weight. I suppose she has, despite this week's gluttony. Good for her, he thinks. Another few pounds and she'll look much better.

No, Mr Briscoe, you're not allowed to think that. It's none of your business how she looks, how much she weighs. She's not doing this for you. You're there to teach her English.

The surge of protectiveness takes me by surprise. Women are not just there to be looked at, I think, and it's a thought Julia would approve of. For fuck's sake. I'm spending too much time in her head. Need to be around someone who gets me. Need to escape.

Chapter Thirty-Six

I expect to appear near Helen, at home or in hospital, but this is a mass of blue. Tiles and splashing and laughter. A swimming pool.

I know this place. It's not too far away from the school, this leisure centre that no one uses for leisure. Julia's mother has a membership here, though she hasn't had much of a chance to use it since Grace was born. Deb's mother uses the gym here, powering her way through workouts so she can stay in shape for her new boyfriends.

Half the pool is roped off for adults determinedly making their way up and down the lanes, mostly saggy-fleshed pensioners. The other half has kids taking a swimming class, a couple of instructors with whistles around their necks keeping an eagle eye on things.

My parents stopped me from coming to places like this. Dad spoke to receptionists and managers, filling them with lies about how sick I was and how doctors had insisted I not be allowed to engage in strenuous exercise, and that I didn't know how to do anything in moderation.

Moderation is for the weak. For other people. I watch one grey-haired woman, all wobble beneath the sheen of her navy swimsuit, doggy-paddle her way to the deep end. Why am I here? To make me disgusted at how slow she's moving, make me wish I could dive in and cut through the water like a fish, sleek and fast, burning away fat with every stroke?

I can't see the point of it, but when I try to leave, I'm pulled over to the edge of the pool, to the entrance to the changing rooms.

'Imogen,' a woman in a smart-but-cute blouse with trousers – classic primary school teacher attire – says to the girl just around the corner, 'come on. Everyone else is already out there and having a great time.'

I can't get around the corner. I push and push and it's like being back at my house.

No response. 'Imogen. What's the problem? Your teacher last year said you were a great swimmer.'

A jolt. I'd forgotten that. Imogen at the beach, the last holiday I remember, racing down to the water's edge to splash around. I see Imogen at three, in a different swimming pool, with orange armbands keeping her afloat, and me holding onto her anyway, just in case, her big blue eyes lighting up with delight as she kicked and bobbed.

The teacher taps her foot against the wet tile. 'Okay, I'm going to have to call your parents about this.'

'Fine,' a sulky voice comes. A teary voice.

Leave her alone, you bitch. Or give her a hug or something. Don't be like this.

I step inside the teacher-brain, because it's all I can do. She thinks about how she knows Imogen has had a tough time of it lately, that she knows she's lost her sister ('lost', like I disappeared down the back of the couch), but also that this is just a lot of hassle she could do without.

126

That's my sister. Not hassle.

An echo, then, of Imogen knocking on my door. And I can't be here. I can't, I can't, I can't. I wrench myself from the magnetic pull of this space, go back where I belong. Helen. Helen is sitting in a chair, pulling at her sleeves. The specific room isn't familiar but the situation is. Counselling. Joy.

I assess her counsellor. Female, grey hair, mid-sixties. Reminds me of Dr Fields, but is not her, for which I am very grateful.

'You mentioned your friend Annabel,' the counsellor prompts.

Clearly I have spectacular timing.

'Yeah,' Helen says heavily.

Why are you talking about me, Helen? Why are you wasting precious seconds of this session talking about me when you could be explaining about your stepfather and what he does to you? Is he still doing it? That's what you need to tell them. Tell them. Keep telling them until they listen.

'Tell me about her.' A nice open-ended invitation there.

'What do you want to know?' It's good to see Helen hasn't totally given in to this crap.

'Where did you meet?'

'In hospital.' Helen smiles, a little. But seems sad. 'We used to give each other tips.'

'About food?' the counsellor checks. Like she doesn't know.

'Yeah.'

'Annabel's anorexic,' she says.

'No,' Helen snaps. 'Annabel *was* anorexic. Was. Past tense. Then she had heart failure. And then she died.' She thinks of the coffin. My coffin.

127

The counsellor takes a moment. 'It's one of the outcomes of the disease,' she says solemnly.

Oh, screw you. You think Helen doesn't know that? You think they don't tell us these things in hospital, listing them off and looking all serious and sounding like they're coming from far away? You think we can't hear them? We hear them. We just know, deep down, where there is truth and beauty and purity, that they're wrong.

'It's unfortunate,' she continues, 'and very sad. I know you must be very upset about her death.'

'I'm not upset,' Helen hisses.

No. She's not. She's angry. She's angry I proved that they were right. She's angry that I'm gone.

Helen, Helen, can you hear me? I know she can't, I know I've no access, but I try anyway. I have to. *It's okay. Remember how we wanted to carve away everything so we could just be? This isn't what I wanted exactly but I wasn't wrong. I need you to know we weren't wrong.*

'What would you say to Annabel if she were here right now?' the counsellor wants to know.

Don't give in to this crap, Helen. You don't have to say anything. They want you to get fat, they want you to lose control and be just like them. You don't need to do what she says. You're stronger than that.

Helen closes her eyes. 'Annabel, have you ever considered –' Her voice goes all shaky.

Don't say it don't say it.

'– that you might have a bit of a problem with food?'

And then she starts to cry.

128

Chapter Thirty-Seven

Wrong. Wrong. *I was powerful, Helen. I was powerful and you're jealous, you're jealous I didn't give in to them, that I was stronger than you.*

We taught each other all our best tricks.

I'll teach them to Julia. I'll show her.

After Imogen, after Helen, dealing with Julia's lunchtime cravings is easy in comparison. Her stomach growls. *You don't need to eat,* I snap at her. *You're too fat already. No chance of starvation.*

'Heya,' Gavin says to her after one of their afternoon classes, 'are you hanging around later to go through the articles?'

She nods. 'Yeah – see you there?'

He grins, and despite herself there's a stupid flutter in her belly. They've avoided deep, meaningful conversations over the past few weeks, but they click over the newspaper stuff, once they have it laid out in front of them. It's *nice*, is what it is: she's getting used to being around him, just the two of them, in a way that isn't just two people chatting at a party with other people drifting in and out of their conversation.

After school, in the office, he picks out some indie band for them to listen to as they work. 'This is really good,' he says, scrolling down through a piece by one of the first years.

'Yeah, I know. Except way too many adjectives.'

'I bet he has Mr Briscoe. Remember that thesaurus exercise we had to do?'

Julia shakes her head. 'No, I – oh, wait. Yeah! That was painful.'

'I think you mean excruciating, or possibly agonising.' Gavin's face is solemn.

'Debilitating.'

'Grievous.'

Julia's impressed. 'Vexatious,' she says triumphantly.

Gavin holds up his hands in defeat. Grins.

Back to work, and they're both now in sufficiently good moods to sing along to the music.

'They're really good,' Julia says.

'Yeah, they did a gig here last weekend, it was brilliant. Really impressive live.'

Julia's not sure what to say to this. 'Who'd you go with?' she asks, and then wants to take it back instantly.

'Ah, just the lads.' This is the truth – it was Gavin and Frank and a mutual friend of theirs from another school – but Julia's paranoid. She imagines Gavin and Sally holding hands. (A quick tap into Gavin's head tells me this is not the thing to worry about. Both he and the mutual friend did some random kissing of random girls towards the end of the night, as Frank shuffled awkwardly and checked his phone and stared straight ahead at the band.)

130

She makes a non-committal noise, a little acknowledgement that she's heard him, and then asks him to proofread the piece she put together at lunch to replace Deb's. This is not quite the stuff love stories are made of, she thinks, but when they finish up she's disappointed. She can feel it in her chest.

'See you tomorrow,' Gavin says, and for a second it seems like there might be a hug, but there isn't.

'See you,' she echoes.

At home, she is at the computer, checking the news of the day, when the Gavin-stalking begins. She doesn't call it that, but that's what it is. She is grateful it's dark outside; this feels like a night-time activity. *Not like you're looking at porn, Julia, good grief.*

But it might as well be, for her: it feels illicit and wrong but also giddying to click through years of photos. Plenty of pictures of him with Lorraine, but there are group shots, too. Gavin, Will and Frank at the park one summer. Click. Gavin, Deb, Patrick, Julia – some school event. Click. Lots of people in this one. A party. Gavin with his arm around Lorraine. Patrick in the middle of telling a story, his hands blurry. Will and a thin, fair-haired girl, make-up hiding how bad her skin is. Click, and then Julia goes back.

If I could start shaking I would. There is something destabilising in me, something tearing at me. That photo.

It's me.

I hardly even remember that party. Everything – everyone – else seemed grey and distant for so long. Julia frowns at the photo – she knows she's met the girl, but she's not sure if it was just that night, if it's just some girl who was with Will for a while. And then it clicks: the girl who used to be in school with them, who was often out sick . . . Andrea? Anne-Marie?

Annabel. Annabel McCormack. When it comes to her, Julia checks her name on Facebook but can't immediately find anyone who might be her. Of course, there are people without profile pictures of themselves – cats or cartoon characters – so she might be this girl or that one, all hidden to the public. She tries to remember if they were told about Annabel leaving, or if she's seen her around since; maybe she's repeating the year after missing so much school.

She goes back to the photo, curious to see if it'll remind her of someone she might have passed by in the corridors, but instead what she sees is something she wants. Thin. This is not an airbrushed photo of a model. This is a girl she knew once, if vaguely, a real girl.

And our memories collide and I'm back there at that party. With Will, who I don't know that well apart from the sex, but that keeps him happy. I'm tired, thinking about going home, and all these people seem so vibrant and energetic. Gavin and Will talk sports and his girlfriend, Lorraine, gives me a conspiratorial eye-roll. It's one of those moments where I know I should think that boys will be boys, and just run with it, but I've never been able to be like other girls.

Behind me, Deb, who always eats a chocolate mousse at break time, understands exactly how to be one of those girls. 'Do you think he likes me? I should go talk to him, right? I should just go over there and start chatting and see what happens.'

'Of course he likes you,' her best friend Julia says. 'Don't freak out.'

132

I turn around to watch as Julia grins. Julia, slim in a red dress. Her hair is down, her eyes bright. She nudges Deb towards Patrick, and then notices me. 'Hey, Annabel. How's it going?'

'Good,' I say.

'Having a good night?'

'Yeah.' I feel I should say more. I don't know what to say, what I can add to this conversation. I am not Julia, full of life and energy and opinions. She starts talking to Will about work experience, which everyone's just finished up a week of; she is full of the buzz of a newsroom. I fade in and out, my memories of a grey office already hazy; what did I do all week, exactly? Gavin and Lorraine join in, earnest and eager.

I have nothing to say. I nod. I think about how many calories there are in an apple.

Once the conversation shifts and the group breaks up, once it's just Will looking at me again, I say, 'I'll be back in a minute.'

I go upstairs, find a bathroom. Look in the mirror. Look away. And then there's a voice outside, a giggle. 'Yeah, I'm at the party . . . it's going okay . . .'

I open the door. It's Julia, her back turned to me, one hand in her hair. 'I miss you, too,' she says, her voice breathy. A pause, a laugh that is not quite a girlish giggle but sounds older, knowing. 'Yeah, okay, give me twenty minutes to get there.'

She doesn't see me. I am barely aware of her then, because seventeen-year-old me doesn't know that one day I'll be this girl's spirit helper or whatever the hell you want to call it. Downstairs, I pass by Deb and Patrick, lips locked, and when I return to Will he puts his arms around me and says, 'Let's get out of here.' I know what he really means, but it's fine by me.

Now, Julia stares at the picture again and wonders what happened to Annabel. They hardly spoke, she remembers; she was the quiet type and didn't get involved in any of the things Julia spent her time on. But she'd probably know if she was still in the school . . . she must have moved, perhaps been gently encouraged to try out a less stressful environment. Not unheard of; Julia remembers seeing certain less desirable students vanish after their exams in third year. She's about to jot down notes for a potential story about this, when the photo calls to her again.

Look at her there, so thin, Julia thinks. Look at her. Look at her.

She looks. I can't. I can't.

Except. Except. It all collides for me suddenly, in a glorious rush of realisation. Julia's earnest Women in Leadership stuff, and Lorraine getting her article in the paper, and Helen and me swapping secrets.

This is what they mean by epiphanies. I am almost thinking in exclamation points.

Julia needs a mentor. She needs a role model. She needs –

She needs to be inspired. By me.

DECEMBER

Chapter Thirty-Eight

Recent search history from Julia's browser:

    'homelessness christmas dublin'

    'how to help homeless christmas dublin'

    'annabel mccormack'

    'annabel mccormack richmond school'

    'annabel mccormack dublin'

    'calories in bananas'

    'best low-calorie snacks'

    'dermot keenan irish news'

    'lorraine carolan irish news'

'annabel maccormack'

'annabelle mccormack'

'annabelle maccormack'

'annabel mac cormack'

'best calorie count apps'

Chapter Thirty-Nine

I am not an easy girl to find online. Being dead doesn't help, of course. Nevertheless, journalistic Julia has sent friend and follow requests to various Annabels online, and two of those are undoubtedly winging their way into an email account I can't incorporeally check. I wonder how long it will take before it shuts down, or whether hopeful and barely literate con artists will keep trying to wrangle bank details out of a dead girl indefinitely.

There's only one thing she has skimmed over and not clicked through to, thinking – like I used to, I suppose – death notices don't apply to teenage girls. Vaguely at the back of her mind, *that* Annabel McCormack is as far removed as the one she finds a reference to on an American genealogy site, who died over a hundred years ago.

This week, the last issue of the newspaper before Christmas, Julia's been keeping to the plan: no lunch. She doesn't quite think, Annabel wouldn't eat lunch (though she wouldn't), but there I am hovering behind her eyelids. Me with Will at that party. Thin. Thin. Thin.

(Not even at my lightest, but still something for her to aspire to, for now.)

In class, Julia makes notes for the articles she has yet to write, and hopes the teachers don't call on her. There are benefits to being a good student even by the already-high Richmond School standards: she can get away with a few rounds of not raising her hand to offer an answer or opinion and no one feels the urge to make sure she's still engaged with the material.

Deb slips out of their shared classes without talking to her, palling around with Lorraine instead. New girl Maria's been watching this, getting traumatic flashbacks to her last school, an all-girls hell-hole, when she's not being groped by Patrick in the corridors between classes.

'Hey, Julia,' she says, catching up to her at the end of the day, 'you up to anything this evening? I'm having a couple of people over to watch a movie if you want to come.' Or at least she is as of about ten seconds ago.

Julia's tempted, but she has the paper. 'Sorry, I've got to get this issue of the paper sorted.'

Maria nods. She gets it: she can tell Julia's not just brushing her off. 'Sure, no worries.'

'Maybe over the weekend or something?' Julia suggests.

'I can't,' Maria says apologetically. Genuinely. 'I'm in this Christmas play next week and we've our final rehearsals all weekend.'

They look at each other and grin. Julia realises it's the first time she's smiled all day. Maybe all week. 'Busy girls,' she says.

'Good thing there's no important exams this year, right?' Maria says.

Julia laughs, and then Maria joins in.

'Good luck with the paper,' Maria says once the laughter stops and they're just a second away from an awkward moment.

'Thanks. Good luck with the play.' Julia's about to turn away, and then adds, 'Hey, send me on the details. I'd love to go see it. Or get someone to review it for the paper, even.'

'Get someone kind,' Maria says. Another grin. She's sunshine, this girl. I wonder if she knows that she's only at this school because a girl died.

The good mood, the optimism of potential new friendships, clings to Julia as she unlocks the newspaper office. Her inbox loads on the computer screen. Maybe, despite flaking out last week, Deb's got her stuff ready for this week – maybe she spent all of lunch writing it and not hanging out with Lorraine. Maybe Sally's actually submitted the piece she promised to do via text message on Tuesday. Maybe the world is a place full of people like her and Maria, who take commitments seriously . . .

The rush of disappointment comes hard and fast, followed by a sense of inevitability. She can't depend on Deb. Can't trust her. Julia finishes her mug of coffee and leaves the door open while she jogs down to the kitchen to make more. Last issue. Last issue of the calendar year, anyway. She has this. She can do it. She can do it.

When Gavin passes by, he looks in – they haven't made specific arrangements for this week but he figures they don't need to, at this stage. But she's not around, so he messages: *Still need me for newspaper stuff today?*

It's the wrong question to ask. Need. It sends her into a spiral of insecurity – is that what he thinks, that she *needs* him, like a clingy pathetic delicate helpless creature? – followed by indignation. She replies with: *It's all good!*

Insight from the spectre at the anti-feast here: she'd be a lot less sensitive about Gavin's word choice if she didn't still have the memory of that kiss, that potential, that hope, in her heart.

Gavin shrugs, moves on down to the computer lab to play around with the video editing software. He's got some raw footage from school matches that he wants to take a look at, maybe arrange into a short documentary if he has enough stuff. There's a lot you can do with a smartphone, but he wants it sharp, professional. For a moment I imagine what Gavin could do with his body if he applied this ambition to it, rather than depending on his semi-regular gym visits, but the thought quickly bores me: I've never been that interested in men's bodies.

On her way back upstairs to the office, Julia texts her parents to remind them she'll be home late tonight. Her dad's the first one to reply this time. He has a standard *OK!* response ready to go. He's just on his way home from work, texting in the car even though he knows he shouldn't; like many of his colleagues he commits many minor infractions of the law on a daily basis. He is thinking about the girl today, two or three years older than Julia, caught up in this morning's domestic assault situation. The boyfriend was the one to ring the police, but as soon as they arrived it was clear they were both at fault. Things smashed everywhere, both of these kids – he thinks of them as 'kids' even though they're legally not – with blood on their faces. Both of them still stumbling and drunk from the night before, the stench of it off them . . .

So every time he gets a message from his daughter keeping him posted about her whereabouts, he thanks God (sorry, Julia's dad, not sure he has much, if anything, to do with it) he has a daughter like Julia. Someone who's managed to get to almost eighteen without ever causing him any trouble. He's lucky, he knows; he can only hope that things with Grace will go as smoothly. Harder being an older parent; Grace wasn't planned but it's easier – if only slightly – knowing that at least he and his wife don't need to worry about their elder daughter.

Meanwhile, that elder daughter they think is so great downs another cup of coffee. She has a second one ready to go. Efficient. She's all about the efficiency. The rush starts to hit her. She types and rearranges and formats, trying not to let the empty space deter her. This being the last issue hasn't prompted everyone to give themselves one big push before collapsing, like you might before an exam; it's more like the last day of school where there's not a chance of getting any work done.

The clock says eight twenty-seven. Too soon. She needs more time.

'I'll be out of here in a few minutes, don't worry,' she says to the caretaker when he stops by, smiling, and then a few minutes later locks the door from the inside and turns out the light. The blinds on the window that look out onto the corridor are already closed, but she sinks down to the floor anyway. The adrenaline kicks in when she hears the footsteps along the corridor, and then the turn of the doorknob. The movie version would have the door swinging open, and the caretaker brandishing a breadknife, and everyone would learn a valuable lesson about the dangers of being a teenage girl on your own after dark, but he just nods and moves on.

Staying @ Deb's for the night, hope that's ok! Jx

Her mum and dad receive the text and reply in the affirmative. Then she gets to work. She's in the zone, caffeinated and buzzy, convinced she can do anything.

Chapter Forty

Gavin is at school early on Friday morning. Unusual for him – he's not a morning person, which is not on Julia's list of his admirable qualities but I think should be. You might call this early arrival destiny, you might call it fate, or you might call it getting out of the house before the plasterer arrives to fix the ceiling in their downstairs bathroom. At any rate, he's there shortly after the building opens up, along with a handful of others. Will's there in supervised study up in the library, and Maria and Carolyn are among the crowd in early-morning detention, a particularly beloved punishment of Mrs Kearney.

Gavin's there heading up to the computer labs when he notices the light in the newspaper office is on already, and he's there to nudge open the door to reveal Julia sitting on the floor, her knees pulled up to her chest, her fingers massaging her temples. Next to her, the photocopier is churning out papers.

'Hey,' he says.

She looks up. Her eyes reveal both the quality and quantity of sleep she got last night – a couple of hours, her head on the desk, her neck at an awkward angle. 'Hi,' she says.

He closes the door behind him. 'So. When you said you didn't need any help . . .'

'Gav. Don't.' Exhaustion is trumping her righteous sense of self-sufficiency.

'I'm supposed to help you with all this stuff,' he says, guilt creeping up. 'Come on. It's my job.'

She says nothing.

He sits down next to her. She props her elbow up on her knee, rests her chin on her hand, turns towards him. 'Hi,' she says finally.

'Hi,' he echoes. He taps his shoulder. 'Come on. Nap time.'

'I'm not a child,' she mutters, only half irritated, and then sighs and gives in, resting her head on his shoulder. She's so tired. Her eyelids drift shut, and Gavin notices the apple scent of her shampoo, notices the way strands of hair are falling out of her ponytail.

It's actually kind of a cute moment. Which is exactly what Sally thinks when she opens the door, planning to apologise to Julia for not getting her stuff in – surprising revelation, she did genuinely have internet issues but has the piece done and on a memory stick if there's still time to squeeze it in – and instead finding her voice vanishing into the air.

Julia looks up first. 'Hey, Sally.' She's too sleepy to be grumpy.

'Hi,' she says coldly.

Julia waits for Gavin to shrug her off, throw out a typical this-isn't-what-it-looks-like line, but he just does his nod-smile thing. Sally spins on her heel and storms off, slamming the door behind her.

'You're not going to go after her?' Julia asks.

Gavin shakes his head. 'Nope.'

'Come on, Gav, she's upset, she probably thinks –' Julia doesn't want to say it out loud, in case it sounds too ridiculous.

'What?'

But it looks like she doesn't have a choice. 'She might think you're cheating on her with me or something.'

'I'm not *with* her,' he says.

'Oh.' And then, 'Does she know that?'

Gavin sighs. 'Yeah, of course she does. We weren't ever together, we just . . .' He gestures into the air.

'Fooled around a bit,' Julia supplies.

Gavin looks sheepish. Says nothing. Then, 'Well, yeah.' He's a little proud, if he's honest. It's an ego-boost, after years of being in a relationship, to know that other girls find him attractive.

'And what about Carolyn?'

'Carolyn?' Gavin's almost forgotten that. 'Carolyn's just . . .' He wants to say 'up for it', but thinks it might sound sleazy. 'Come on, you know what she's like.'

'And is that what you're like now?' It's a little sharper than she intended. 'Kissing whoever crosses your path? Who's convenient?'

'Julia.' To give him credit, he gets exactly what she means. 'That wasn't what I was doing with you at the party, okay?'

'This isn't about me,' she says, lying through her teeth. It's easy to argue this on behalf of others. 'It's just not a great way to treat people. What if Carolyn really likes you? And Sally's just gone off in a huff there.'

'That's not my fault.' He gets up now, leans against the wall.

'It kind of is.' Julia recognises the power imbalance, stands up too so she's not looking up at him.

'It is not. She was the one who decided to storm off.'

Julia shrugs. 'You could've handled it better.'

'I'm not going to *handle* her.'

'I didn't say *her*, I said *it*.' Julia is pedantic.

They're glaring at each other again, another classic almost-kiss moment. Will they, won't they . . . ? No, they won't.

Julia cracks this time. 'Look, I know you're just out of a relationship, I get it. I just think you need to be careful about using people as your –'

'Sorbet girls,' he says, over her 'rebounds'.

She flushes.

Confession: Gavin is growing on me. He's not saying it in a mocking way, not trying to make her feel uncomfortable. He's wondering, now, what her story is.

'Julia . . .' he says.

'Do you know what it's like to be with someone you really – you admire, you *love*, and find out you're just this – this *palate cleanser* for them?' Julia's voice cracks a little.

Gavin looks at her, realises he's never paid much attention to her relationships. Thinks about who it might be. And thinks about the girls, the girls he's kissed at gigs or in nightclubs, the girls he's upfront with: he's not ready for a relationship. 'That's not the deal with these girls,' he says finally. 'I'm not leading them on. I wouldn't do that.'

Julia wants to say: Gavin, you're lovely, you're kind, and when you kiss a girl you can be pretty sure she'll want more from you, because who wouldn't? But she's already too raw.

There's silence.

'Come on, I'll help you fold these,' Gavin says, indicating to the stack of newspaper sheets the photocopier's spewed out.

Julia doesn't need any help. So she thinks. But I know she does. From me. And maybe from him. Maybe just for this. So she lets him at it, and I don't try to talk her out of it.

Chapter Forty-One

I was never good with help either. But it always came from the wrong places. A pseudo-concerned teacher at school. The first doctor my mum brought me to. And then Dr Fields. Dr Fields, who always looked for the big explanation. 'You couldn't control your life changing every few years,' she said to me once, with her saying-wise-and-important-things face on. 'You were put into a new school, a new location, and you couldn't do anything about that. What you could control was what you put into your body.'

'That's it?' I said, so full of disdain for her I would have crushed her if I could. If my fists could close easily. 'That's the best you can do?' Plenty of people moved around lots. It was not the end of the world.

'Was it hard for you, to make new friends?'

I glared. 'What makes you think I wanted new friends?' I was strong. I was different.

'You didn't want new friends.'

I sat in silence.

'Did you miss your old friends?'

'This is beyond stupid.'

'Annabel –'

'There's no reason! I don't have a reason, okay?' Tears at the back of my throat.

It was inside, not outside. It was always like this. I could remember being seven or eight, pulling my school blouse against my belly, wondering if I looked fat. The fear of it. The terror.

'Annabel, I'm not saying that was what caused your eating disorder. There's a lot about the brain we still don't fully understand.' Not that it stops you from prescribing drugs, I thought. 'But they can come from something in your life that's making you unhappy and that you need to control. They can start that way. And sometimes identifying that can help us make you better.'

'Better according to who?'

'Annabel.' That tone.

'I'm not sick. I'm not broken. I don't need you to fix me.'

I needed to fix myself. I *was* fixing myself.

Imogen asked me one day not long after that, 'Why don't big girls get hungry?'

'We just don't,' I said.

It was a lie. But we always lie to children, don't we? How could I tell her that it wasn't about not being hungry. It was about not giving in to it.

'Mum still gets hungry.'

I shrugged. 'She's different.' It made me feel sick to look at her, at any of them. My parents and their middle-aged spread. Imogen with her soft cheeks, soft arms, soft legs.

'She says it's 'cause you're sick.'

'I'm not sick.'

151

Her eyes, still baby blue, were starting to fill up with tears anyway. 'I don't want you to die.'

'I'm not going to die, Im.'

'Swear?'

'I swear,' I said. Impatiently.

'What'll we do for my birthday?' she said, hands on her hips. Another way of seeking the same promise.

'Whatever you want.'

We always lie to children, don't we? Imogen's twelve today.

Chapter Forty-Two

'Tis the season, almost. Christmas, Christmas. Twinkling lights, goodwill to men, blah blah blah. Screaming children flinging themselves on the floor of the toy shop because they can't have everything right now. Pervy old men playing Santa Claus, asking the kids if they've been good this year. People stressing out about money, food, presents, family, travel. 'Tis not the season to be jolly. 'Tis the season for too-high expectations of other human beings.

Julia counts down the days to the Christmas holidays, which includes not just everyone's favourite face-stuffing competition but her birthday, too. A time for treats. She thinks: selection boxes. Cadbury's Roses. Quality Street. Ferrero Rocher. The apple pie that her aunt makes. Her dad's Christmas pudding, with thick cream.

Oh, Julia. No. No chocolate. No desserts. Now, let's look at bread. And meat. And milk. Drink lots of water, it'll help you feel full.

I'm getting through to her. My voice in her head every time her stomach growls: *Remember, every time you say 'no, thank you' to food, you say 'yes, please' to skinny. Have another bottle of water. Strong. Be strong.*

She's a smart girl. She can memorise facts and figures for exams, keep up with whatever's happening in national and international news, analyse material and make connections quickly. It is no trouble to memorise calorie contents of different foods.

As the holidays draw near, she keeps to herself. No newspaper meetings to go to, no reasons to interact with people, so she spends breaks and lunches in the library catching up on homework and not eating. It's not until the second-to-last day of school that Deb comes to find her. 'Hey, *there* you are.'

'Hi,' Julia says warily. She's been mostly avoiding Deb since finishing up with the newspaper stuff, still annoyed about the push to finish early and then the not bothering to even submit what she promised.

Deb's not going to acknowledge any of this (or say sorry directly). Instead she says, 'So listen, you're coming to my party tomorrow night, right?' Social butterfly that she is, she's arranged another gathering for the sixth years at her place.

'Um,' Julia says. She got the message – a group one, not personalised – and has been holding off answering, feeling far away from all the enthusiastic responses from others. (This is one of the benefits of counting calories. It's a world of its own.)

'Everyone's going to be there, come on. You deserve a break.'

Julia bites back the retort about *not having anything else going on in her life other than the paper apparently*, and instead shrugs. 'I'll see, I might have to babysit.' Baby sisters are a convenient excuse, she thinks.

'How about tonight, you want to come over? We can catch up.' Meaning Deb can rant some more about Sylvia's pregnancy, and the suggestion that she might be this child's godmother, as though she wants to even acknowledge anything to do with the bitch who broke up her parents' marriage.

Julia makes a point of checking the calendar on her phone, even though her social life is minimal these days. It's never been particularly hectic anyway, but she's been out of the loop the past few weeks. Tonight is the one day she actually has something on. 'Actually, I'm going to a play.'

'Oh. What's on?'

'It's the local theatre group – they're doing *A Christmas Carol*.'

'Oh, right. Maria's in that.'

Julia nods. 'Yeah, she got me the ticket.'

Deb is slightly put out at this, that Julia already has this bit of information, that she – gasp – has other friends. 'Okay. You don't want any company or anything?'

Julia does, actually. She'd have maybe skipped it if Maria hadn't told her she'd put a ticket aside for her already. But the way Deb's phrased it makes it seem like she wants to be let off the hook. 'It's fine,' she says.

Fine, as they say in therapy, is a four-letter word.

Chapter Forty-Three

A Christmas Carol. The ghosts of Christmas past, present and future. Julia has the soundtrack of *The Muppet Christmas Carol* playing as she sifts through her wardrobe trying to find something to wear for the play. She stands in front of the mirror, already lighter and better.

She is not suddenly thin. Don't be ridiculous. It takes work. Willpower. But I can see she might get there one day. I think about butterflies emerging from chrysalises.

She holds up a high-waisted black velvet dress, something she found in a charity shop a few months ago, and decides to try it on. As she wriggles into it, she sings along with the music, with the Muppets lamenting how mean Scrooge is, and Imogen flashes into my head again. She loves this movie. The Christmas holidays officially start with Imogen and me watching it, Mum and Dad popping their heads round the door at regular intervals to smile indulgently. *Yes, we're watching it again. It's the greatest Christmas movie ever made!*

Stop it, brain. I watch Julia in the mirror, tugging at the dress. It hides a multitude of sins, but she's pulling at it anyway. Then takes it off, and stands there in her underwear. Glares at her reflection. The next dress she takes out of the wardrobe is her Christmas dress from a year ago. She looks at it on the hanger, red and slinky. There's no way in hell it'd fit her now. It looks laughably tiny, like a Barbie dress.

Now this is what I don't understand. She should be looking at this with longing. With heartbreak. She could fit into that once upon a time. Returning to it would be an important step in the right direction. But she stares it and suddenly starts tearing. Or trying to. Ripping up clothing is harder than it looks. So she gets scissors, from her drawer – starts cutting it up, chop chop chop.

Tell me I don't have another Susan on my hands, tell me she's not going to take those scissors to her skin next. But her mind's on matters beyond cutting; she takes the slivers of the dress, gathers them up in her arms and shoves them in a plastic bag. Then that goes at the back of her wardrobe, beneath old school reports and copies of the paper.

There are plenty of things in her wardrobe that don't fit any more, but the dress is the only one subjected to the scissors, and there's a brick wall up around the 'why'.

She goes back to looking at herself in the mirror. You can lose hours that way. Then, finally, because the play starts in twenty minutes: skirt and baggy jumper, covering up everything. *It will do*, she thinks. Wearily. *It will do.*

Chapter Forty-Four

Some thoughts on *A Christmas Carol*:

1. Local theatre groups are less appalling than you think they might be, or that Julia fears they'll be, but there is still at least one person in the production who shouldn't be allowed on the stage. The woman playing Mrs Cratchit mumbles her lines, while Tiny Tim delivers his lines far too enthusiastically for a sick little kid.

2. Charles Dickens really loved sick kids, didn't he? But he probably never met any. Hospital wards aren't full of brave, inspiring invalids. They're mostly cranky. Tired. Sick. Or don't want to be there. Shouldn't be there.

3. Maria is good. She's playing Belle, Scrooge's long-lost love, and Julia notices the way she changes how she moves when she comes on the second time, when Scrooge sees her with her big happy family, in her

new life. She's glad she came, now, instead of hanging out with Deb or staying at home alone.

4. It's easier for Julia to feel happy for Maria than Lorraine (who has a piece on exam stress in yesterday's *Irish News*), to be proud on her behalf, and I wonder if that's to do with Gavin or the shared field or something else entirely.

5. Ghosts have so many more exciting powers in stories than in real life. I start to feel slightly resentful at not being able to take Julia flying through the sky or time. False advertising.

6. Even though there are no Muppets in this production, Imogen would love it.

Chapter Forty-Five

'You were brilliant,' Julia tells Maria at what passes for a cast party for a local theatre group; there are teas and coffees and biscuits set out in the community centre hall across the road.

Maria's in a post-performance daze. 'Thanks,' she says, but it all feels unreal, like she's still waiting to go on stage.

Scrooge comes over to hug Maria, tell her she was terrific, and Julia realises he looks familiar. She tries to make the connection – he's someone's parent, but they mostly blur together – and then she spots Gavin chatting to the woman who played Mrs Cratchit.

'That's Gavin's dad,' she says to Maria when Scrooge heads off to praise the rest of the cast, and Maria nods.

'Yeah, Gavin helped us out with some of the sound stuff,' she says. 'He's a good guy.'

Julia's torn between swooning inwardly and trying to figure out how many pretty age-appropriate girls there might have been in the cast that Gavin could have kissed. 'Yeah,' she says.

'I really like it here,' Maria continues. 'I mean, you've got a fair share of nasty people, but there's a lot of decent humans, too. You know? It's really –'

She stops. Julia's smiling at her. Maria's face reddens; she hides it in her hands.

'I talk crap for about two hours after being on stage, just ignore me,' she says. 'I'm basically drunk on acting right now. Indulge me.'

'I'll hold your hair back while you throw up all that positivity,' Julia says solemnly.

Beneath Maria's laughter there's something else: relief. The relief of being liked. And now I feel like an idiot: she's not at the Richmond School because of its good reputation, eagerly waiting for any place to open up so she can soak up the extra-curriculars and get involved. She's there because they had a place and the girls at her old school were making her life hell.

'Maria! You were fabulous.' That's Mrs Cratchit now, no longer mumbling, and Gavin's there beside her. The actors get into a discussion about something that happened backstage, a near-disaster with the costumes, and Gavin smile-nods in his way.

'She's a bit old for you, isn't she?' Julia murmurs, nodding towards Mrs Cratchit.

Gavin smiles. But Julia's still going, thinking about Sally storming off.

'Don't tell me you've worked your way through all the girls your own age in Dublin,' she says.

Good-natured though he is, he feels this is unfair. Yes, he's been out more weekends than not since the break-up; yes, there have been girls in nightclubs and at bus stops. But it's only a bit of fun. A distraction. 'Not exactly how I'd put it,' he says tightly.

'So how would you put it?' Julia wants to know.

'What people do when they're single.' He's trying to be nice. Why does he have to justify this – the thrill of it, the feeling of being liked, the initial buzz before it all wears off and he's the guy who can never quite be good enough for his girlfriend? Ex-girlfriend, he corrects himself.

'I don't think it really counts as single if you've that many girls on the go.'

They are no longer talking quietly; Maria and Mrs Cratchit are witnessing this.

'They're not *on the go*,' Gavin says. Never the same girl twice, although working with Sally on the newspaper has made that more difficult. The irritation – or is it hurt? – is audible now, and Julia backs off.

'Okay. Fair enough.' She pauses, and her focus shifts: from the girls who might be falling for him to Gavin himself. 'I just think you might want to try being properly single for a while.' She touches him on the arm, lightly, so he knows she's more concerned than critical. 'Relationships can be really intense. You need to take time and figure out who you are without that person, you know?'

'Yeah, but they're also –' Gavin begins, and speaking of intense, their two witnesses are feeling it and Maria tugs Mrs Cratchit away to go see if they can find pink wafer biscuits. 'They *help* you figure out who you are. If you're with someone, they can make you . . . be your best self.' Saying that aloud makes him blush a little. Cheesy. Too personal.

Julia doesn't know what to say. 'Is that . . .' She tries again. 'Was that how you felt with Lorraine?'

Gavin would be immensely appreciative of an interruption right now. Where's his embarrassing amateur actor father when you need him? 'It was for a while. Not lately, though. We just kept fighting, over stupid stuff.'

They remember that fight, the hug in the kitchen. Gavin remembers more: a whole montage of Gavin-and-Lorraine arguments. With his video-editing brain, he actually remembers it this way; if I were so inclined I could probably dive deeper into his mind and find out what angsty rock song he'd have playing over the clips.

'Are you okay?' Julia asks, her voice low.

Gavin goes straight into nice-guy mode. Cheerful smile. 'It's fine. Are you going to Deb's party tomorrow night?'

'Yeah, I suppose.'

'Great,' he says.

'Great,' she echoes.

It is a relief for all concerned when Gavin's father chooses this moment to start a singalong, out of key though he may be, and the entire room joins in.

Chapter Forty-Six

'I hear congratulations are in order.' The voice comes out of nowhere. Julia spins around, and call-me-Dermot is standing behind her, minus a pregnant Sylvia.

Julia blinks. She wants to ask what he's doing here at Deb's – Deb's mum's, really – Christmas party – but knows it'd be rude. Her brain freezes up.

Let's step inside Dermot's head for a second: he's here ostensibly to drop off Deb's Christmas present. He and Sylvia are heading off to Tenerife for Christmas itself, and work has been so busy (one of the things Dermot writes about is food, which is rather crucial at this time of year; he's also ghostwriting – what a stupid phrase – a biography and taking on as much work as he can get, even stuff that he privately considers beneath him, with the new baby on the way) that he hasn't been able to get over here until now, two days before Christmas and the night before their early-morning flight.

But, yes, he is also conscious that this is the night Tracy is having a party, and he's heard whispers that she's met someone new, and he can't stop himself from finding out who it is. Some strange competitive urge, the sort of primal thing that you'd think would be buried, if you were to look at him.

Julia's still standing there in silence. It's only been a few seconds, but long enough for him to help her out. 'Editor of the newspaper. Well done.'

'Oh,' she says. 'Yeah. Thanks.' She wonders if it was Deb or Lorraine who passed on this bit of news. Imagines Lorraine's email, and Dermot's response, reminding her that there are brighter and bigger things for her than a school paper.

He looks her up and down. Notices her. Notices her in the way a forty-three-year-old man should not notice his teenage daughter's friends. Admires her curves, by which of course he means her breasts, the dip between them visible at the neckline of the black velvet dress she finally decided was acceptable. I edge away from his thoughts, his pervy-old-man thoughts.

'And you, too,' she says. 'Congratulations on the – on the baby. That's great.'

No, it's not. There's a tight knot in her chest and she can't breathe and how dare he be happy and standing here talking to her like it's all okay.

He looks at her solemnly. Puts his hand on her arm.

Don't touch me, don't touch me, don't touch me, she wants to scream but she can't. They're in the middle of a party and why isn't anyone interrupting them? But she can't scream. Make a scene. No. Can't do that.

Her heart is thumping like nobody's business.

'Thanks, Julia,' he says. 'I really appreciate that.' All meaningful and serious. He is looking at her breasts. He has a

165

flash – no, she has a flash – no, they both have a flash – of his hands there. Then on her thighs.

Get away from him, Julia. Get away. Right now. RIGHT NOW.

She smiles weakly. She wants to go. She wants to listen to me. But she can't.

The weight of his hand on her arm.

Another flash: the weight of him on top of her. Her gasp as he –

JULIA.

Chapter Forty-Seven

My own memory, this time: Helen. Helen telling me.

Helen all blasé, like, of course her stepfather would do that, no big deal. Me not knowing what to say.

Bastard, I thought.

But also: a feeling of betrayal, creeping inside my unworthy bones. There it was. Helen's reason. Her big explanation. Even if she didn't tell it to Dr Fields, she had one.

Julia has a reason, a something, thefuckingbastardrapedherfuckhim and I want to save her and I hate her all at the same time.

Dermot. He lifts his hand from Julia's arms when Tracy calls from across the room theatrically, 'Is that Dermot over there?' (Tracy, incidentally, is both irritated that he's turned up and delighted that she's just got her hair done and also that her new boyfriend is an inch taller than Dermot, and yes, she knows it's petty. Tracy, incidentally, is someone I kind of want to punch right about now.)

Dermot smiles a little at Julia before he turns to go greet his ex-wife and the new man in her life. Julia's heart is still calming a little. She wants –

No. Don't eat anything. No. You're better than that. Don't let this turn into another bingeing session. You're stronger than that. Don't let him get to you and ruin everything.

And for the first time ever, Julia answers me, even though she doesn't know it's me she's addressing: *So what the hell am I supposed to do to make this go away? Right now. I need something right now.*

If there were a treadmill nearby I'd be pointing her to that. Run it out. Run it all away. But there isn't.

Deb comes over, two drinks in hand. Alcoholic – vodka mixed with Fanta Orange. Holds one out to Julia. 'Heya. Were you talking to Dad? He wanted to say congrats about the newspaper. I showed him the last one . . .'

She keeps talking but Julia zones out. Takes the drink.

Julia, do you know how many calories there are in –

Knocks it back. Wonders where she can get another.

Oh, for not-God's sake. At least ditch the Fanta Orange, if you're going to get hammered. Insane amount of sugar.

Don't get me wrong. I get it. I get that she's allowed to be upset, that there's a reason, a *cause*, and she needs something. I just wish it wasn't this.

Discovery: she can't hear me when she drinks. Or maybe she can, and it's just easier to ignore me. Am I even needed here?

Don't do anything stupid, Julia. Please.

(But what's going to happen to her that's worse than what Dermot did to her?)

I step away from the Christmas party, back to my house. All the lights are on now. They're home. Everyone's home. There's tinsel on the Christmas tree – Imogen's insistence, Mum hates it.

They'll have a great Christmas this year. No arguments about Annabel not eating her turkey and ham and butter-drenched mashed potatoes. No waiting for her to finish her dinner. No Mum in tears, no Dad yelling. No Imogen watching like a hawk to make sure the food goes in Annabel's mouth and not in her napkin.

No grumpiness behind closed doors about the heating bills because it's forever too cold in the house for Annabel even with several layers, always so cold and shivery. No Annabel messing things up.

Is that why you sent me to the hospital? I ask the house. *Did you know I would die there? Did you know?*

Answer me!

I would say it's killing me not to be able to get a message through to them, but, well, you know.

I can't turn back time. I can't undo what happened to Julia. But I can make her thin. It's the only skill I have that can help her. And then the channels of communication slide open for me. Then I can finally tell them.

Tell them they were wrong, that they should never have sent me to hospital. I was in control, that's all. I wasn't sick. I didn't have any reason to be – they even knew that in there, they *knew*. It was a choice, a lifestyle, a goal.

My family shouldn't have sent me to hospital. I was fine. I was strong. I was on my way to perfection. They fucked it up, and now –

Now all I want to do, all I can do, is *tell them*.

Tell them just how utterly and completely pissed off I am with the lot of them.

Chapter Forty-Eight

Back at Deb's, where I am pulled against my better judgement, Julia is experiencing the wonders of alcohol. Drinking is not a brand-new thing for her, but it has always felt like something that requires a decision: to drink or not to drink. Not something to be reached for when in pain without thinking about it.

(She's always felt that there's something weak about drinking when upset, using alcohol as a crutch. She doesn't make the connection yet: food has been her crutch for so many months now. Since Dermot, since – that. Dermot, who along with his pregnant wife has left the premises. The remaining adults are in the dining room, across the hallway, trying out a bottle of scotch someone gave Tracy at work.)

Now, though – oh, she's revelling in it. She sits on a couch next to a gloomy Maria. 'Hey, what's up? Don't be sad. You were in such good form last night.'

Maria offers up a weak smile. 'Thanks.'

'So sadness is not allowed,' Julia declares.

'Patrick broke up with me.' It takes both me and Julia a moment to remember that Maria was technically going out with Patrick, seeing as he didn't even turn up to see her in the play.

'Oh. Oh. That's awful.' Julia is overcome with the awfulness of it. Julia is a little tipsy. 'He's an idiot. He can't even use apostrophes right, you know. True story.'

Maria giggles, despite herself. 'I'm better off alone, in that case.'

'Exactly! Exactly.' Julia takes another gulp of her drink.

The sadness swoops over Maria again. 'But he was so nice,' she says, resting her head on Julia's shoulder. She thought, she really thought, he was one of the decent humans at this school.

'Nice is not the same as good,' Julia says firmly, remembering the conversation with Deb all those months ago.

'That is wise,' Maria says. This is what Maria is like when actually drunk, rather than stage-drunk; I realise she has also recently (as in, in the last half an hour) become acquainted with the notion of alcohol as a cure (albeit a temporary one) for a broken heart. 'Julia, you are *wise*.'

'I would put it to you,' Julia adds, 'that a truly good guy is hard to find.' Lorraine is passing by, en route to the kitchen, and Julia calls out to her. 'Lorraine! Good men. Do they exist? We're conducting a survey.'

'Sure.' Lorraine shrugs.

'Not nice men,' Julia insists. '*Good* men.'

'What's the difference?'

'Nice is like . . . Gavin.' She wouldn't dare say this if she were sober. 'You know, like he wants to seem all helpful and nice but really he's just . . .' She waves a hand vaguely.

'Just what?' Lorraine is on the defensive now. She hasn't bitched about Gavin, even though everything's still awkward between them – not ugly, just a pretence that everything's okay and delightful and not hideously fake.

171

'You know, with the girls, and –' Julia stops, not because it's occurred to her that she shouldn't mention to Gavin's ex that he's kissed other people, but because she doesn't want to talk about the attempted helping out with the newspaper stuff. She doesn't want to seem weak.

Lorraine's stung. She's had her own encounters – late-night things that are never going to go anywhere, even though she still gets texts (which she ignores) from two guys who want to see her again – but they've been lacklustre. And she doesn't like to think of Gavin being with anyone else. 'He's allowed to have girls, Julia,' she says coldly to cover it up. 'We're not together any more.'

'Yeah, but he doesn't love them. I mean, he *loved* you. You had a serious long-term proper relationship and it was all great and lovely and he's lovely . . .' She's drifting now. The edges of life are fuzzy now. Everything's lovely. It's safe and cosy and it's okay to say anything.

No, it's not, it's really not.

'But,' she continues, 'I think he's maybe a little too charming, you know? Which is nice, but not good.' Julia's drifting from the specifics of Gavin to her theories about all men – definitely not something she would let herself do without alcohol in her veins.

Lorraine is slightly lost. She frowns. 'He's okay. He's not my favourite person at the moment, but he's not – evil.'

'I didn't say evil,' Julia says, irritated.

'Well, you implied it.'

'Hey, guys –' Maria tries to break in.

'I'm just saying.' Julia's huffy now. And determined to prove to Lorraine that she hasn't won.

'Well, don't.'

'Guys, guys, don't fight,' Maria says, but it falls on deaf ears.

'You don't know him, Julia,' Lorraine continues, tiny and elegant, hands on hips. 'So maybe you should keep your fat mouth shut.' As if her emphasis on 'fat' isn't enough, she looks her up and down. Not like Dermot. Like she's – well, she's looking at Julia like Julia looks at herself. And thinking all the things that Julia thinks. And letting this be written all over her face.

You're not allowed, Lorraine. No.

'Lorraine!' Maria says. 'That's not on.' Funny, she thinks, how much easier it is to say this to someone when they're being a bitch to someone who isn't you.

Lorraine gives her the evil eye, too, and then turns and walks away. She's not sure where she's going exactly – dramatic exits work better if you've mapped them out beforehand – but then she sees him. Gavin.

'Hey,' she says, all flirty and knowing.

For Julia, it's like everything's happening far off into the distance.

'She shouldn't have said that,' Maria says. 'That was *so* out of line. Are you all right?'

Julia shrugs. 'She's right. I'm fat.' Very zen, drunk Julia is.

'You are not,' Maria says. Automatic response. She knows fat is bad. Then she looks at Julia. Really looks at her. 'You are so pretty,' she says with a sort of wonder.

Well, she's kind of drunk.

Julia is hardly listening. She's looking over at Gavin and Lorraine. Lorraine's got one hand perched on a jutting-out hip, and her face tilted up towards him: her standard in-public-with-Gavin pose. Is he smiling at her? Julia can't tell.

Well, if Gavin and Lorraine want to foolishly slide back into a relationship even though they were having all those fights, let them at it, she thinks magnanimously. In fact, she's going to tell them.

They're not planning on sliding back into a relationship. At least, Gavin isn't. He's remembering the last time he was here, for Deb's birthday, right after it became public knowledge that he and Lorraine were over. It feels like a lifetime ago.

'How's it going?' Lorraine asks him, all smiles.

'Cool,' he says, shrugging.

'Good. That's good.' She's a little tipsy. He can tell.

'You okay?' He's already planning on taking her by the elbow and getting her outside for some fresh air. (Note: he genuinely means 'fresh air', not making out with her. Interesting.)

'Yeah,' she says. 'I'm good.'

Riveting conversation here. Four years of this? No wonder they split up.

She leans in. 'Do you miss me?'

Gavin doesn't know what to say. Yes. Yeah, he misses her. But is this going to turn into one of those things . . . 'Do you miss me?' he counters.

She giggles. 'Maybe.'

This is the point at which Julia appears from behind Lorraine's shoulder and says, 'I just want to say, guys, I think it's great that you're back together. Congratulations.'

Gavin gets the sense that either there's some elaborate practical joke being played here or this is a madhouse.

Lorraine makes a face at him, and it's not one he likes. Her sneering face. It doesn't suit her. 'Make her go away,' she mouths, which he thinks is rude.

'Thanks,' he says, 'but, uh, we're not back together.'

'Well, you should be,' Julia says, unfazed. 'You can make each other better people.' She doesn't mean it in a nasty way. She's remembering Gavin talking about relationships. But it doesn't come out well.

Lorraine spins around. 'Go *away*, for fuck's sake.'

This is the point at which the rest of the room starts to pay attention to what's going on. They look up from their drinks and little snacks and their conversations and phones and eye up the trio – Gavin's eyes flickering back and forth between a furious Lorraine and a matter-of-fact Julia. More than one person thinks: oh God, here we go again, having flashbacks to the Gavin/Lorraine squabbles they've all witnessed over the years.

'There's no need for that,' Julia says. Mellow. Placid.

'You're still there! I'm trying to have a conversation with my boy—' Lorraine cuts herself off.

Gavin would like it very much if they could all politely pretend that they didn't hear that, and move on. Unlike many boys of his age, he believes the appropriate response to hearing a fart is to develop selective deafness rather than to snicker or create a scene. He feels something similar should apply here.

Julia disagrees with this sentiment. 'But he just said he wasn't your boyfriend.'

Lorraine looks like she's ready to throw a punch. In fact – oh, there she goes. Out comes the little fist. Right into Julia's stomach.

This is a step beyond anything anyone's ever seen before – usually Lorraine tilts her head and tells Gavin coldly that she'll talk to him outside. This has everyone gasping and not quite believing it, like something they're watching on the TV.

Julia moves to hit her back, but the blow to the gut is doing something to her, and she puts her hands over her mouth instead. It's churned up her insides, which are already pretty well churned from the drinks, and she's about to –

She lurches from the room, feeling it at the back of her throat, and oh there it is in her mouth and she's pressing her fingers against her lips so tight but some of it is spilling out, so she has one hand wet with bits of vomit and the other trying not to let it seep through and get onto the floor, and then she's in the bathroom and it goes into the sink and onto the floor a bit and some onto the mirror and the wall, force behind it.

The door's still open and she now kicks it shut, embarrassed that people have heard (and they have – there's a couple outside in the corridor wincing at the sound and being put off their kissing) and also conscious that she now needs to clean this up before anyone sees. The humiliation. And it's all Lorraine's fault. She wouldn't be puking if she hadn't been punched like that.

But now she feels like some stupid drunk girl. She shouldn't have said anything to Gavin and Lorraine, what was she thinking? They'll be so smug, now, both of them. Smugly together.

Julia rinses her mouth with tap water and starts rolling out the toilet paper to clean the place up. There's a knock on the door. 'I'll be out in a second!' she calls, trying to sound airy. All is well, she's not a mess, it's all fine.

'You okay?' It's Maria.

'No,' Julia says honestly.

'Do you want me to get you anything? Water?'

'I'm fine.' She's using up the better part of a roll to get all the bits of vomit, and finding it completely disgusting, and wants to curl up into a ball and die (but not really because she doesn't know what dying is, really), but apart from that, it's all fine.

When Julia emerges from the bathroom, eyes slightly bloodshot – the puking will do that to you, never went in for it myself – she just wants to slip away before anyone sees her. Go home and read a good book or maybe watch a DVD. Maria's still waiting there. 'Hey. Are you really fine or . . . ?' She knows there's no such thing.

'I'd be better if Lorraine hadn't punched me.'

'I can't believe that actually happened. Does she normally do that kind of thing when she drinks?' There's nothing like a bit of violence to sober people up.

'Not usually. I must be special.'

Maria squeezes her arm.

'Julia!' Deb says from the doorway of the sitting room. 'Come in here.'

Julia shakes her head. 'No, I'm just going to –'

'No, come on, Lorraine has something she wants to say.'

The rest of the room are still watching but pretending that they're not. Gavin stares at the floor, and Maria goes over to reassure him that she checked on Julia. Lorraine is beckoned over by Deb, who looks pointedly at her.

Lorraine clears her throat. 'I'm sorry for hitting you, Julia.' More accurately, she's sorry for causing a scene and for losing her temper in public. She's sorry she looks like the bad guy.

Deb turns to Julia, expecting a gracious acceptance. Julia's not in the mood. 'You're actually not,' she says. 'Don't bother.'

'Oh come on, she's said she's sorry,' Deb says to Julia's back. Julia ducks behind the couch, like she's hiding, but emerges a moment later with her handbag and coat. 'Julia, come on, you're not going, are you?'

'Yeah, I'm going,' Julia says, exasperated.

'You can stay here, stay in my room if you want,' Deb says. She doesn't want Julia to go. She's worried, and she's not used to being worried about Julia.

Really, you stupid girl? You didn't notice anything going on between her and your creepy father, then? Some friend you are.

'I'm going home,' Julia says, louder this time. Why won't Deb just listen to her? Why can't she just leave?

On the other side of the room, in a glorious move that he's not aware of, but it's beautiful, Gavin steps just out of reach as Lorraine's hand reaches for his arm. She grabs air instead, and for a magical second it looks like she'll fall flat on the ground, but she steadies herself. He's moving towards Julia. 'Walk you home?' he asks.

Say yes, say yes, say yes. Is any of this starting to come through to you again now that you've thrown up everything inside you?

She gives a little shrug, which is not quite a yes, but not quite a no either. And off they go.

Chapter Forty-Nine

There's nothing like cold night air for making you feel like real life is intruding again. Julia thinks: at least she doesn't need to go into school next week. At least it's the holidays and she can hide away at home for a while and not think about the embarrassment of it all.

'I'm a mess,' she groans.

Gavin shakes his head. 'Nah. It happens to all of us.' He means throwing up after a few drinks. It's not a terribly unusual occurrence for someone to be sick at a party or on a night out. Gavin himself may have found himself slumped over a toilet bowl at a nightclub recently (after getting himself involved with three different girls in the space of four hours – a productive night, if you want to look at it like that).

'Getting punched by Lorraine happens to all of us?' Julia says, and then starts giggling.

'No, I mean . . .' Gavin starts, as though there's been a genuine misunderstanding. Then turns to look at her, and sees that she's joking rather than out of it. 'It was an unexpected turn of events,' he says instead. Grins.

'Yeah,' Julia says. 'She doesn't like me.'

Gavin wants to interrupt her, but she keeps going.

'And she thought I said you were evil. Which I didn't say. I said there was a difference between nice and good.'

Gavin's skin gets prickly. 'Right.' He feels like he's come in at the end of a movie. 'What's the difference?'

Julia is realising she may have said too much. She's also realising it's cold out, and Gavin is walking her home, which is – nice? Good? Both? 'It's nothing,' she says.

'What's the difference?' he repeats. On edge again. What is he like in Julia's head?

'Don't listen to me, I'm drunk and stupid and . . .' Julia trails off.

'I'm just curious.'

'Well, why are you walking me home? Which you don't have to do.' She realises she should have said that at the start. Before they left Deb's road.

'Because . . . it's what you do,' Gavin says.

'That's not an answer.'

He thinks about how to word it. 'It's what you do when you want to make sure a friend gets home in one piece.'

'Are we friends?'

'Yeah, of course.' He's surprised.

'You don't just feel sorry for me?'

Gavin laughs out loud, and then realises she's serious. He stops walking, puts his hands in his pockets. 'Why would I feel sorry for you?'

'You just act like –' Julia tries to think of the right way to put it. 'You act like you're trying to save the day. Like you need to. With the newspaper, and now tonight, walking me home.'

'Is that such a bad thing? I just want to make sure you get

home in one piece.' He puts his hands on her shoulders. Warm hands. Safe hands. 'Okay?'

'I'll be fine.'

'Look, what if . . . something happened, and – I'd feel like shit.'

'Exactly!' she says, her voice getting louder. 'It's about you. *You* feeling like shit. You want to make sure you look like the nice guy.' She looks him up and down, at his wide-eyed bewilderment. 'No, it's worse – you want to *feel* like a nice guy. Knight in fucking shining armour. No wonder you get all the girls before you toss them aside. Well, look, I don't need rescuing, okay?'

'I don't want to – I don't –' He doesn't know what to say. It all stings. What's wrong with trying to be nice? Trying to be a decent guy? What the hell does she expect from him? He's doing something wrong by not becoming a monk after breaking up with his long-term girlfriend, he's doing something wrong when he walks a friend home to make sure she's okay.

'Just leave me alone,' Julia says.

Every nice guy – good guy? – has a breaking point. Gavin walks away, and thinks of the perfect line when he gets back to Deb's house: 'You need to be rescued. From yourself.' It's always the way, isn't it? You think of the right retort too late to use it.

When she gets home, Julia crawls into bed and pulls the duvet over her head. She can't think about what she said to Gavin – but it flashes across her brain on repeat and she squeezes her eyes shut. She is a crazy person, she thinks. He's just trying to be nice.

Then she remembers: he is invested in seeming nice. Thinking of himself as a nice guy. The potential rescuer. She thinks about Dermot, at Deb's birthday party. And then she's not allowed to think about it any more, any of it.

181

Chapter Fifty

Julia's phone the next morning: *Home okay?* (Deb); *you okay?* (Frank, surprisingly); *Really hope you got home okay. You are AMAZING. Hope you realise that & feel better tomorrow. Mx* (Maria, possibly still tipsy).

She fires off quick, reassuring replies, and then gets Gavin's number up on the screen. She hardly ever uses it for anything apart from newspaper stuff. For social occasions, Deb's usually the one to organise everyone. But now something's needed. An apology. She was too intense last night, too caught up in the humiliation and the alcohol and the way Lorraine looked at her.

He didn't have to walk her home. And she didn't have to be rude to him. But she was also right about some of it –

This goes on for quite a while. Text messages are composed, revised and deleted. This is the kind of thing you obsess over only when you really like someone. Love someone, even. I have never done this. Not with Will, not with the boy at the school before that whose name it takes me a while to remember. Philip. That's it. We didn't keep in touch. He is hazy and not quite real to me. An overexposed photograph.

I never thought highly of them. I never wanted them to think well of me – me, not just my flesh-and-bone container. If there was anything to like.

She rearranges the words one more time, contemplates the emoji options.

Just send the damn text, Julia.

And then: *and think about how much better this is all going to be when you're thin. You'll understand, when you're there. How it's like nothing else. You won't worry like this when you get there. I promise.*

She is still dithering when I go check. Just to see if it's working yet. To see if I can get through to them. The Christmas tree lights twinkle, that much I can see from outside the house, but there's no sign of anyone. Mum will be cooking, maybe, and Dad might be out doing some last-minute present buying, and Imogen will be curled up in front of the TV marking the first day of the Christmas holidays. I can almost hear her singing along to the music.

I stare up at the house, and then it happens, like some kind of reverse Christmas miracle: a letter floats down in front of me. Imogen's writing.

Dear Santa,
This Christmas I would like you to make me thin.
Yours sincerely,
Imogen.

Oh, Imogen. You're too old to believe in fairy tales now, surely? Twelve years old and you still think Santa Claus can work wonders? No. He doesn't exist. You're the only one who can make it happen. You know my secrets. You know it doesn't just happen. You watched. You know.

I'm disappointed in my little sister.

No. Not disappointed. It's something else. I can't tell what.

Like I can't quite catch my breath, but I don't have any to catch.

Chapter Fifty-One

A selection of text messages sent over the Christmas holidays:

Julia to Gavin: *So sorry about last night. Not in need of rescuing, but no need for rudeness. Thanks for walking me home.*

Gavin to Julia: *Almost home!* ☺ *Glad you're okay.*

Julia: *Wasn't eaten by lions or anything!* ☺

Gavin: *Cool. Didn't get into any more fights?* ☺

Julia: *Trees looked a bit menacing, but they know their place.*

Gavin [Christmas Eve]: *Happy Christmas Eve* ☺

Julia: *You too. Hope Santa's good to you!*

Gavin [Christmas Day]: *Santa is a legend! Hope you got everything you wanted* ☺

Julia [from outside her house, taking a brisk walk to burn calories and also get away from the stash of chocolate]: *Yeah – loads of good stuff! What did you get?*

Gavin: *New laptop (parents), some good editing software too.*

Gavin [following an exchange in which Gavin raves on about the video editing software and Julia mentions some of the things she's planning to buy with the gift certificates her parents got her but not the diet guides she's already ordered]: *Sleep well* ☺

(Of note: it's the first time he's ever texted that to a girl who wasn't Lorraine. Also of note: he realises it, and has a moment of panic.)

Julia [the next morning]: *Just saw this. Aww* ☺ *Hope you slept well too.*

(Followed by feeling slightly warm and gushy towards him, which she tells herself to snap out of.)

Gavin [on Julia's birthday]: *Happy birthday!!* ☺

Julia: *Thanks! How'd you know it was my birthday?*

Gavin: *Brilliant memory* ☺

Julia: *So, Facebook?* ☺

Gavin: ☺

Gavin [two days later]: *You going to Patrick's New Year's party?*

Julia [who was included in the general invitation to their class, but has declined, not because Patrick's dumped two of her friends in the past two years, but because she wants to avoid everyone after the scene at Deb's party]: *Nah, family thing* (Same excuse given to Patrick. Not at all true. Her dad's working New Year's, and her mum is planning on an early night.)

Gavin [disappointed, but telling himself it's because the more going, the merrier]: *Cool. We'll miss you though!*

Julia [taking a deep breath before sending]: *Remember, just kiss ONE girl at midnight, not ALL of them!* ☺

Gavin [after much redrafting and rewording and strange heart-pounding sensations]: *Hahaha. Giving up for New Year* ☺

Julia [one minute after midnight, New Year's Day]: *Happy New Year. Hope that resolution works out for you* ☺

Gavin [a quarter past midnight, after her text has come through, delayed by everyone in the timezone texting and calling at the same time]: *Happy New Year* ☺

> Observation: at home, receiving this message, Julia
> feels oddly empty (good feeling, run with it). It feels
> generic, like the sort of thing he's sending everyone,
> and she's embarrassed now for texting him. It looks
> like she thinks they have some kind of connection
> whereas he's just . . . Gavin, nice to everyone. In a
> generic, general, pleasing-everyone kind of way.

At Patrick's party, half of the sixth-year class at the Richmond
School are dancing the night away. (Maria's not in attendance,
for obvious reasons.) Several things have already been spilled
on the kitchen floor. Patrick's parents go ballroom dancing
and are at a hotel a hundred miles away, under the impression
that Patrick is having 'a few friends' over. Patrick himself is
fairly drunk at this stage, contemplating texting either Maria
or Deb or both of them, and Will is trying to talk him out of
it. His reasoning is more to do with Patrick not needing the
hassle and how he'll regret it in the morning, but I approve
of the behaviour anyway. Patrick doesn't seem like a catch.

Meanwhile, Frank of the girl-angst and photography skills and
Carolyn of the Gavin-kissing and sex-toy-gifting are upstairs
in the spare room engaging in activities that have previously
only ever been solo pursuits for Frank. Lorraine is sprawled on
Patrick's bed with two girls from the student council, all three
lamenting the unfairness of their teachers and how stressed
they are about exams and what they're going to do next year.

And Gavin, nice guy, has chatted to everyone there and
been polite and friendly and is now sitting outside on the front
step on his own, his phone in his hand, rereading Julia's texts.

JANUARY

Chapter Fifty-Two

Three days before she goes back to school, Julia's at the computer – of course – going through the emails from various social media websites. Friend request accepted from Annabel McCormack – who turns out to be thirty-two and one of those people who is smart enough to have everything private but dumb enough to accept friend requests from total strangers. She sighs, and returns to the others, and then up it comes, when she's looking at Annabel Mc, an account I suddenly want to be able to get into. Have people done that hideous thing of grieving at the dead person, like they can actually read it? Has Susan shared one of her crap poems and been praised for it?

Up on the screen in front of Julia there's a link to Imogen McCormack, friend of Annabel Mc. And when she clicks through she can't see much information – it's all private – but the profile picture is –

I can't look straight at it. Something like gravity pushes it out of sight. I suppose even a photo seems like contact, and I'm not allowed that. But I know what it is. Me and Imogen from a year ago, making silly faces at the camera. She has her tongue out and I have an exaggerated pout. I am hiding behind her, my arms circling her from behind, my head poking out over her right shoulder.

(I remember thinking she was too fleshy, too much.)

Julia clicks the button and waits. She stares at the picture. She's not looking at Imogen, and I hate her for that a little bit. She doesn't know how lucky she is, to be able to. She's looking at the girl who seems happy, the thin girl with her arms around her little sister. She's looking at her inspiration.

Chapter Fifty-Three

'These are dangerous,' Julia's mum says, nodding towards the opened tin of chocolates on the floor, taking another orange one out and unwrapping it.

Family bonding time: the Jacobs family, Grace included, are watching the *Back to the Future* trilogy. Grace is not quite appreciating the complexities of time travel and is mostly being entertained by Julia making funny faces at her and tickling her.

'The diet starts tomorrow,' her dad agrees, helping himself to two more.

It's all good-natured, all light, but Julia's angry all of a sudden. 'Come on, you're not actually going to go on a diet. You never do.'

Onscreen, the imagined and now inaccurate version of 2015 plays out, while her dad says, 'I might. You never know.'

'First time for everything,' her mum says. Pauses. Then. 'Julia, you don't need to take everything so seriously.'

Have you met *your daughter, lady?*

Julia's embarrassed already. She has tears in her eyes, which she's desperately willing not to fall; she stares at Grace instead. 'Yeah, I just – I don't like when people talk about their plans and never follow through.'

'We all do it,' her dad says. Cheerful. Like he's explaining something important to her about the world. 'We're going to paint the upstairs bathroom one day.' Turns to his wife. 'Remember that?'

'We're actually going to do that, Tom,' she says.

'Sure.' He winks at Julia, tries to get her in on the joke.

'No, really, I must give them a shout tomorrow and get a quote . . .'

And suddenly they're in domestic-land, and I try to nudge them. *Look at Julia. Tell her she's lost weight. Tell her she's doing well.*

But Julia's still in baggy clothes, still eating dinner with her family. When they sit down that evening, for her dad's spaghetti dish, she eats. Small bites. Her plate seems too large. Her parents' servings seem excessive. Grotesque.

She tries to remind herself that they don't eat together very often, even over the holidays. She can control her own dinners most of the time. But still. She can't finish.

'I'm full,' she says with her plate half-cleared.

Her mum shrugs. 'Filled up on chocolate? I'll put it in the fridge for you and you can have it later if you like.' She's already forgotten the conversation earlier, and forgotten – or maybe never noticed – that Julia hasn't touched any of the Christmas chocolate stash lying around the house.

Julia's lucky not to have suspicious parents. My mother would have rooted through the bin at the end of the day to see if I'd thrown food away. Julia's mum doesn't think to pick through the crumpled tissues to the leftover food beneath, emptied out of its clingfilmed bowl. I have to admit I'm a little jealous.

Chapter Fifty-Four

Julia's *feelings* (Dr Fields would be so proud, except that she's not writing them down – her beautiful new notebook is only for recording what she eats) about going back to school: mixed. Getting back to the newspaper, and being away from the Christmas junk food supply in the house for most of the day – they're both appealing prospects. On the other hand, she's reluctant to be in the same building with Lorraine, and not sure about Gavin – she both wants to see him and doesn't.

She likes the thrill of her phone buzzing and a message from him arriving, the warmth that floods through her when there's something that makes her smile. Her admiration for his correct placing of semi-colons in reports about sports or politics has nothing on what goes through her when she sees one followed by a closing bracket, winky-facing its way into her heart. But that is safe, contained in her head and her phone.

Nevertheless, she's panicky the night before the new term, worries racing through her head: what if everyone's laughing at her behind her back, still talking about what happened at the party?

A more horrifying thought: what if Gavin's playing some kind of game, texting her, and even though she hasn't said anything embarrassing, what if he's showing her messages to other people and they're all laughing about it and thinking what a stupid/boring/dull/unfunny/uncool/un-everything person she is?

You're wasting your time worrying about this. You can't control Gavin. You can't control what the rest of them think of you. You know what you can control, right?

She does. Sets her alarm for early the next morning. And then in her baggy T-shirt and school tracksuit bottoms, out she goes into the dark, cold morning. There are glamorous runners out already, all too visible in these well-lit suburban streets, in tight, sleek pinks and greens. Julia hates them. The unfairness claws at her chest. Those girls with their tiny stick-arms and tiny thighs, effortlessly pumping their arms and legs, wearing unnecessary sweatbands around their foreheads (matching their outfits, of course, of course).

You can be like them soon. Use it. Power through. No pain, no gain – everyone knows that.

She launches into a run, all fire and determination, her feet thudding along the ground. There's the small satisfaction of passing an older jogger – silver-haired, tracksuited, nothing tight or revealing in sight – but then she feels it, the ache in her calves, the burn in her throat.

Keep going. Power through.

She's coming up to a set of traffic lights, and there's a solitary car winding its way down the road.

Keep going! Get across! You can easily get to the other side before he gets here.

She slows, stops at the lights, gasps for breath.

You stupid, lazy, pathetic bitch. Is that the best you can do? Do you think this is supposed to be easy? Do you think it doesn't happen without any effort, without pushing yourself until it hurts like hell?

I need to stop, she thinks, so defensively I know she can hear me, sense me.

What you need is to get into shape. What you need is to stop thinking you deserve to keep shovelling food into your body if this is the best it can do.

The pedestrian lights go green, the little walking man lit up against the night sky. She sucks in a breath and runs across.

Keep going, keep going, keep going.

When she gets home she's weepy, eyes stinging at her bulk, the bulge of her belly, the thickness of her thighs, the speed at which she becomes out of breath. Red-faced, she slinks to the shower and turns up the water to maximum heat.

She has a beautiful fantasy about the hot water scalding the fat off her bones, leaving her light and airy. Instead her flesh turns red. So much flesh. So much of it.

And she's hungry. She's so hungry, and she's thinking about warm, buttery toast . . .

Of course you're hungry! Of course you want it. But you can't let yourself have it. Can't let yourself start. You know the rules.

She's aching for it. She's telling herself, you need to eat, people are allowed eat, people need to eat, it's not a bad thing.

But it is for you. It is for you.

She thinks about the pictures: Annabel at the party, Annabel with her sister. She thinks: thin. She thinks: no pain, no gain.

She puts on her school uniform, her stomach growling.

Chapter Fifty-Five

At break time, she distracts herself by talking to Maria about the Christmas holidays: Maria, like Julia, spent most of her time at home glued to the computer, although in Maria's case it involved watching movies on Netflix and researching anything she can find about the audition she'll have to do for her preferred college course in drama. And then at lunchtime it's the newspaper meeting, and Julia's optimistic: she's got through the whole morning without anyone mentioning the party, without Gavin and his mates pointing and laughing at her. It's going to be a good year.

And then. 'What time is it?' she asks irritably, even though she knows: twelve fifty-three. Eight minutes after the newspaper meeting was due to start.

'Will we just get started without them?' Gavin suggests. The missing 'them' includes Frank (who has the best of intentions of getting there but has been pulled aside by Carolyn for a moment), Will (whose panic about college has kicked in and is currently in the library) and a handful of others (including Sally). It's Deb, Gavin, Julia, a fourth-year girl, and a first-year boy. That's it. If *The Richmond Report* were a flimsy two-page newsletter then maybe this would be acceptable. But it's not. It is one of the things the school prides itself on. Julia can practically recite the lines from the prospectus: *There is a strong tradition of student journalism at the school, with many notable journalists, broadcasters and commentators having first made a name for themselves on* The Richmond Report.

'This can't be everyone,' she says.

'It's the first day back,' Deb says.

'What's that got to do with it?'

Deb shrugs. 'People might have forgotten. And Frank's probably busy with Carolyn, and did you hear the latest –'

'I'll text the guys,' Gavin says, getting his phone out.

'No, it's fine,' Julia says. 'Don't bother.'

At this moment, the two other students in the room are exchanging awkward looks and conducting a conversation via facial expressions about whether they should leave.

Gavin's fingers tap away. 'They're probably just –'

'I said, don't bother,' she snaps. This is the last thing she wants: Gavin swooping in to sort things out for her again. If they're only turning up because Gavin says so, what's the point? She's the editor, she's the one in charge.

Gavin very slowly and very deliberately puts his phone back into his pocket. Says nothing.

The silence hovers in the room and the first-year boy is overcome with a desire to laugh that he knows he mustn't give in to. Deb speaks just in time, impatient, bored: 'Julia, come on, what do you want to do?'

Julia wants to do something that will make Gavin stop looking at her like that, like she's a stranger. Something that will settle the beat of her heart. 'Okay. New year, new plan. This week's issue is going to be about fresh starts. We'll run things on New Year's resolutions, study plans, diets, exercise, all that stuff. And we're also going to run a piece about looking for new representatives, new contributors . . .'

She hands out assignments. She'll do diets. She can do that.

'Sports . . . Gavin,' Julia says to Gavin's right shoulder, 'can you do something about exercise, general benefits, staying motivated . . .'

'Yep,' he says tightly. That's all he says for the rest of the meeting. They brainstorm ideas for features, settling on a piece about privacy and public figures, jumping off from a dodgy tweet sent by a local politician over the break. Julia looks to Gavin and waits for him to volunteer, as does Deb. It's right up his alley, exactly the kind of story he likes. Her eyes meet his, and she's so ready for the offer that it takes her a while to process the fact that he's not saying anything.

She wonders: if she just directly asks him, will he say yes?

(He will. But she won't ask, and he knows it.)

'Okay, I'll do that one,' she says. Adds it to her long list. 'That's it, see you all next week. Stories in by Thursday morning at the absolute latest.' She tries to smile brightly. Be encouraging. Act like she doesn't want to go on some kind of murderous rampage.

Gavin is the first to leave, and with him vanishes all the fizz of their communications over the holidays. Then the others. Deb hovers. 'What's going on with you and Gav?'

'What? What do you mean?' Julia aims for a sort of cool, remote surprise that anyone might have detected any kind of tension there. She doesn't quite make it.

200

'You're acting weird. Did you have a fight or something?' Deb runs through the possibilities in her head. 'Oh, he didn't hit on you when he was walking you home that time, did he?' Deb is aware of some, but not all, of Gavin's dalliances since the Lorraine break-up.

'Don't be silly,' Julia says. 'He'd never go for me.'

'Do you *want* him to?' Deb's mouth is slightly open here. 'Is that what's going on here?'

I suppose you have to give her credit where it's due, because as far as I can tell, that's completely what's going on here. But where Julia could open up and giggle about how cute he is, how funny, how charming, she freezes.

Deb is her best friend. But she's also Dermot's daughter.

'No. I'm just saying, Gavin wouldn't ever – make a move. There's nothing, it's fine. Look, I'm going to go see if I can find Frank now. I'll talk to you later, okay?'

She is a strong, confident leader, she tells herself. She is not in need of rescue. She is not in need of Gavin on his white horse. She is in control. She is in control.

Chapter Fifty-Six

Julia runs into Frank on the way to the kitchen. For coffee, not food. His face falls. 'Julia, shit, I'm so sorry.' He really is. He's caught up in a Carolyn fog, the thrill he feels when she's around.

'Frank –' Julia starts, ready to snap, and then thinks better of it. She needs Frank on board. And he does look apologetic. 'Don't worry about it.' They talk through what images she needs, and Frank nods and smiles. His mind is elsewhere, reliving how worried he was that Carolyn wouldn't want anything to do with him after the New Year's party and how the constant messaging and hanging out since makes him feel like he could do anything.

It's extraordinary, the way some people feel when they believe themselves loved. Is it real, any of it, or just some hormonal chemical surge that can't be trusted?

And along comes Will, speak of the devil, and I know more than ever that I never loved him, or that he never loved me. Not even close. 'I can't,' he says, even before Julia gets a chance to open his mouth. 'I've too much to do.'

'Come on, Will, we all have a lot to do,' she says.

'I can't,' he repeats. He's mid-storm-off when Julia calls after him.

'Will! This isn't about the paper.'

He turns. Suspiciously. 'What?'

'You know your girlfriend from fifth year?' Julia's almost afraid to say this. Is it too obvious she's trying to be that thin, trying to be her?

Will looks blank. Then says, 'Which one?'

Lovely, Will. Thanks. You were no prize either, you know.

'The girl who only came for a while and then left – I think she moved or was out sick a lot or something. Annabel.'

Another blank look. Now I'm starting to really get pissed off. 'Oh yeah. I think she might have moved or something.' He doesn't have a clue. If I had fists I'd be clenching them.

'You don't have contact details or anything for her?'

Will takes out his phone and checks. 'Nope, sorry. It's a new phone, I lost all my old contacts.'

Julia's disappointed. 'Do you know anyone who would?'

Will shakes his head.

Frank screws up his face. 'Oh yeah, I remember her. She was really quiet. Kind of hard to talk to.'

Says Frank. *Frank*. Frank whose experience with girls was up until very recently limited to pictures on the internet. Who the hell does he think he is, passing judgement on me?

'I just wanted to try to track her down,' Julia says. 'You know, for an end-of-school round-up piece.' This last part is a lie, but it sounds plausible.

Will shrugs, and then the bell goes and they're all off to class. Julia looks at her newspaper to-do list, and watches the homework mount up. First day back and already the teachers are piling it on. But she can do this. Her stomach grumbles. She can do anything. She is strong. She agrees to help out with Careers Day, because it's two months away and she will manage it. She says yes to running a big feature on the work of the Environmental Committee in the paper next week, to coincide with Green Week, and she'll proofread their booklets, too, why not? (She realises too late she has failed to ask if printing so many booklets is really the best thing for the environment.)

She is exhausted by the end of the day, but she gets up early the next morning, goes for her run, smothers the ache in her belly. I am careful not to praise her too much. *Fat bitch. You're only doing what you should have started ages ago.* I know she needs to hear this.

And if I get tired of saying it, that's what I have to remind myself: she needs to hear this. Dermot is her reason for flab, for bulging, for eating her feelings. I need to be her reason for control. For strength.

Chapter Fifty-Seven

'Annabel,' the Boss says/thinks in that way that lets me know she's disappointed in me. 'Let's hear how it's been going since the last time we checked in.'

Can she tell I'm losing hope? Yes, Julia's running, restricting food, all that good stuff, but I'm getting nowhere. I still can't get inside my house. I can't even peer in, I've discovered; the second it looks like someone might be at the window I'm pushed away. Visiting the hospital girls is no problem. I can go visit Susan, read her terrible poetry, watch her take out all her razor blades and then put them away again with a little noble tilt of her head, so proud of herself. I can see Helen, eating dinner with her family, one bite at a time. But any hint of a glimpse of Imogen or Mum or Dad – forget about it.

'It's fine,' I say.

'Fine is –' she starts, and then stops herself.

'A four-letter word,' I finish. Shrink-speak. Fine is not a feeling word, it's a placeholder, a politeness. 'You sound like Dr Fields.'

'The psychologist in the hospital,' the Boss says. Like I don't already know.

'Don't tell me you know her.' Is there some collective for women, regardless of their life status, whose sole purpose seems to be to spout therapist-talk in my direction?

'Only through you.' She pauses. 'I used to be one of them.'

'A psychologist?'

'No, Annabel, a Capricorn. Yes, a psychologist.'

This is not surprising. Not exactly. Just that I never thought about her being anything other than what she is now. 'Were you any good?'

'At times. Other times, not particularly. I was depressed.'

'How depressed?'

There's something floating on the air that might be described as a rueful laugh.

'Are you telling me this so I can *relate* and *learn*?' I ask. The thing about therapists – they are selective with what they tell you about their personal lives. Or they're supposed to be. You're expected to tell them everything. They give away nothing, unless they think you might benefit from it in some way. Very manipulative. They want you to trust them so they can creep inside your head and screw you up.

'What do you think you might learn from it?' She's making fun of me now.

'I think you might want me to identify with having *suicidal tendencies*.' I would spit the words out. If I could. If I could.

'You didn't kill yourself,' she says. Gentle now. 'You were sick.'

I wasn't sick.

I wasn't.

I wasn't. That girl in the picture was fine. It might be a four-letter word, but fine is fine as far as I'm concerned.

Do you want to live, Annabel?

I try to shake it off.

'Christmas must have been hard,' the Boss says.

'No.' Lie.

'It'll get easier.' But I suspect she's lying, too.

I used to imagine this. Not quite this. I didn't have a concept of the Afterlife, if this quite counts. Didn't believe in ghosts. Used to tell ghost stories to Imogen just to freak her out, when she was little. Before I started explaining about calories and before she started telling on me. But now don't I look silly. If you'd asked me flat-out I'd have said there was nothing after death. Nothing at all. But I didn't really think about it. Not this.

I thought about floating.

I thought about light. Pure. Clean. Raw.

I thought about being free.

Statement of obviousness: I'm not feeling it. I'm really not.

'Come on,' she says. 'Tell me about how Julia's doing.'

Julia.

For some reason I don't want to talk about the food. I don't think she'd understand.

'There's a boy,' I say instead.

'Go on.'

'She likes him.'

'Does he like her?'

I miss the ability to shrug. 'He's a boy. He thinks she's nice, but, you know. She's fat.'

'Is that important to him?'

Is she for real? 'You've got to be kidding me. His last girlfriend was this tiny little thing . . .'

'And what happened there?'

'They broke up.'

The Boss waits. One of those expectant pauses. I know them well.

'I know what you're thinking,' I say irritably. 'Just because Lorraine was thin doesn't mean they were happy. Which you're then going to extrapolate into some big thing about how it's more important that we're comfortable in our own skins, blah blah blah.'

'Well,' she says.

'Julia's been eating her feelings since . . .' I almost don't want to say it out loud.

'Since?' Of course she can't let it slide, of course there's the prompt.

'Since this creepy asshole raped her,' I snap.

The Boss is silent for a moment. 'Okay.'

'Okay what?' And already it is too like those sessions in the hospital, seeing that glimmer of hope in their eyes when a boy or man was mentioned, their disgusting fizzy anticipation at finally identifying the origin of this alleged illness. 'It's not something I have personal experience of.'

'I didn't say that.'

'Okay.' I mimic her tone.

'It sounds like something important that Julia needs to deal with.'

'She is,' I say impatiently. 'I'm helping her. It's just not happening fast enough.'

'Things take time.'

'This is taking too long.' I don't mean it to sound like a whine, but it does.

'You could always give up,' she reminds me.

Give up or keep going. Give up or keep going.

Neither. I want to do neither.

I can't decide. When did I lose my ability to choose?

'Think about it,' she says finally, when maybe a minute or maybe an hour or maybe a day has passed.

Whenever it is next dark, I am outside my house. Then outside the hospital. Then at my grave.

Beloved daughter and sister.

Lies. Such lies. If I was really beloved, they wouldn't have made me go to the hospital. They would have respected me, instead of telling me it was wrong and that I was sick. They would have left me alone.

If I could spit. Oh, if I could spit on this grave.

Chapter Fifty-Eight

Maria is the one who finds her. Thursday afternoon, after school ends, Julia is alone in the newspaper office trying to breathe. In and out and in and out – but it's like her lungs aren't working any more. I can relate, Julia. The paper is half-empty. The paper due to go to print tomorrow morning.

'Hey, what's up?' Maria says.

'I can't do it.' Julia's eyes are manic. 'There's too much and I can't do it and everyone keeps flaking out and quitting and . . .'

'Okay. Okay. Calm down.' Maria says it even though she knows 'calm down' is one of the least helpful phrases ever invented. She looks at the computer screen behind Julia, which is opened up to an email.

Unfortunately I must resign from the newspaper as I cannot continue to meet the unreasonable expectations of the new editor, it says, with Sally's name at the bottom.

'Sally from fifth year? You're better off without her,' Maria says. She doesn't really know whether that's true or not, but it feels like the thing to say.

'It's not just her. It's everyone.' Julia wonders if this is what it feels like to have a nervous breakdown or if this is just simply how failure tastes. There's pounding in her chest and a dizzying sense of not-good-enough swirling around her. And then tears.

'Oh God, Julia. Hey. It's okay.' Maria grabs her, hugs her. 'It's okay.'

Julia lets herself sob for a moment, and then orders herself to stop. 'Ugh. No, I'm sorry. I feel like – such a hysterical girl, you know?'

'Shocking news, lady, you are a girl.' Maria grins.

'Yeah, I know, I just don't want to be –' Julia tries to phrase it as precisely as she can. 'I don't want to be the kind of girl who gets upset over nothing, who turns everything into a drama.'

Maria shakes her head, her heart aching. How long did it take her parents to accept that she was seriously unhappy at school and not just a diva? 'I don't think you are. If you're upset you've probably got a good reason to be. This newspaper stuff seems really stressful.'

'Yeah,' Julia says heavily.

'Okay. So. My spelling is appalling, but let me know what else I can do.' She settles herself at the next desk.

'No, no, it's fine.'

Maria raises an eyebrow. 'I've a couple of hours before I need to get home. What can I do? Is there anyone else I can rope into helping out?'

Julia opens her mouth and then closes it again.

'I know Deb's gone off swimming,' Maria continues, 'but Will might be around.'

Julia's waiting for her to say that one name. And then the burn of it gets too much. 'Do you have Gavin's number?'

211

'Gavin! He's a pet.' Maria is pleased with this. 'I'm going to call him. And make coffee.'

'Maria?'

She's almost out the door. 'Yeah?

'Thank you.'

Chapter Fifty-Nine

Maria hangs out until half five, helping out where she can, and then it's just Julia and Gavin, alternating roles of good cop/bad cop as they send messages to anyone who promised a piece and hasn't yet submitted it.

Some observations on the newspaper office between six and nine that evening:

1. Gavin very kindly doesn't mention that, once again, Julia told him this morning it was fine and all under control and there was no need for him to stay after school. He doesn't ask her why Maria asked for his help instead of Julia. He's starting to get how Julia works, starting to understand how much she'd love to be able to do all this by herself.

2. Julia thanks him for coming along, and hopes he knows there's an apology in there, too. That she really does appreciate him.

3. Some of the late pieces do actually come in, between

six-forty-two and seven-twenty-seven. Julia and Gavin argue, half argue, over whether to include these pieces. He thinks she's cutting off her nose to spite her face; she thinks she needs to establish her authority. He thinks she's going to want these people on board for the rest of the year and should keep them on her good side; she thinks that it's because she has to work with them until May that she needs to show them deadlines are serious business. He thinks she needs to fill the paper; she thinks they're better off having a shorter, better-quality issue. They compromise, picking out the best of the late pieces and coming up with a paper slightly shorter than the usual. They don't admit it out loud but it's satisfying to reach that compromise, like something's slotted into place as though it was made to fit.

4. They take a break and Julia shows Gavin Sally's email. He bursts out laughing, even as Julia launches into a rant about commitments and flakiness. They co-write a quick piece about that topic, mentioning no names, in the slot where Sally's material would have gone. He likes seeing Julia laughing, what it does to her eyes when she's found a way to transform her irritation.

5. Over the course of the three hours, Julia thinks about kissing Gavin four times.

6. When Julia's caught up in something, and there isn't food directly there, she doesn't eat, doesn't think about it. And when her stomach starts rumbling she's embarrassed, like she shouldn't ever be hungry. Gavin offers to get her something from the vending machine (chivalrous), but she shakes her head, her cheeks turning red.

7. At this stage, Gavin has thought about kissing Julia seven times. When he sees her looking embarrassed, it's time number eight, but it's the first time he imagines looking into her eyes before it happens, holding a clear, steady gaze.

8. They're kicked out at nine, when the school has to be locked up. They're almost there, and agree to meet at eight the next morning to finish it off. For a second, outside the school, it seems like there might be a hug, or something more, but then Julia says, 'Thanks,' and he says, 'No problem,' and then they go their separate ways, into the night.

It occurs to me, as a sense there could or should be something more hangs over that space outside the school where they've parted ways: if Julia's problem with food started with a bad guy, then a good guy should be part of my plan to help fix her.

Chapter Sixty

The next morning Julia's relieved but sheepish. She's the editor. She should have been able to handle it. She doesn't want to seem weak. She arrives into school at seven, has everything ready to go by the time a grumpy – not a morning person, remember? – Gavin turns up.

'Morning,' he says, pushing the door open. 'Sorry I'm late.' Five past eight. He is conscientious.

'It's okay,' she says, turning around in her chair. She smiles in what she thinks is a bright and capable way. I suppose it is. But put-on. 'I'm nearly finished.'

He looks over her shoulder. 'Wow. How long have you been in?'

She shrugs. 'Got in a bit early. Couldn't sleep.'

He feels useless now. And grumpy. (See above re: mornings.) 'Right. Good.'

Julia senses the grumpiness, then starts getting grumpy herself. It was good of him to stay last night, when she was tear-stained and desperate. But she needs to prove that she can do this herself. She's not going to depend on anyone, especially not a (*man*, she thinks, then corrects to *guy*).

216

'Yeah,' she says. 'It's almost ready to go to print.'

'To bed,' he says irritably. 'You put it to bed.' Newspaper terminology.

'People don't actually say that any more,' she says dismissively. She knows that in fact they do, but she needs to say something to stop her cheeks from burning. Bed. Gavin. Her mind is linking the two things and she wishes it'd stop.

He changes tactics. 'Next time I won't bother getting up early to do you a favour.' This is the moment he becomes aware of his own grouchiness. Normally his nice-guy brain is switched on, and he wouldn't dream of complaining about something he'd done because he felt it was the right thing to do.

Julia's jaw clenches. 'Next time? Thanks. Nice to know you have so much faith in me.'

'Hey, I'm not the one scaring people away from the paper every time I open my mouth,' Gavin says, and then immediately wishes he'd kept his shut.

'I – it's not my fault they're flaking out. I thought you got that.' Julia thinks back to the piece they wrote last night, how good it felt to be laughing beside him. Now the sting. The betrayal. She feels idiotic.

'You're right,' Gavin says. 'Forget I said anything.'

'No, I can't forget it. What did you mean by that?'

Gavin would very much appreciate it if a giant tornado swept through the school right now and took him somewhere far, far away. 'Some people think you take it too seriously,' he says finally.

'Taking something seriously isn't a bad thing,' Julia says.

He looks at her, a bit shaken but determined, and realises he agrees with her. 'No, it's not. You're right. I just don't think everyone's as passionate as you are. You're –' He lets out a breath. 'You're special.'

It should be a compliment, but it sends panic through Julia's veins. 'I'm not,' she says quietly. She turns back to the computer screen.

Gavin understands how compliment-fishing works. This doesn't feel like one of those occasions. Julia is not a girl he's trying to chat up for the night. 'Is there anything else left to do?' he asks instead. He waits. Then: 'Do you want me to just leave you alone?' It comes suddenly, and it's not something he's used to saying. Leaving someone alone instead of stepping in makes him feel powerless.

If he hadn't asked, or if he'd asked in a way that wasn't as gentle, in a way that made it sound like a punishment, she'd have told him to go. Instead she says, her voice still soft, 'No. Stay.'

He steps a little closer. His hand rests on her shoulder, and she takes a little shaky breath. Her head turns, her fingers reach up to touch his, and for a second there they are: just looking at each other, and it's the safest and scariest thing either of them has felt in a long time.

'Newspaper,' Julia says finally, with a little sheepish smile.

'Let's get on it,' Gavin says. Nods. Thinks: shit. Shit. I like her. I really, really like her.

Chapter Sixty-One

For the next two weeks they're back to their usual routine: Thursday evenings together, and messaging each other throughout the week. They swap interesting links, and sit next to each other the day their guidance counsellor explains how to fill out their CAO applications, listing off the courses they want to do in college in order of preference.

Drinking game, Gavin scrawls on a page of his A4 pad. *One shot every time she says 'order of preference'.*

Julia adds, *One sip! Otherwise we'll be on the floor.*

By the end of the talk, they've filled a page with their drinking game: finish your glass when she reminds you that it's the six best subjects that are counted, not all seven or eight.

I wonder what I would have on my list, if I was going to college. Not psychology, I quickly decide. Even though I am starting to understand – maybe even relate – to Dr Fields's frustration with me for not doing what she wanted me to do. Because as I watch Julia and Gavin walking together, I want to scream at them to hold hands, or to do something to acknowledge the whatever-it-is building between them.

219

Instead, Gavin goes to the library to do his homework, and ends up kissing Trish, the fourth-year representative for the paper. The librarian catches them and crosses her arms, not impressed. 'From now on,' she says to Gavin, 'you'll sit right here anytime you're in the library.' She taps a desk right under her nose.

Trish quite rightly deduces that this is due to Gavin having been in this position before. The shine of an older boy being interested in her vanishes, and she flounces off.

Trish is not at the next newspaper meeting. Julia receives a weirdly intense and vague message about her not being able to be on the staff any more because of a personal interaction with someone, and she doesn't want to name names, but she feels very hurt and upset and . . .

It's on Julia's mind as she looks around the room, taking in the changes to the staff. Will's here today, but he's been floating in and out for the past couple of weeks, depending on his level of study anxiety. (While Gavin and Julia were swapping notes at that talk, Will was trying to calculate his likely grades and worrying about failing maths.) Deb still turns up, but usually late and glued to her phone. Maria's started to come along and to contribute TV and film reviews; Julia is grateful for this and for the fact that her spelling isn't as bad as she claims.

'Anyone know any of the fourth years particularly well?' she asks. 'We need a new rep.'

'I'll cover their section this week,' Gavin offers.

'Cool, thanks.' It genuinely doesn't occur to Julia that he's doing anything other than being Nice Gavin – *Good* Gavin, she corrects herself – until afterwards.

'Listen,' he says, looking a little sheepish, 'I think Trish is upset with me. We had a bit of a misunderstanding.'

And then, idiotically, he actually relates the story as though he's expecting her to laugh along with him at the drama of it all.

Julia stares at him. 'Library Romeo,' she says.

He grins a little bit, and then realises it's not a compliment. 'Hey, it's completely ridiculous. We were just talking, and one thing led to another, and then we were caught . . . I think she's probably more embarrassed by that than anything.'

Julia's not buying it. 'How many girls is that now? Six? Seven?'

He counts back silently. The nightclub girls. Then the handful in school – Trish. Sally. Carolyn. Julia. He looks at Julia now, actually waiting for an answer. He doesn't want to sound sleazy.

'Not more than that,' she groans. 'Gavin, are you into double digits?'

He considers attempting a wink here. Resists. Thankfully. 'Maybe,' he says coyly.

'And what do you get out of it?'

He feels this is a stupid question with an obvious answer. Says nothing, but it's written all over his face. He gets girls. The attention, the intimacy, the fun. It's *fun*.

'Like . . . is it making up for not having Lorraine any more?' She genuinely wants to know, but when she sees the way his expression jumps from jovial to shocked, his mouth slightly open and his eyes hard, she regrets asking.

'You been with anyone recently?' His voice – oh, you wouldn't recognise it. Not the easy-going social Gavin, not the persuasive speaker. It's too sharp around the edges.

'Not recently,' she says quietly.

'So.' He says it like it's the end of the conversation.

'So what?'

'So FUCK OFF.'

It's funny how just certain words said loudly can bring tears to your eyes. Like a reflex. Julia looks at him and he's gone all fuzzy. Makes it feel even more like he's a stranger.

'You don't have a clue,' he says. No. No, of course it doesn't make up for not having a girlfriend. It doesn't make up for anything. It's its own separate thing – fun, distraction, light. What you do after having been with the same person for years.

'Don't I?' Julia says.

He looks at her. 'Some people actually *like* having a bit of fun. Not everyone freaks out and thinks a kiss is a big fucking deal and runs off like a crazy person.' He's been carrying that hurt around for a while.

Julia's bright red. And upset.

Come on. Stand up for yourself.

'It's not *crazy* to want to avoid being sucked into your web of using people just to try to get over your ex,' she says. 'Which is what you're doing; you're using people, you're not actually – you don't care about them, you don't give a shit, you just want some stupid slut to grope.'

Instant regret for Julia: use of the word slut. It makes her think of Deb and Sylvia, and she hates that. Hates the association with Sylvia, and then the word itself: only for the girls, never for the guys. She wants something harsh and cruel and she hates that there's no other word that seems to fit.

'You including yourself in that? Stupid slut? You're lucky anyone wants to –' He stops. Stops himself. Too far, Gavin.

'Lucky anyone wants to what?' she says. 'What, Gavin? Lucky anyone wants to grope me? I should feel so fortunate that the almighty Gavin was so kind and considerate as to want to feel me up.' Her teeth are gritted.

She doesn't look pretty here. Her face is patchily red, her hair is up in that wretched ponytail, her belly sticks out, the uniform's drab and she has tears in her eyes. But she's not standing down. Not giving in and trying to soothe him.

She looks . . . fierce.

'Yeah,' he says defiantly. She's a fucking head-wrecker, that's what she is. He's furious and shaky and hurt, beneath it all. She stopped that kiss. She won't let people in. She looks at him like he's this horrible person and he wants her to understand, to know that he's not a bad guy, that he's not leading these girls on, that he wouldn't be –

That he wouldn't be doing any of it if she'd just *kept kissing him.*

And Julia laughs. Laughs right in his face.

The bell goes for the end of the lunchbreak, and he stares at her, hard and cold, his own cheeks reddening now, before storming out.

Chapter Sixty-Two

Gavin spends Thursday caught in a will I/won't I about staying after school with Julia. The main thing that does it (he thinks) is that there's so much work to do – proofreading, fact-checking, finalising the layout – that it wouldn't be fair to leave it all on Julia's shoulders.

The actual thing that does it, for those of us able to tap into people's brains, is that he wants to see her. He likes these Thursdays with her.

'Hey,' he says.

'Hi,' she says tightly, glancing up from the keyboard before returning to typing with a suspicious intensity.

'I'm sorry about –' He's not quite sure what he's sorry for, exactly, only that he is.

'You know,' she says quickly, still staring at her screen, 'it's an abuse of power, messing around with one of the kids on staff.'

That's the last thing he was expecting to hear. It's like a punch. 'I didn't –'

Did he? Was he pushy? His mind spins back to that day. They were talking, and flirting, and then – did he put her in a situation where she felt like she had to go along with it?

Julia's unnerved by the silence. She turns around, looks at Gavin's face. And as soon as she sees it, she wants to hug him.

'I hope I didn't make her feel . . .' he starts, voice quiet, doing the most amount of overthinking of a kiss anyone in the history of humanity has ever done.

'Gav. You wouldn't.' She shakes her head. 'I'm sorry. That was my own – stuff – talking.' He doesn't realise that this might be the most personal thing she's ever admitted to him.

He doesn't know what to say. Defensiveness and worry are battling it out in his brain. 'It was just a kiss,' he says, and then hates how that sounds. 'Oh, for fuck's sake, Julia, I wouldn't do anything with anyone that they didn't want. I wouldn't.'

'I know. I know.' She stands up, moves closer to him. 'I know, okay?' Her hand rubs his arm.

'Friends?'

'Yeah.'

But they're too close. Too close to be friends, and it's too much, and then they're both leaning in and lips are on lips and there's pressing and holding and arms around each other. The kiss is magic and glitter, dissolving the world around them, and their thoughts blend and blur: oh, this. This. This.

Chapter Sixty-Three

The day after their kiss, their endless kissing, Julia's kicking herself over a typo in the paper, a TK left where there should be a figure that she was going to go and check. She leans against the wall of the office, groaning. 'I can't believe I missed it. I read that piece over and over again, and I missed it, I can't believe . . .'

Gavin says, 'Hey, it's all right, it's one tiny mistake.' He's right up next to her, his face so close, and Julia kisses him again, because this is Gavin and he's right here and she wants to kiss him, but . . .

'Mmmph,' she says.

He steps back. 'What?' His eyes seem to have grown; she looks into them and it feels like she might be safe.

'I . . .' she starts. She's had a sleepless night, a weird mix of exhilaration and fear running through her.

'What?' he says again, but this time with a smile, and leans in to kiss her neck.

'Gav.'

'Mmm.' His lips on her skin are too beautiful. She doesn't deserve this, she thinks.

'This doesn't mean anything, right?'

Gavin's nodding along in agreement until he actually hears her, then freezes. Stops kissing her. Steps back, looks at her. 'Oh,' he says.

'It doesn't, right? I mean, this is just another one of your rebound flings . . .' Julia waits for him to agree. If she is a sorbet girl then at least she'll know. Protect herself.

'No,' he says. 'Julia' and 'fling' are not two concepts that fit together in his head.

'It's okay,' she says, making herself laugh a little. 'I don't want you to get into something where you're making promises you can't keep. This isn't like that. It's okay.'

'It's okay,' he repeats.

'We can do this without it being a big thing,' she says. Like she's trying to reassure him.

He doesn't want to be reassured. Doesn't even really get why she's trying to reassure him of this. But then she leans in, kisses him, and that's that. Everything else vanishes.

Don't get too happy, Julia. We've still got a lot of work to do.

227

Chapter Sixty-Four

People with new, exciting love interests – still secret for the moment, still limited to shenanigans in the newspaper office rather than hand-holding in the corridors – often lose focus on the things that really matter. Julia falters a little as the days go on: skips a morning run, eats lunch, finishes her dinner. Accepts the offer of half a chocolate bar from Gavin one day after school, even though she hates eating in front of him.

These are small setbacks. I try not to take them personally, but it's hard. The next time she's on her computer consulting the pictures of me, now saved to a folder alongside articles and tips and other images – ribs and bones jutting out from under translucent skin – I push at her. *Remember Annabel*, I tell her, even though it feels ridiculous to talk about myself in the third person.

The next day she finds herself knocking on Mrs Kearney's door.

'Julia, come in. How are things?'

'Fine.' Julia hovers at the door until Mrs Kearney indicates she should sit. 'I just wanted to ask you a question for a piece

I'm doing for the paper. Is there any way of getting contact information for students in our year who've left the school?' She has her good-student voice on.

Mrs Kearney purses her lips. 'What's this for?'

'Well, it's our last year here, and I'd love to do a feature on how we've all got on over the past six years at the school, a now-and-then piece, and it'd be great if we could include people who started out with us, or who were here for a year or two . . .'

Mrs Kearney is not an idiot. There are already warning bells. Not specifically related to me. She just doesn't like the flavour of this. 'Oh, I don't think that would be appropriate, Julia.'

Julia would normally accept this. But she needs to know. About that girl in the photo, the girl at the party, the thin girl. 'So it's not possible to get contact information for them?' she asks.

Mrs Kearney frowns. 'It wouldn't be appropriate,' she repeats, her irritation visible now.

Julia stares at her. 'Did Annabel McCormack get expelled?'

Silence. Mrs Kearney is shaking her head – not to say no, but to despair of what exactly has happened to Julia Jacobs that she's coming in here with bizarre conspiracy theories. After some tut-tutting she says, 'Julia, we can't discuss confidential information about past pupils with students. You know that. Students leave the school for all kinds of reasons. This is not a suitable topic for the school newspaper to be looking into. Do I make myself clear?'

'Crystal,' Julia says sharply.

'Watch your tone.'

There are potential responses swelling up inside her, but Julia knows when to stop. She inclines her head slightly, just the tiniest hint of deference, but then leaves without apologising.

A dead end, she thinks, and I would almost laugh if I was alive.

That night, she checks again: Imogen McCormack has not yet added her as a friend. But she does, Julia sees, have the option to receive messages from anyone, so that's the button she hits now. *Hi, Imogen. I used to go to school with a girl called Annabel McCormack, who's in your profile picture – guessing you're sisters? I'd love to catch up with her – can you pass on my contact details?*

She imagines meeting Annabel. She imagines, though she doesn't realise it, being like Helen: looking for the secrets or tips that the thinnest girl might share, if you asked nicely. If she felt like you were worthy to share them with.

FEBRUARY

Chapter Sixty-Five

Julia puts on her serious face for the camera. 'Hello, my name is Julia Jacobs, and when I grow up . . . wait, that sounds stupid.' She shakes it off, starts again. 'My name is Julia Jacobs and I'm hoping to be a journalist.'

Behind the camera, Gavin grins. He likes the alliteration of it. Likes how solemn she's being.

Early February. A week and a bit into what Julia refers to as their palate-cleanser fling. Gavin's putting together a short video for Careers Day, with a copy of it to go into a time capsule the student council are working on. Julia's his first subject. Partly because she's so sure of what she wants to do, unlike him – his list of potential college courses is mainly parent-influenced and he's sure he'll change his mind before the summer – and partly because she's there, over at his house, sitting on his couch.

(Julia's on his couch, he thinks, in his house, where despite being Mr Nice Guy he hardly ever invites people. Somewhere in their brains they are both a little unsettled by how normal this is, already.)

'Wait,' Julia says. 'I'll do that again. My name is Julia Jacobs and I'm working towards becoming a professional journalist.'

'PMA,' he says with a grin.

'Crucial,' she says, looking serious, until the corners of her mouth twitch.

PMA stands for Positive Mental Attitude. It's a phrase their guidance counsellor loves – take two sips every time she mentions it, from their drinking game – and has now become an in-joke for the two of them, to be used half mockingly. Couples. Spare me. (There is no etiquette book for how you should gracefully react when the girl whose spiritual welfare you're – somewhat insanely – supposed to be concerned with gets a boyfriend, but I'm probably supposed to be more supportive than this. The cutesy stuff is just too much, though.)

'And what about journalism appeals to you?' Gavin asks, keeping the camera focused on her. He's got a decent enough camera function on his phone, but for this he prefers actual cameras. It feels sort of old fashioned, but he likes it.

'Well,' Julia says, and she's about to launch into what she's practised in her head for years, refined over the last few months – a whole speech about the importance of the press and reporting and questioning and awareness – when she sees the way his fingers are holding up the camera, the way the top button of his regulation school uniform shirt is open, the way he's just *there*, and she stops. 'The boys are cute,' she says instead, shrugging, and she smiles.

He laughs, puts down the camera and puts his arms around her. She's happy, but also sucks in, wishing she was tinier, thinner. She's lost some weight but it's not enough (never enough) and she thinks: at some point in the future, she will be thin and everything will be perfect. Everything will slot neatly into place.

This is the plan.

'You're cute,' he says. 'Actually, no, I misspoke. You're beautiful.'

She blushes. She can't believe him. Not yet. 'Gav, stop it. I'm not.'

'Stop fishing.' He kisses her neck. Breathes her in.

'I mean it. I'm – ugly, I'm fat. You even said it yourself.' There it is, she thinks, out on the table.

Everything freezes. 'Julia. Hey. Hey.' His eyes fix on hers. 'I never said that. I didn't say anything about that. God. You're gorgeous. I love your body.'

I love your body.

This is not the first time someone has said that to her.

A flash: *I love your body.* And another: *Has anyone ever told you how special you are?*

She won't let me in enough for me to identify the speaker, but I have a pretty good idea. Call-me-shithead – I mean Dermot.

'I have to go,' she says.

I try to reach her, but the words have done something to her, turned the beauty of the day into something ugly and warped. The low, after the high, is too much. She cracks. The newsagents, with its special-offer three chocolate bars for the price of two, is too tempting. The leftover Christmas chocolate is too tempting. The six-pack of crisps in the kitchen cupboard. A toasted cheese sandwich – no, two – no, four. Carbs. All the fucking carbs.

There is one good thing. She's been on the Annabel plan for so long that her system has forgotten how to handle the binges. So it's easy when she feels queasy, to help the process along, to slide her fingers into her mouth and reach for the back of her throat. Not even digested yet.

When she's finished, she goes to the computer and sends another message to Imogen.

235

Chapter Sixty-Six

Text messages between Julia and Gavin over the weekend:

Gavin: *Are you okay? Worried about you. x*

Gavin [twenty minutes later]: *Just let me know you're home safe. Please?*

Julia [half an hour later]: *Sorry for freaking out.*

Gavin: *No worries. You know I really do think you're beautiful. x*

Julia [unsent]: *I want so much to believe that. x*

Julia [unsent]: *You're beautiful. So so crazy about you.*

Julia [unsent]: *I just really really really don't want to be your sorbet girl.*

Julia: *You're too nice to me* ☺

Gavin: *Nice or good*??? ☺

Julia: *Don't start. See you Monday. x*

Chapter Sixty-Seven

It takes until the third message to get a reply. And like the photos, I can't see the words. Just Julia's responses.

Oh my God, I'm so sorry to hear that. I hope I didn't upset you.

It sounds awful.

No, it's okay!

Seriously. I'm here anytime you need to talk about her. ☺

It's only after those messages that she revisits the death notice, which doesn't say anything about anorexia, the term Imogen uses. The term everyone used, I suppose. (I don't object to the term, just the context: like it's a disease instead of a lifestyle.) She thinks: so that's why she was so thin.

She thinks: I could never be that disciplined.

She thinks: I want to know more about her.

I think: don't upset my sister, Julia.

I think: she's not going to tell you the right things. Just the lies my parents have fed her.

I think: I don't know what to think.

Chapter Sixty-Eight

It's exhausting. I forgot that part. How strong you need to be, to keep it up: the running and the limiting what you eat and the constant, constant awareness of that ache that you know you can't let yourself give in to. And Julia has other commitments. She has homework and babysitting and mock exams, the practice run for the real thing at the end of the year. She has her friends – well, Maria – and her sort-of friends. She has Gavin.

She is not yet at the point where none of this affects her. She feels everything too deeply. She breaks down sobbing one morning, mid-run, because she is not yet thin and it feels like she never will be. She sees another piece by Lorraine in the *Irish News*, about young people's engagement with local politics, and her heart is a painful stone in her chest. She could have written that. But Lorraine is better than her.

Every time Gavin kisses her, Julia worries that he's thinking about how much tinier Lorraine is. Every time he does something kind – leaving a tiny teddy bear in her schoolbag on Valentine's Day, which is in the middle of their exams and Julia's pretending to ignore (stupid commercial nonsense) – Julia wonders if it's just him falling back into old habits, doing what's expected of him as *a boyfriend*.

And then there's the Monday late in February, after their exams and mid-term break, when Deb doesn't show up to the newspaper meeting for the third time in a row, and Julia snaps. Stalks off to find her afterwards, and finds her leaning against the wall of the little sixth-year kitchen, talking to Lorraine.

'Where were you?' Julia demands.

Deb steps back. 'Here. Calm the fuck down.'

'It's Monday,' Julia says.

'Yeah, thanks, I know.'

Lorraine says nothing, just watches this unfold. Perhaps a little smug. Perhaps thinking how much better she'd handle this.

'So why weren't you at the meeting?'

Deb groans. 'Julia, I'm wrecked. We've just finished exams, for fuck's sake.'

'Yeah, I know, I did them, too. They're mock exams. As in, not actually the real thing.'

'They're still exams,' Deb says. Her arms are crossed, her eyes are steely. 'I don't want to screw them up. My mum'll kill me.'

Lorraine decides to step in here. 'Come on, Julia, it's just the school paper. You're taking this way too seriously.' Implied: Lorraine would never have got this upset about it. Lorraine has perspective. Lorraine has connections in the real world now.

Something snaps in Julia. 'Fine. I guess we're done.'

'Hey, I didn't say I wanted to quit the paper,' Deb says. 'I just meant –'

'No, I mean we're done. You and me. Done.' Julia's staring at Deb, but it applies to Lorraine, too. This is where it ends, she thinks. This is where she gives up on being helpful without it being appreciated, on being dismissed when it suits people.

Deb stares at her. 'That's a bit dramatic, isn't it?' Cold now. Even a little sneery.

'Julia, you're being really immature about this,' Lorraine says, with a tiny pseudo-sympathetic wince.

Julia gets very calm. Very quiet. 'Dramatic and immature. I see.' Eyes on Deb. Ice. 'Dramatic like someone who's spent the last year turning every single conversation around to her parents splitting up? Or immature like someone who'll put up with listening to this shit mostly because your fucking asshole father is getting her stuff into the newspapers?'

She walks out, leaving Lorraine going, 'Oh my God, where the hell did that come from?'

Gavin catches her on the way to class. 'Hey. Did you find Deb?'

'Yeah,' she says. Like a zombie.

He slips his hand into hers. 'How are you doing?'

'Grand,' she says vaguely. But inside: *What have I done what have I done what have I done?*

She thinks about the salty tang of a packet of crisps or the reassurance of bread or the crunch of cereal. About the smoothness of chocolate squares melting in her mouth. That will make everything okay.

No, Julia, no it won't.

He's reaching towards her, for a kiss, for comfort, and she can't breathe, she needs to get out of here.

Tell him. Tell him about Dermot.

'Hey,' she says, 'I have stuff to do so I'll see you later, okay?'

'What stuff?'

'Just – stuff.'

He is suspicious. Rightly so. Her face is flushed, her eyes panicky. 'What's going on?'

'Nothing. Nothing's going on, I just have to go. I'll see you later.'

More of the same. Her secret food stash is in her locker. She races there, empties it into her school bag. She wants it all and now but knows she has to find a secret place. Her heart is pounding.

Don't do it, Julia.

She can almost taste it all. She doesn't know where she'll start. She darts back up to the newspaper office and locks it behind her, the turn of the key reassuring her.

Weak. You are weak. Weak, pitiful, pathetic.

When you are really hungry, you don't care.

When you're starving, all you want is that food inside you.

If you are strong you will parcel it out. Tiny mouthfuls. Leave some on your plate, quieten that place inside you that is screaming for more.

If you are weak, you will shove it all down your throat as fast as you can until there's nothing left.

I can't help her once she starts. I shout and shout but she doesn't want to listen. I have to wait until she stops. Until she's ready to hear me again.

This time it's harder. She can't wait for nausea to hit. She has to do it herself. Her fingers jabbing hurt more this time, and when she throws up it reminds her of the Christmas party, but when it's over and she's rinsed her mouth there's something else there. Relief. Redemption.

Chapter Sixty-Nine

Hi Imogen, it's me again. I meant what I said about it being okay to talk to me about Annabel. Actually, I'd love to hear more about her. Would it be all right if we met for coffee (or hot chocolate or whatever) sometime soon? My treat. Julia x

I am not privy to this meeting. Of course. Julia is nervous the way she is before parties, figuring out what to wear. She feels oddly like she is competing with a dead girl.

Maybe she is.

I try to imagine if Imogen would tell Mum or Dad that she was meeting a strange girl. I wonder if she would say she was going to the cinema with friends, or going shopping – does she still hang out with the same bunch of friends? What were their names? I scrabble for details.

They meet in a cafe in the city centre. I'm not allowed in. That's how I know Imogen's already in there. I can watch the shoppers instead – groups of girls, giggling together, all with full faces of make-up. A married couple in their thirties, him off to buy shoes, her wondering when they can sit down for a cup of coffee. A younger couple, ostentatiously all over each other.

There's a girl eating an ice-cream cone. In February. She's maybe fifteen, sixteen. With her friends. She swirls her tongue around the edge and one of them makes an obvious dirty joke. She laughs. The air is cold but she's warm in her red hoodie, and happy. I tap into her brain and she's just: happy.

Meanwhile my baby sister is sitting in the cafe with a girl she only knows from the internet. An unsettling cloud surrounds me: this is not a thing that normal twelve-year-olds do. She should be with her friends. Or reading. Or dressing up. Or –

Imogen, Imogen. I hate Julia for being able to see her.

I hate that I can't remember any of her friends' names, because I was too busy – too caught up in my own head – to ever learn them in the first place.

I was strong, I remind myself. I was right and everyone else was wrong.

I was right, I was right, I was right, I was right I was right I was *right*. I repeat it over and over until the words blur together into a meaningless hum.

Chapter Seventy

Meanwhile, Gavin's been concocting a plan. To give him credit, he's no fool: he has two theories, and one of them is that Julia's got another boy on the go, and the other is that she has *issues* (he actually thinks the term) with food and body image. Being an optimist, he's plumping for (unfortunate choice of words) the latter.

He has a whole speech prepared about how he thinks girls are under way too much pressure to be physically attractive but also how he thinks she's beautiful but also *also* about everything else that he likes about her. Because he does like her, he thinks, and part of why he can tell is that her occasional freak-out moments would be too much hassle if they were coming from anyone else.

He needs to enlist someone else's help, and Deb's off the list – no one's talking about why exactly Deb and Julia aren't speaking to one another, which is unusual. Typically Deb would recount the conversation. Lorraine hasn't said anything, but she shoots Julia death glares every so often. (She's thinking about the *nerve* of Julia – to imply she's only being a good friend to Deb because her dad's helping her with her career.

The absolute nerve. Of course, she's growing more sympathetic towards Dermot – she can see the *adult* perspective – but understands that Deb mightn't.)

Gavin spends the next newspaper meeting – the one after the weekend where Julia and my little sister had a conversation I still know nothing about – assessing potential allies. Frank is too awkward, Will is not her biggest fan. And then Maria speaks up about a movie she's going to review this week, and Julia says, 'Oh, I really want to see that,' and his intense, work-minded girlfriend pauses the meeting for a whole minute while the two of them figure out a time that works for them both. Something inside him melts. (He tries not to show it. Julia's still being weird about people knowing.)

He hovers after school on Wednesday. Julia's picking up Grace, and Gavin's planning to spend the evening in the library (in what is still his designated seat, straight in the librarian's line of vision). 'Hey, Maria. Can I talk to you in private? Just for a second.'

Maria gets a strange flutter. It's a weird thing to be asked, and even though she's never fancied him, she's heard some of the stories. 'Sure.' They find a quiet corner near the library.

Once it's just the two of them, Gavin feels the nerves kicks in. It's not altogether unpleasant, sort of like a shot of espresso. 'So, uh, yeah,' says Mr Articulate. 'I was hoping you could help me out with something.'

Maria's brain goes to all kinds of places. 'Oh?' Her voice is just the tiniest bit higher than normal.

'Friday night,' he starts, and then freezes. Then unfreezes. He's put a lot of effort into this already, surely it'll pay off and

247

there's no need to panic now? He just needs Maria's help. 'Can you get Julia to the *Irish News* offices at about eight?'

Maria stares at him. 'What?'

Gavin feels his cheeks burning. He's not used to this sensation. 'I just need you to –'

'What the hell are you going to do to her?' Maria crosses her arms, stares at him. She doesn't know it, but it's a classic Julia pose. 'Because this sounds really creepy and screwed up.'

'What? It's not like that. I just want to – we're going to have a picnic, okay? But I want it to be a surprise.'

'You want to have a picnic,' Maria repeats. 'In some offices?'

When she says it like that, Gavin's face falls slightly. 'I just wanted to do something –'

It clicks for Maria even before he has a chance to finish. 'You *like* her,' she says.

And he feels a rush – because he hasn't been able to say this out loud to anyone else, hasn't been able to do much more than nod and shrug mysteriously whenever his friends start going on about how he's probably got a load of girls stashed away somewhere – and suddenly his whole face is lit up. 'I think she's amazing.'

Maria is this close, *this* close, to bursting into tears. Not that she's secretly wishing that Gavin had a crush on her, but because it's just so sweet. He's pulsing with joy.

'That's great,' she says, barely holding it together. 'Oh my God. Does she know? Does she know anything?'

The sensible part of Gavin knows he should probably try to do this sharing as little information as possible. That part of him seems to have run off looking for a snack or something. 'We've been fooling around a little bit,' he says.

Maria shrieks, then calms herself. 'But you're not, like, officially together,' she says, sussing it out pretty quick. Julia's keeping it to herself for a reason.

Gavin shakes his head. 'But –'

'But you want to be. Oh my God. You guys are just – this is just –' Maria's struggling with not letting the pin-pricks at the back of her eyelids go any further.

Gavin is right there with her. Not quite with the tears, but with that struggle to find the right words. 'So you'll help?'

Chapter Seventy-One

Friday evening, and Julia's staring at herself in the mirror again. She's not good enough, not thin enough, and she digs her nails into the flesh on her belly and wishes she could just rip it out, just tear the skin and excavate all this fat. She can see it clearly for a moment, and it makes her want to weep with the unfairness of the world. She is lighter than she has been for over a year, but it is not enough. Nothing is enough.

She reaches for her food notebook, and turns to the back page. There are numbers there. Numbers I haven't seen before.

No. Numbers I haven't seen written down in that notebook before. But numbers I know. My lowest weight. And my weight when I died. Not the same. Close, but not the same.

Numbers Imogen apparently carries around in her head, ready to hand over to strangers. (Why does my baby sister carry those numbers around? I know what carrying numbers in your head means. How can my baby sister, who thinks thinness is something Santa might bring you, be carrying numbers around in her head?)

Julia's phone beeps and she slams the book shut. It's Maria. *Be outside in 5.* Julia's heart pounds, not for the first time that day. She's been hiding from parties for the last while, and now the prospect of going out, even just to keep Maria company at her friend's gathering for an hour, feels like stepping into a dark shadowy alley where bad things will inevitably happen.

Black. She'll wear black. She has an image, suddenly, of vibrant reds, then of vivid greens – bright colours, colours that you are allowed to wear only if you are skinny, unless you want to be ridiculed. She imagines slinky dresses and jeans and her breath starts coming in gasps. She grabs her phone. *I'm sorry. I'm so sorry, but I really can't go to the party tonight. Really.*

Already the guilt is crawling in, but it has to be done. There is no way she can smile and be pleasant at some party, even if Maria begged her to go, even if she promised it was just for a little bit, there's just no way. The screen lights up a split second before the ringing begins, and Julia holds down the power button until it all fades away and the screen goes black. Phone off.

Her dad's just gone to work; her mum's taken Grace over to a friend of hers so that they can drink coffee and have toddler-obsessed chat. So the house is empty – of people, anyway. She still finds herself creeping down to the kitchen like she's afraid someone will catch her.

Don't do this, Julia. You're better than this.

(But my heart is strangely not in it today. Maybe because it stopped working months ago.)

'Julia! I know you're in there!' Maria shouts through the letterbox. 'Come on, let me in.' She pounds on the door, and the surprise of it is what hits Julia most.

Deb wouldn't do this. Deb would be annoyed with her, but not actually turn up.

She opens the door, uncomfortably aware of the fact that she is still not dressed for a party or indeed for any human interaction, with her school uniform skirt still on and a ratty T-shirt pulled over it. 'I can't go,' she says. It sounds so feeble now that Maria's standing in front of her.

'Sure you can,' Maria says. 'It's just for a little while.'

Julia shakes her head. 'I really can't.'

'What is it?' Maria looks her up and down. 'Are you having a crisis about what to wear?'

Julia lets out a sharp laugh. If only, she thinks, if only. 'I'm having a crisis about my fucking *body*, Maria.'

Maria thinks back to that party. Thinks back to how calm Julia seemed about being called fat, so accepting of it, even though it's not a word Maria would ever think to use for her (she does, I suddenly see, view Julia as pretty). Now she looks at her, sees how Julia's jaw is set like rock but how her eyes are starting to fill up and how her hands are shaking. 'Okay,' she says. 'Okay.'

She nudges Julia upstairs to her bedroom, delivering a pep talk en route. 'Okay. Two things you need to remember. The first is: fake it until you make it. Act confident. Act sexy.'

'I can't act,' Julia says.

'Sure you can. Look, we all do it a little bit every single day. We act like we're okay, like everything's fine, and it's not.'

Julia isn't an idiot. 'What's going on with you?'

Maria shrugs. 'Nothing.'

Julia starts laughing. 'Case in point. Come on, what's up?' This is easier than having to think about herself.

'Nothing specific,' Maria amends.

252

Julia stares her out of it.

Maria blinks. 'Look. I spent pretty much every day at my old school being left out of things, or being made fun of . . .' She shrugs again, leans against Julia's bedroom wall. 'It's not important.'

Julia's eyes are wide. Sympathetic. 'I had no idea. God, Maria. That's horrible.'

For a second, I imagine myself there with both of them, in my body, all three of us friends together. For a second I want to be *there* for them. Stupid.

'But now,' Maria says brightly, 'I have great friends. Including one who's going to decide what to wear so we can go out soon, right?' She thinks of Gavin, waiting.

Julia sighs. 'Right. What was the second thing?'

Maria's brain flicks back to her spiel. 'Second thing: you need to accentuate what you have. Everyone has stuff about their body they hate. Everyone.'

Julia's heard this before. 'Yeah, stuff. *Bits*. Not their whole body.'

'Really? You hate your nose?' Maria folds her arms.

If I knew she'd hear me I'd tell her to leave it. Don't go down this road. Julia doesn't hate her nose because it hasn't occurred to her to hate it yet. If you ask her to, if you point it out –

'No.'

'Right. Because it's a great nose. I hate mine. It's too big, it's totally out of proportion. Okay. Feet? Do you have weird feet?'

Julia has never considered them. 'I don't know. Maybe.'

'Bad example. Practically everyone hates their feet. Okay, your hands. Look at your hands.'

Julia holds them out. They're – I want to say pudgy, but that feels wrong somehow. There's something about the word that doesn't quite fit.

'Those,' Maria says, nodding at them, 'are those fancy hands that make the newspaper happen every week.'

'Oh for God's sake,' Julia says. 'So what? That's nothing to do with being – pretty.' The word sounds laughable out loud. So disconnected from her. It's not the sort of word made for girls like her, she thinks.

Maria's phone starts going off. Gavin. She doesn't pick up. 'Of course you're pretty,' she says over the chiming of her ring tone. 'But – come on, Julia, pretty?' She thinks about the girls in her old school, with sleek hair and smooth faces and ugly souls. 'You're smart, and you're passionate, and you're kind, and there are so many more important things to be worrying about.' She looks at Julia's bookshelves, the diet books piled up in front of all the shelved ones, so that only certain words from their titles can be seen: *Women in*, *A History of*, *Political Thought From*.

Realisation, and it hits me maybe at the same time that Julia's figuring it out: Maria's disappointed. She thought Julia was better than this.

Hey. This is important.

Julia turns away. Can't look at Maria. Can't look at herself in the mirror. 'You should go to the party. They'll be waiting for you.'

'I'm not going to some ridiculous party. I'm luring you down to some offices so Gavin can seduce you, or whatever.' Maria is weary now. 'Just get dressed and come on, okay? He's waiting.'

Julia moves like the air is suddenly ten times heavier. There isn't a party. There's Gavin. This is a secret plan of the kind that happens to other people, but not to her, except now it's her turn and why can't she think properly?

She puts on a flowing black top over leggings, sprays perfume on her wrists, smears on eye shadow.

From the train station, they walk mostly in silence to the offices. Maria's feeling it, the weight of that floating sadness about to swoop down on her, the kind that makes her just feel sad about the world. Julia's got this amazing night ahead of her, she thinks, and she doesn't appreciate it, or get it, and she's filled with all this body-image crap that seems like it should be beneath her, and . . .

Meanwhile, Julia is frozen. Nothing to do with the weather, which is mild for February, but because she knows where they're going.

'Oh,' she says. 'It's the *Irish News* offices.'

'Yeah, that's what he said.' Maria consults her phone, where she's got a little map open telling her where she is, where she needs to be. Pity we don't have GPS in the Afterlife. 'Weird place for a date, right?'

'They've got, um . . .' Julia takes a breath. 'They've got this door that goes up onto the roof. It's a great view.' It overlooks the canal, she remembers. Looks out over all the city lights, all the lights and all the people going about their lives.

The last time she was up there she felt like she was floating.

'Sounds cool,' Maria says.

'Yeah. It is.'

'Go, Gavin.'

'Yeah.' Julia knows her voice sounds too heavy. 'He must have really thought about this. It's really thoughtful.' Says the aspiring writer. But Maria doesn't seem to pick up on the repetition.

'He's one of the good ones,' Maria says, sounding much older than she is.

Julia nods, fights back the tightening of her throat.

'He really likes you.'

Julia knows this. She knows this, even if she's not quite sure why. Even if it all feels like something that's about to slip out of her grasp. This is a tightrope she's on and everyone falls eventually, she knows, and fat girls fall first.

A flash, suddenly, as they come to the door of a tall Georgian building with a set of elegant signs, the *Irish News* among them, to the left. Julia wrote a letter to the editor when she was younger, about a piece they'd run during the summer about making sure your kids didn't get obese and got plenty of exercise. *Health is more important than weight*, she'd typed earnestly, fourteen and slender and believing it. She'd included a rant about the dieting industry that had statistics about how much money they made from convincing people that obesity was a big health crisis in and of itself. They didn't include that part, which annoyed her at the time, even though she was pleased to see her name in print.

She's thinking about that now, and it's not making any difference. Her brain puts it in a separate little box and goes back to feeling too fat, too much.

'Gavin? Hey, we're outside.' Maria turns to Julia after he's hung up. 'He'll be down in a sec. Don't tell him I told you, okay?'

'Okay,' Julia says. This feels like going into an exam, only ten times worse. She knows how to handle exams.

The door opens. 'Hey,' Gavin says. Big smile. He's dressed up – not quite venturing into suit territory, but smart trousers and a shirt (clean, ironed) and shined-up shoes.

'I'll leave you two alone,' Maria says quickly.

'Are you going to be okay getting home?' Gavin looks up and down the street. Dark and quiet. This feels like a safe road. But still.

'Yeah, absolutely.' Maria just wants to get out of there.

'Text me when you get home? And listen – thanks a million.'

She nods, flees.

Julia is staring at him.

'Hey,' Gavin says. 'Surprise.'

Her eyes are stinging. 'You're one of the good ones,' she says, and it's like her voice is coming from far away, but Gavin can't tell, he thinks this is all wonderful, and he cups her face and kisses her like there's no tomorrow.

Chapter Seventy-Two

Gavin's mum knows the editor, as it turns out, because apparently half of the Richmond School are linked in some way to this paper, so they get a tour – brief, as there are still plenty of people working – of the offices. On one wall there are photos of various journalists at the paper, past and present, often with famous people; Julia looks through them rather than at them. There haven't been that many additions in the past year.

The phrases rush at me. *I love your body. Has anyone ever told you how special you are? God, I can't believe how beautiful you are.*

Julia's shell is starting to crack. And then they're going through the door, and Julia follows Gavin up the little staircase out onto the roof, and there it is. Like it was yesterday.

Freedom of the press is essential. Without that, you've just got all those guys in power completely unaccountable. The media is . . . You have to respect your writers, but you can't let them take the piss, either . . . Work experience is one thing, Julia, but don't let them take advantage of you. You have to place a value on your work . . .

'Pretty cool, huh?' Gavin says.

'Yeah,' she says distantly.

She's been up here before. Slipping away from a party in her red dress, the weekend after finishing her work experience. 'I miss you, too . . . Yeah, okay, give me twenty minutes to get there.' And after she hangs up the phone, she meets Dermot around the back entrance. He takes her up here, serves up compliments and champagne in plastic glasses.

You're so smart. You're going to do so well, Julia. You know your stuff . . . God, you're beautiful . . . I love your body . . . I can't leave her, you know I can't, but can't we just . . .

And I'm there, now, with her, finally accessing it: Julia can't believe it's happening and she knows it's weird and it's Deb's *dad*, holy crap, but he's handsome and the way he's looking at her, the things he says, it's like she's the only girl in the world. And when he kisses her it's harder to remember all the reasons she shouldn't be doing this. And when he gently moves his hands underneath her clothes she wants it. She gasps. The world around them dissolves.

His weight on her and she gasps and she loves it. Loves him.

That was the first time. Not the last.

'What do you think?' Gavin wants to know, half pleased with himself and half worried she's going to tell him that this is not in the least bit romantic and how the last thing she wants to do on a Friday night is hang out in a workplace, even if it is a whole sexy rooftop picnic thing.

I can't leave her, Julia . . . I have to think of my daughter . . . She remembers that now. Tracy was always just *her*. And Deb was always *my daughter*, like Julia was much older, someone

259

he could talk to about his children instead of being friends with them.

Julia never asked. She was proud of that at the time. She liked Tracy. She understood it perfectly: it was a sexless marriage, a loveless marriage. But it was tolerable, and they had a routine, and Julia never asked him, not once, to leave his wife.

She never asked and then he did. Later. For Sylvia.

There it is, the memory unlocked, still raw and fresh, and I want to cry and yell and slap and do all those things you can do with a body. Suddenly I understand Susan tearing at her flesh: sometimes you need to hurt yourself to make a shock seem real.

'Julia?' Gavin checks.

She is only half aware of his voice. She walks around the blanket he's set out. Actually, there are two, she realises, which is wise because it's February and the ground is cold and she's still got her coat on. 'Is this chicken salad?' she asks, inspecting a plastic bowl with clingfilm stretched over it.

'Yeah.' He looks sheepish suddenly. 'I didn't want – I wanted to make sure it was something you'd eat.'

A flurry of panic in her chest. 'How do you know what I eat?'

Gavin shrugs. 'I pay attention?' He laughs. Of course he pays attention. He wants to know things about her.

She doesn't want him paying attention. She doesn't want him noticing what she's putting in her mouth, judging her for it.

She looks inside the freezer bag sitting next to the blanket. There's wine – white – and she thinks about the calories. And chocolate mousse, so there's no way she's going near that. And next to that, what looks like – yes. Maybe strawberry or maybe raspberry, but definitely sorbet.

'You got sorbet,' she says.

'Yeah,' he says, and he's grinning.

Even without a body I can feel the cold now. Julia's feeling it. She stares at him.

'Because you're my sorbet girl,' he says, like it's another of their in-jokes.

'Is that what I am?' The words are hard to get out.

'Hey. No. God, I – sorry, I thought it'd be funny.' Gavin's disappointed. Kicking himself. He steps a little closer. 'Julia, sorry, it was stupid. Forget it.'

It's too cold here. She doesn't look at him.

'Come on. I'll get rid of it.' He takes out the container and empties the red slush out over the side of the building. 'It's gone. That's what I think of sorbet,' he says firmly.

Another flash, another time: Dermot holds up the spoon to her mouth, gets her to taste it, and she ends up with brain freeze. He laughs and kisses her and then takes her to a hotel where she studiously avoids looking at the girl at the reception desk as they walk past.

He's waiting, now, Gavin, for her response – a laugh or a smile or something to indicate he's fixed a mistake he didn't even realise he was making.

'I should go,' she says.

'What? Come on, don't be like that, sit down.' He indicates the blankets, and he's even got his phone set up with a romantic playlist, and he's been planning this all week and now it's all falling apart and he doesn't know why. 'Julia, I know – I think I know – that this food stuff is an issue for you, but . . .'

He's all ready for his speech, if a little thrown, but she shakes her head. Not listening.

Words, Julia, words might be helpful right now. But she's too far gone, and there's just her racing down the steps, and then down four flights of stairs until she's outside again.

She's going home to eat. To forget.

I don't think I have the energy to stop her, and I'm not sure I want to.

A flash: it wasn't when he stopped seeing her. *We can't keep doing this.* That wasn't when it started. There were tears. There was walking around in a haze. But that wasn't when food started to save her, when it was easier to swallow calories than to think or feel.

Another flash: three weeks later. Deb's on the phone, sobbing down the line. Her dad's moved out. He's left her mum – and for a second it's like a dream come true for Julia – to move in with this bitch Sylvia. He loves her more, Julia thinks. He loves her more. And she understands suddenly, horribly, what she is. Not some great love or temptation. Just something in between courses.

I love your body . . . Have you had sorbet before? Try it . . . We can't keep doing this . . . You always knew what the situation was . . . I'm sorry you feel that way . . . I love your body . . .

Chapter Seventy-Three

Julia's missed calls:

8.14 p.m. Gavin

8.17 p.m. Gavin

8.19 p.m. Gavin

8.25 p.m. Gavin

8.33 p.m. Maria

8.36 p.m. Maria

8.41 p.m. Gavin

9.12 p.m. Gavin

9.15 p.m. Gavin

9.38 p.m. Gavin

9.45 p.m. Maria

10.01 p.m. Gavin

10.33 p.m. Gavin

10.59 p.m. Gavin

11.22 p.m. Gavin

11.48 p.m. Gavin

12.35 a.m. Gavin

On Saturday morning, she retrieves the phone from her bag, deletes any texts and voicemails, and turns it off.

MARCH

Chapter Seventy-Four

'He didn't rape her.' I am blank. I am with the Boss, checking in, and that's all I can think.

'He was older than her, though. He took advantage of her.' Her voice is kind.

I want to shake my head. If I had one. It was legal. Barely. But legal. 'She thought – she thinks –' I don't know how to explain it, except that I understand how Julia sees it now. Dermot is not the big scary rapist who took advantage of her. She knew. She knew when she put on her red dress, the one that lies in slivers at the bottom of her wardrobe, that he might call. She knew when she put on her best black underwear that night. She knew when he called her late, after Tracy was asleep, his voice low in her ear, coaxing her into telling him what she was doing to herself . . . it was exciting and exhilarating and sexy. The aliveness. Her body thrumming with desire.

I didn't know bodies could feel like that. I am jealous of her, even though it hurt her afterwards. Even though hearing that he'd left Tracy for someone else was like a knife.

I don't know how to fix her. I don't know if my way is working. I don't understand what it is to love or lust after someone like that.

And if I can't fix her, then I can't tell my family what I think of them, can't tell them they were wrong, that I wasn't . . .

Do you know how exhausting it is, never being able to sleep? It's been months, months of this, and I just want to sleep. One fucking good night's sleep, is that too much to ask for?

'What are you thinking, Annabel?' The Boss is gentle now. Shrinks! Honestly.

I am thinking it's high-level dysfunction, that Dermot is a fucking creep, but that she loved him, or thought she did. I am thinking this isn't about what happened to her body but what happened to her heart.

But it's all mixed up together. You don't get to be just a body or just a heart or a mind or spirit or whatever the hell you want to call it. Unless you're me, of course. Lucky, lucky me.

I miss my body.

I don't.

But.

I hate this.

'She's an idiot,' I tell the Boss.

'Is that really what you think?'

'Yeah,' I say, like I'm sulking, and maybe I am, and that's it. This meeting is over. I wish myself away. Not home, to lurk outside Imogen's window. Not back to Julia's, or to watch Gavin or Maria or any of the others. I need someone who understands.

In a soothing pale-green room, Helen is talking. Helen, Helen, why are you actually talking to her?

'I think I might want to do psychology,' she says.

The counsellor lady nods. Bet she's loving this.

'I know you're not supposed to go in there trying to fix your own problems,' she continues. 'But I think it helps, if you've been . . .'

I watch her face. She's trying to think of the right words. I know this look of Helen's, only I haven't seen it used on counsellors. With adults. Only us, late at night, trying to find the words to put on the things we couldn't tell them.

The counsellor waits patiently. They do this. Some of them are worse than others. They'll sit there for ages, waiting for you to talk. Great job, getting paid to sit there in silence. They probably plan their weekend in their heads, figure out what they're going to have for dinner, what they're going to do.

'If you've been in the dark place,' she says finally, with a bit of a laugh.

It wasn't dark, Helen. It was pure and it was light and you were almost there, so close, and now . . .

She's put on weight. I can see it in her face, even though she's covered herself up in baggy clothes. The bone's vanishing from sight. She's not fat, not Julia, but she's not what she was. She's . . .

The word that is coming to mind is *more*.

Not grotesque. Just more.

There is more to her now.

And I don't want to be here any more, don't want to be around this.

I hate this. It's not fair, any of it.

Chapter Seventy-Five

Julia Jacobs, editor of the school newspaper, gets mostly As and a couple of Bs in her mock exams, which don't even count, and she doesn't tell anyone. Not Gavin, not Maria, not Deb, not her parents. She goes through the meetings on autopilot and doesn't look anyone in the eye. She sits in class and takes notes and does her homework. And then she thinks about food and how much she weighs and how much exercise she needs to do and how fat she is and this goes on and on and on.

I just feel so guilty all of the time. This morning I went out for a run but I know I could have gone faster, and then I ate lunch even though I know I shouldn't, especially after going over my allowance yesterday.

She is still messaging Imogen. I want so much to know what the other side of the conversation looks like. It eats – ugh – away at me.

That's a really good idea, I'm going to try that. Stay strong. x

What's a good idea, I want to know. What's Imogen saying? What does she even know? Maybe she's just regurgitating all the stuff our mother used to say. Advice for healthy eating. Not that she was right about any of it, except –

270

I don't know what to think any more. If I could cry. Do you know what a relief crying is? I remember it and it's like knives all over, not being able to do it. The hurt all building up and then the release.

I want Julia to cry, to tell someone about Dermot – because she still needs to talk about it, no matter how grown up she thinks she was at the time, no matter how ready, because it has left scars on her that no one in her life even thinks to look for.

I want her to tell Gavin, but she's ignoring his texts, his messages and everything he's said that isn't directly connected to the newspaper. He's back on the kissing-every-girl-in-sight train, only his heart's not in it. If Julia just explained, I know he'd understand. I know. She used to think he was a good guy, not just nice. She's right.

But she's ignoring everyone: she won't talk to Maria any more, except at meetings, and Deb and Lorraine aren't speaking to her. She keeps conversation with her parents to a bare minimum. Even when her mum asks if she's okay – running water doesn't always cover up the hacking sounds of throwing up – she says she's fine, just maybe ate something dodgy. Her mum puts her hand to her forehead to check her temperature but doesn't think to ask, *Is there anything you want to tell me about sleeping with your former best friend's father that might have felt right at the time but in retrospect was clearly incredibly fucked up?*

Why would you?

Yeah, sometimes I do that too. I know it's not the same but it's such a relief. xxx

What? What, Julia, what do you do? What do you do that my baby sister does also? Click obsessively through photos of Gavin while still ignoring his messages? Stay up late doing homework?

My death notice is bookmarked now. Today, today exactly, it's been six months. Six months since I died.

In the house that used to be my home, even though I can't see in, I can hear my mother's scream. 'Imogen, for the love of God, eat your dinner!'

Her sobs are quieter. I have to strain my incorporeal ears to hear them.

Chapter Seventy-Six

A Thursday in mid-March. Julia's in the newspaper office, and Gavin is in the computer lab, proofreading and then emailing copies on to Julia, without comment. This is how they do it, these days.

There is something fuzzy in the air, she thinks, but she's getting used to feeling that way. She's losing weight – not fast enough, she thinks, but it's happening. Last weekend her aunt and uncle came over, told her she was looking fabulous – but then again, they always say that. She can't take these things seriously. She knows she is not good enough.

The only person who understands is –

No. Julia. You can't think that. Imogen doesn't understand. Just because she was my sister, she doesn't –

I don't know. I want Imogen to have someone she can talk to. A big sister, now that she's 'lost' hers. Every time Julia types a message, part of me thinks that I would probably say exactly the same things. Wouldn't I?

Didn't I? (Isn't this exactly what I wanted, for Julia to understand?)

Her phone is on the desk next to the computer, and there's

a new message from Imogen, which of course I am not allowed to access, and another one from Gavin – she checks that one first, hoping it might be something personal. It isn't, and she's weirdly disappointed and relieved simultaneously. It is easier this way.

Even if Gavin thinks – thought – that he liked her, Julia is just a sorbet girl. He'd realise it eventually. Find a better girl. Better, prettier, thinner.

A knock on the door, although it opens before she has a chance to answer. 'Julia?'

She spins around in her chair to see Mr Briscoe there with a sheaf of papers in his hand, and then the fuzziness in the air increases, and the corners of her vision are dark suddenly, and then she's on the floor.

'Shit!' Mr Briscoe says, setting down his papers. He freezes for a moment then, because he knows he has to help her but is also terrified of touching her. Not, it must be said, in case he hurts her, but because he is conscious he is a male teacher alone with a female student and any physical contact should be avoided. He leans out into the corridor, checks if there's anyone else there – a nice lady teacher to come along and help out – but there isn't.

Julia's come to by the time he starts trying to pull her up to a seated position. 'I'm fine,' she mutters, her cheeks red. It's always embarrassing when people witness it. I remember that now.

'You fainted!' he says, like she hasn't figured that out. 'Will I ring your mum or dad and get them to pick you up?'

'No, it's okay,' she says.

'Or I can ring your GP . . .' He's trying to think of what the best thing to do is. If it were during the school day, the PE teacher would be on hand for dealing with any health crises, or the reassuring school secretary would have something wise to say, but there's only a handful of staff still in the building.

'It's fine,' she says again, sharper this time. And then she uses the great excuse that gets teenage girls out of any awkward situation with male teachers: 'It's just my time of the month.'

And despite having heard this before from many students, some more trustworthy than others, he suddenly finds the carpet extremely interesting. I should be glad he's leaving her alone. I should be. But I feel like he's an idiot, all the same.

When Julia tells Imogen about this later, still tapping away at the computer in school, I suddenly know the story Imogen will tell her. Her first period. Ten and a half – too early, really. I wanted to hug her and reassure her, but she scowled at me and stormed off into my room. Opened my wardrobe. She started flinging things out onto the bed – years' worth of sanitary towels and tampons, purchased regularly by our mother for me and hardly ever needed. But it was one of the things she watched out for: if the supply in the bathroom was regularly raided, she could breathe a little easier, become less watchful.

'You don't know how it feels!' she screamed at me, and then of course our mother came running, and saw, and knew, and there was another doctor's appointment, another panic about whether there was a hospital bed available, and all the while Imogen was there, sobbing half with the physical pain and half with the other kind, the kind that – I've discovered – clings to you even after you die.

Julia goes home and doesn't tell her parents about the fainting. That would make them worry. Make them notice.

I know exactly how she feels, only I find myself whispering, pointlessly, into her parents' ears that night: *Notice her. Look at her.*

Chapter Seventy-Seven

The Easter holidays come as a relief. Mondays are becoming exhausting – dealing with people. Being in charge of the newspaper. All she wants to write about right now is food. She reads some of Dermot's old work online, perusing it like pornography. He has a way of describing restaurant meals like sex. (I am pretty sure this is deliberate, a way of trying to make himself seem desirable and cool, but I also know I don't think about either food or sex like normal people do.)

When she wakes up on the first Sunday of the break, there's a 2 a.m. message from Gavin. *Julia just want to say I still think your amazing & really wish yuod given us a cahcne because we had SOMETHING xxx*

She deduces, rightly, from the spelling and the hour that this is a message sent under the influence of alcohol. But she presses her finger against the screen of the phone anyway, fondly, before remembering that she can't take this kind of nonsense seriously.

Gavin probably sent the message and then turned around and kissed a beautiful blonde creature, she thinks. Wrongly. (He was over at Will's house going on about Julia, gesturing dramatically, while Will and Frank looked on in slight terror and bewilderment, until Gavin fell asleep on the couch. They are all going to pretend it never happened. Will is also going to deny all knowledge of the black-marker doodles that appeared on Gavin's face during the night.)

On the third day of the Easter holidays, her mum says, 'So we booked the hotel.'

'Hmm?' Julia looks up from the computer to where her mum's hovering in the doorway of her bedroom.

'Down in Wexford. Thursday to Sunday.'

It takes Julia a moment to remember that this is one of those things – like New Year's diets – that her parents have been talking about but that she suspected was never going to happen. A few days away 'somewhere nice' for the whole family.

The change of plans alarms her.

They travel down in the car, her dad driving while her mum shuffles through the music on the car radio and sings along. It's not a particularly long journey, a couple of hours, but they stop on the way anyway. 'For a bite to eat,' her dad says.

That's the moment when Julia realises that she's facing four days in close proximity with her family. Her parents with time off, not racing off to work or making dinner. Grace is not enough of a distraction under these circumstances.

'You haven't eaten anything all day,' her mum says at dinner that night, after Julia orders a salad. No dressing. 'Get something more substantial.'

'I'm fine,' Julia says.

Grace is under the table, and her dad has ducked under to rescue her and place her in her special high chair. As he sorts that out, Julia's mum checks her forehead, then the glands at her neck. 'You need to eat something more, pet. Keep your strength up.'

'I'm fine,' Julia repeats, staring at the table, her eyes stupidly blurry. Something like guilt creeps around me. I try to shrug it off.

Julia's mum conducts one of those parental eye-conversations with her husband, urging him to back her up.

'Have some of my chips,' he says.

'I'm fine, Dad,' she says, her voice getting colder.

They don't understand, she thinks. They're trying to undermine her. She can't let it happen.

There is a look on her mum's face I have seen before. It's like a stab to the gut. Julia swallows, air and saliva. 'I'm just not hungry. I think it's exam stress. It'll wear off.'

This is plausible. This is normal. This is nothing for them to worry about.

They don't think that Julia could ever become a girl like me. They're not scared enough. Why aren't they scared? Why aren't they screaming at her, like my mother, *Julia, for the love of God, eat your dinner*?

I know vomitting is only for the weaker girls, but right now, if I had a body, I somehow know I would want to be sick.

Chapter Seventy-Eight

Poor exam-stressed Julia survives the rest of the time away with her family by engaging in Annabel-sanctioned tricks, handed to her – I realise – not just by me, but by Imogen. When she does eat a full meal, it's fingers down the throat.

I wonder if Imogen does this too. I want to see her so badly. Except I know. I *know*, okay, fuck right off. I can't communicate with her, with any of them, until I've completed my mission. Saved Julia.

I could ask the Boss for help, except I can't. She's one of them. She is like Dr Fields. Dr Fields with her *I'm here to help*, except she wasn't, not at all. If she'd really helped then – then I wouldn't be dead, would I?

Except. Except I didn't want her help, but I didn't need her help, but I – I had it under control and if I'd been allowed to keep up my plan instead of sugar water forcing its way into my veins then my body wouldn't have been under so much pressure that it – that it –

Julia. Focus. I need to focus.

The first day back at school she gets the schedule for Careers Day. She is on the list to chair a panel of recently graduated

Richmond students talking about their college courses, and also to interview one of their guest speakers. Guess who.

She shakes for a bit. Then gathers herself. She is Julia Jacobs. She is strong. She just needs to know how to be stronger. Needs something more. Needs to take this to the next level.

Hey, Imogen. Remember that girl you met at the funeral who was in hospital with Annabel? Do you have her name or contact details or anything? Jx

Chapter Seventy-Nine

'Thanks for meeting me,' Julia says, all professional. Another cafe, one of a chain of coffee shops, and one I'm allowed to see inside this time.

Helen is in a grey jumper and jeans. She looks younger than Julia, but she's not. A few months older, actually. She looks at Julia and doesn't assess her the way we always used to: there is no criticism, no satisfaction at being thinner. Instead she says, 'It's okay. I'm glad you're doing the piece about Annabel.'

This is the story Julia's handed her: she's writing a belated obituary for the school paper. And a whole thing about eating disorders. Julia nods. 'I think it's an important topic,' she says. 'Can I get you a coffee or something?'

'I'll get it.'

'No, no, seriously.'

'Okay. Hot chocolate, please,' Helen says, deferring to the girl with her grown-up aura of footing the bill. A Dermot trick, I guess. And what on earth is Helen doing drinking hot chocolate?

And then the panic comes when Julia sets it down in front of her. This is the Helen I know: fearful of the sugar and all the other crap in that mug.

She forces herself to take a sip. And she is proud of herself for doing it.

'So,' Julia begins, 'you were in hospital with Annabel? That's what Imogen told me, anyway.'

Helen nods. 'Yeah. We were –' She doesn't quite know the word.

'Friends,' Julia prompts.

Helen laughs suddenly. A sharp, awful laugh. 'I don't know. I don't think that's the right word for it. We were too fucked up to be real friends.'

Like a stab. Then I realise what she must mean. She was jealous. That must be what she means, right?

'What do you mean?' Julia's intrigued now, her journalistic nose hungry for details. For secrets.

Helen looks at her like she's an idiot. 'Well, gosh, let's see. When you're trying to recover from an eating disorder, the last thing you need is someone reassuring you you're not actually sick.'

The word *sick* jars with Julia. With me, too.

'But maybe she didn't feel like she was sick,' Julia says tentatively.

'Which is kind of part of the actual illness,' Helen snaps. Pauses. 'Sorry. I shouldn't have come. I don't want to talk about her.' She sets down her hot chocolate. Opens her handbag. Flings two notebooks on the table, with bits of paper spilling out of them. 'I kept those. From hospital. Take them. Write your piece about Annabel. Just don't mention me.'

'Helen!' Julia calls after her, but not overly enthusiastically. She has what she came for.

283

Julia. Go after her. For fuck's sake. Make sure she's okay.

The truth is I don't know if I would have chased after Helen either, when I was alive. But now I do. Now I follow her running down the road, looking frantically for somewhere she can hide – maybe, I think, to throw up the gulps of that hot chocolate she swallowed. There's a fast food restaurant up ahead and she ducks in, keeps her cool until she locks herself in a bathroom stall upstairs.

And then she folds into herself, and the noise that comes out of her is beyond human. It's a howl.

Despite the betrayal, I wish for my arms. To tighten them around her. *I love you. I've got you. You're safe.*

APRIL

Chapter Eighty

'Okay, Annabel. How's it going?'

Silence.

'Do you want to talk about Julia?'

Silence.

'Is there anything else going on you'd like to discuss?'

I don't want to be at this meeting. She must know that. 'No.'

'Are you sure?'

'You know.' I almost growl the words. That's why she's pushing. She knows about Julia meeting Helen. She knows about Helen . . .

'What do I know?'

The sound-thought that comes out of me is like Helen's howl.

'You seem angry.'

'No shit.'

'What are you angry about?'

Silence again.

'Annabel.'

In therapy when you refuse to talk they can remove some of your privileges, if you're in hospital, or they can refer you

287

to someone else. I'm not sure what the Boss can do here. But I do know the great technique they all rely on: waiting.

It's easier to wait out a fifty-minute session than eternity.

'Helen said I was sick,' I finally burst out. 'And Julia –'

'Do you think Julia's sick?'

Yes.

Maybe.

I don't know.

'She's doing what she needs to feel strong,' I say finally.

'Right.'

'But . . .'

'Is it working? Is it healthy?'

I know the answer she wants me to give. I know. But I can't.

'Maybe not, but it's not like she's *sick*. It's just . . .' Normal. What we do. What I did.

'Just what, Annabel?'

'I can't do this,' I snap. I hate this. I hate her. I hate Dr Fields, I hate my parents, I hate Dermot, I hate Imogen, I hate Julia, I hate Helen, I hate . . .

'Who are you really angry at?' the Boss asks.

But I'm already moving away.

Chapter Eighty-One

Julia thinks about backing out of the Careers Day thing, even with those notebooks filled with calories and food and thoughts and chants. Motivation. Inspiration. She even says to one of the student council types, 'I'm not sure I'm the best person for this . . .' and is buttered up properly, with talk of how good Julia is in front of an audience and how of course she's exactly the right person to interview Dermot Keenan about careers in journalism.

Networking opportunities, she thinks, his voice in her head.

Careers Day is a Wednesday, and it's for all the senior students: the fourth years go because that year is a chance to *find yourself* or whatever; the fifth and sixth years go because they're the Leaving Cert students preparing themselves for the exam that'll determine their college choices. (The Richmond School is not a place one attends if one is not planning to go to university.)

The morning is about college: first up, their guidance counsellor provides a seminar about Managing Your Time at College. Julia catches Gavin's eye at one point and they exchange just the tiniest of smiles before looking away awkwardly. He is still a little embarrassed about the drunk message he sent, and more embarrassed about her not replying to it.

Julia slips backstage a few minutes before that session ends to make sure all the Richmond past pupils are there – they've already run through the questions via email. She introduces everyone, with the year they graduated the school and what they're doing or did in college: there are five of them, all aged between twenty and twenty-five. This is an attempt to make Careers Day relevant and exciting. Or something.

Gavin's filming it all, or rather, all the bits that involve actual guests and not just their guidance counsellor rabbiting on. He watches Julia through the camera lens. She's bright and confident, but there's something empty. Something hollow.

He wants to pull her aside at break time, tell her she did a great job, ask her if she's all right, but he can't find her. She's in the girls' bathroom, shaking.

After the break the roster of speakers from now until the end of the day goes up on a PowerPoint presentation. A representative from Richmond's student council opens the proceedings, already mentally updating his CV with his public speaking and organisational skills. Julia eyes up the list. Four men, one woman. For God's sake, she thinks, irritated, and do you know what? It's the first thought she's had all day that's about the world and society and not about food or her body or Dermot Keenan.

It's like how she was before – before me.

Except she wasn't okay then either.

I don't know what to think. I want to help her. I just want – I want to scream. I want to punch. I want to tear things to the ground.

Julia's stomach growls, demands to be fed. Real, genuine body hunger. Julia and food. Food and Julia. It was a tangled mess before I got here. But.

I want to slap her.

She stares blankly at the first speaker, who Will's interviewing, explaining what the day-to-day life of a solicitor is like. Gavin, witnessing it all through the camera, thinks about how unhappy this guy sounds.

A tug on her sleeve. 'Julia. You and Mr Keenan are up second, come on backstage.'

He smiles when he sees her, and she hates herself for thinking it might be genuine.

Oh, Julia. And the urge to slap fades. If only I could be there in person to tell her she can do this. She can get through this. *Screw him, Julia. Screw him over.*

'So,' she says brightly, addressing a spot on the wall behind him, 'I'll ask you all the obvious questions: how you got started, what makes a good feature . . .'

'That sounds perfect,' he says. The smile is still there. Warm. Real.

Fuck him, Julia. Fuck him. And something flows through her and she looks directly at him. 'How's Sylvia?' she asks.

Her voice sounds sweet. Her eyes are fire.

Chapter Eighty-Two

All Gavin can think is how the solicitor guy on stage is going bald and still sounds like he's waiting for his life to properly kick off, like the time in the future when everything settles into place is still ahead of him. He seems like someone with regrets.

Gavin's sensible, parent-approved first choice of Business and Law in college starts to feel like a tie where the knot's just that little bit too far up, pressing against his windpipe.

'Thanks so much for that, Mr McCarthy,' Jenny from the student council says. (Gavin tried to kiss her last week at a party and then chickened out and sat on the stairs, telling himself to stop obsessing over Julia.) 'And thanks, Will, for such great questions. Next up we have a name that I'm sure is familiar to many of you from the morning papers. Dermot Keenan is a journalist whose work has appeared in *The Irish Times*, the *Independent*, the *Examiner* and the *Guardian*, along with numerous magazines. He was a regular columnist for the *Irish News* for several years, and has also . . .'

A bell's going off in Gavin's head now, and he's not paying attention to Jenny listing off the radio and TV work.

The *Irish News*. That column. Restaurant reviews. He remembers because Deb always knew where the best new places to eat were, not that it made any difference to them at fifteen, sixteen. Gavin's never seen the point of food writing anyway. Waste of column inches, especially the lavish way people describe things like pastas or oysters or desserts.

Dermot Keenan was very good with desserts. Mousses and pavlova and . . . sorbets.

It occurs to Gavin that there are a whole range of ways to think about rebound relationships, pulled from books and pop culture, but Julia thinks in terms of food.

Sorbet.

They appear on the stage together, from the right-hand side, Julia and Dermot, and he does the tiniest little touch at the small of her back to direct her into her seat and she flinches.

It's the tiniest of things. Microscopic. There are teachers sitting in the front row, supervising, and two more leaning against the back wall, all trained to spot impropriety, and no alarm bells go off. You wouldn't notice, unless you knew Julia. Unless you really knew her. There's a flicker of fear until she puts on her brave face.

Gavin sees it. He's thinking about Julia's brave face, and how he doesn't believe it because this is a girl who stays up all night working on the newspaper and who runs away from him when she's upset and who kept insisting they had a palate-cleanser relationship even when he was kissing her like there was no one else in the world.

There's something here. He doesn't know quite what, but it feels tangled into this whole mess, and he wants to be up there with her, holding her hand or maybe just sitting next to her.

'Mr Keenan,' Julia begins, and I can tell, and I bet Gavin can, too, that the formality briefly unnerves her. Call-me-Dermot looks surprised, too. Only for a second. They are both good at public faces, if you don't know what to look out for. 'The face of journalism has changed dramatically since you were starting out – we've the internet, social media, blogging, a decline in print media, just to name a few. What do you see as the biggest challenge facing aspiring journalists these days?'

Dermot blinks. Thought he might get a 'tell us a bit about yourself' to kick off. Then he chuckles. 'Starting off with an easy one, then!'

Julia smiles. Her face feels frozen. And then. She doesn't let him off the hook. She waits, therapist-style, for him to speak. *Good girl. You can do this.*

'I suppose there are a lot of challenges these days, Julia, it's very true,' Dermot says.

He dislikes this topic, because it reminds him of the challenges facing him. It used to be easier, this job. Not easy, but easier. He misses the stability of having columns, rather than pitching and hoping for the best. Today is supposed to be an ego-boost, about presenting him as a success.

Gavin watches Julia as Dermot talks. She looks haunted, he realises (oh, Gavin, if only you knew). It does something to him.

I push. I push and I push at her. I am Annabel McCormack and maybe a bad influence, but I am angry and fierce and she needs me right now.

294

'There's an expectation now, for people starting off,' Dermot says, 'that they'll do a lot of work for free. Which is disgraceful.'

'People need to be paid for their work,' Julia says, nodding along. 'And yet, with this expectation in place, is it the case that if you're insisting on being paid, you won't get your foot in the door somewhere? What advice would you give to anyone sitting here today who might want to go into journalism?'

A flicker inside her: she knows what he's going to say to this. She's heard all the advice before, delivered confidently to an audience of one. She's soaked it all up with big eyes and been impressed. She's gone to bed with him.

'Well, you need to get paid,' Dermot says. 'You need to put a value on your work.'

'But if the current norm is to work for free when you're starting off,' Julia reminds him, 'is there not a sense that you might be shooting yourself in the foot?'

Yes, thinks Dermot but doesn't say it. 'Well, the current norm needs to change. That's a given.'

'So how can we do that, here?' Julia lifts a hand, indicates the audience. 'How can all of us, here, help to change that?'

The teachers perk up, waiting for something inspirational. This must be planned, they think. This will lead to something marvellous.

Dermot opens and closes his mouth. It is clear for a moment – only a moment – that he is stumped, and pissed off about it, and then he begins to speak. 'I think everyone here needs to value their own work,' he says. 'Regardless of whatever profession they're working in. And to value the work of others. That's how we change things.'

Someone at the back starts clapping, but then stops when it doesn't turn into a big clap from all the audience, and there's laughter. It isn't mean – it's just recognition of one of those things, one of those awkward moments.

Dermot is even managing to keep a smile on his face.

'Obviously that's not terribly helpful,' Julia continues, raising an eyebrow. 'Do you think that your generation had it easier?'

'I wouldn't say that –' he begins.

She looks pointedly at his greying temples. And that's the moment. That is the moment when she realises, really realises, that Dermot Keenan is old enough to have known better. 'But, come on,' she says. 'Obviously you're in a different situation to everyone starting out now. Do you think it's even possible for your generation to offer up helpful advice to the young people of today?'

When she says 'your generation', it's like flicking paper pellets: not the worst injury in the world but definitely leaving a bit of a sting.

'Julia,' he says, with a little laugh – this is how he's going to play it now, I realise, and try to impart that knowledge to her. 'You're making me sound ancient.'

'Oh, Dermot,' she says, with a little laugh of her own. 'You're not exactly as young as you once were, let's be real here!' She is charm. She is poise. It sounds so innocent that even Mr Briscoe, watching from the front row, doesn't think to read too much into it – although Mrs Kearney is grinding her teeth and preparing a lecture for Julia on how to treat guests to the school in a respectful manner.

Dermot forces a smile. 'I suppose that's true. But I've years of expertise behind me . . .'

'Of course!' Julia says brightly. 'That's why you're here. And you've a history of mentoring young journalists, isn't that right?'

He looks as though he doesn't quite understand the question, but recovers. 'Well, when I was working for the *Irish News*, I always took an interest in the work experience programme,' he begins.

'I remember,' Julia says. Her tone shifts. Darkens. 'Tell us more about that.'

His eyes meet hers. Jesus Christ, he thinks.

'Do you think, for example, programmes like that lend themselves open to abuse?'

A gasp from someone, followed by a giggle. In the front row, Mrs Kearney is beginning to get worried. This is definitely not appropriate, she thinks.

'I don't quite follow you,' Dermot says, trying to remain calm.

'Putting undue pressure on unpaid workers, I mean,' Julia says smoothly.

'Oh, I see. Well, as I was saying earlier, we need to ensure that, eh, that people don't find themselves under pressure to work for free . . . I wouldn't quite count work experience in that same category, mind you.'

'So the work experience programme would be for – people who are still in school?'

He nods.

'People who are probably more vulnerable, in many respects. Do you think they might feel under pressure to do anything inappropriate? Especially young women, if they're faced with –'

A red-faced Mrs Kearney leaps to her feet. 'Julia! My office. Now.'

Julia's face is pure innocence. 'I'm sorry, Dermot,' she says unapologetically. 'Censorship and schools. You know how it goes.'

Dermot watches her leave the stage, unsure of what to do. Someone starts clapping. Jenny from the student council comes out and says, 'Thank you for your time, Mr Keenan. Next up we have . . .'

Chapter Eighty-Three

'What the fuck was that?' Deb demands.

Julia turns around, en route to Mrs Kearney's office. And her face is like nothing Deb has ever seen before. Not on Julia. She thinks of a lab experiment they had to do in science a few years ago, where they learned the hottest kind of flame wasn't the orange you see in fireplaces. It's white. That's Julia's face.

'Necessary,' Julia hisses, and marches on.

She doesn't even make it to the office. Mrs Kearney grabs her by the arm and says, 'Right. Whatever this is about, you need to apologise to Mr Keenan. That's no way to speak to a guest at this school. Then we'll talk.'

Julia is escorted to the staff room, where Dermot has been handed a cup of coffee and a biscuit. He looks up, alarmed, to see her.

'Miss Jacobs has something to say to you,' Mrs Kearney prompts.

Julia looks at her. Fearless. Fearless because I am there with her, cheering her on. 'Give us a moment, please.'

'Julia, I don't think that's appropriate.'

Julia shrugs, crosses her arms, waits.

Mrs Kearney falters. She's like the rest of them: going through the guidelines for this sort of thing in her head. She doesn't really believe Dermot Keenan would ever do anything to Julia – his daughter's best friend, for God's sake! – but she's spoken to him at parent-teacher meetings, and wouldn't be surprised if he's guilty of a few overly flirtatious comments.

'I'll be just outside,' she finally says. There's no one else around; everyone else is teaching or supervising Careers Day. She taps her foot, not quite believing she's been banished from her own staff room by Julia Jacobs.

Inside, Dermot stands up. 'That was a bit much,' he says. There is still a bit of a smile there. It is easier to charm women than to chastise them, to get them back on side.

Julia, you can do this.

She looks at him. She looks at him. Stares right at him. 'I'm sorry you feel that way.'

He blinks, and it's not so much that he remembers his own line thrown back at him as he deduces what's going on. 'Julia,' he says gently, and I realise there is a fondness for her beneath all the wrongness, 'I hope you're not still upset about . . .'

He trails off in the hope that he doesn't have to actually put words on it. Some journalist. She's good, though. She waits. 'About . . .' she prompts, after a silence.

Good. You've got this.

'Come on, Julia, you know what I mean.'

'Do I?' Giving him nothing. I'm so proud right now I can almost taste it and it's delicious. This is what she needs to do. Not this crazed eating/starving/exercising/panicking cycle, I finally, finally realise. In this moment, she is glorious.

'Julia.'

'Dermot.' There is something sing-song about her voice. Something mocking. 'Tell me you're not going after Lorraine these days.'

That's like a slap. Makes him feel ugly. He's not, actually. 'She's practically a kid, Julia, Jesus.'

Julia puts her hands on her waist. Her school-uniformed waist. 'Really,' she says.

'You weren't – you weren't a kid.' It's part praise – *you're not like the others* – and part a terrified question.

'I wasn't,' she agrees. Almost cheerfully. 'But I bet you haven't mentioned me to Sylvia, have you?'

Now the fear. He remembers it well – always there at the back of his mind, that she'd tell Tracy. And now there's someone else she can tell. He looks at her, his eyes big and frightened, and suddenly she wants to laugh. She holds it back.

'What do you want from me?' There's not much he can offer. Connections, maybe. That's it, he realises; she wants him to put in a good word for her at one of the papers, even though there's not much going for anyone there these days . . .

And then she can't help it. The laughter explodes from her. 'Nothing,' she says, through gasps. Nothing. Nothing. There is nothing he can offer her that will undo any of this, but that look of fear – it's all she needs. That power.

The man who broke her is standing in front of her and instead of cowering or hurting, she's laughing at him.

He attempts a smile, attempts a fix, but he's angry now. He feels small. Stupid. She's making a fool of him.

Mrs Kearney raps once on the door. 'Is everything all right?'

301

Professional face. Dermot nods and says, 'Thanks for the coffee, Linda.'

'Oh – you're very welcome.'

'I'm sorry we had to cut your interview short.' Mrs Kearney makes dagger-eyes at Julia. 'We really appreciate you coming in.'

'Don't worry about it,' he says, forcing himself to chuckle. 'My pleasure.'

'I'll walk you out,' Mrs Kearney says. 'Julia, I'll see you in my office in five minutes.'

When Mrs Kearney returns from handshakes and smiles with Dermot, who they both know very well will be never coming in again to do anything for the school, she takes a deep breath before entering her office, thinking she'll need a very large glass of wine this evening.

Julia sits calmly, legs crossed. There is something about her that makes her look older, wiser, despite the schoolgirl uniform.

'That was – hugely inappropriate,' Mrs Kearney begins. 'Careers Day is not the time or the place to ask a guest at our school about – about –' She doesn't want to finish the sentence. She shakes her head. 'Do you understand that?'

Julia has a response all planned, but as it turns out she doesn't need to use it.

'I *know* you understand that, Julia, you're a smart girl. So.' She doesn't want to ask the question. She knows she has to. 'Is there anything you need to tell me?'

Julia looks at her, startled.

And Julia is breaking my stupid, worthless heart by being surprised at this. That someone has noticed. That someone knows she's not okay.

'No,' she says finally.

And the voice, softer than she's ever heard it, goes, 'Are you sure? You can tell me, or you can tell one of your other teachers . . .'

Julia almost laughs at the idea. I was stupid, she thinks, but not a child. Not a child. 'This isn't anything you need to report,' she says, and in that moment Mrs Kearney doesn't quite understand but guesses it's her initial suspicion – a bit of flirtation that made the girl uncomfortable when she was off doing her work experience. Doesn't it happen everywhere? She feels united with Julia in a kind of world-weariness.

And yet, and yet. 'I might suggest to your parents that it'd be a good idea for you to talk to someone,' she says. Then, carefully, 'Sixth year's very stressful, and you've a lot on your plate. Is that all right?'

She means a shrink, of course – they always do – but Julia nods and thinks about her own someones to talk to. She has nothing to tell Mrs Kearney. But she has something to tell *them*.

Chapter Eighty-Four

It's only on her way back to the assembly hall that she starts shaking. She's barely aware of passing by students in the corridors, or of Lorraine tutting at her as she goes by – it's not about her, or Deb, or anyone. Not any more.

It's a little like she's floating far above all of this. There are people looking at her like she has two heads, and then she's brought back to earth by Maria squeezing her hand. 'Julia. Hey.'

'Hey,' Julia whispers, conscious that there's still a speaker on stage – Carolyn's interviewing a doctor. And suddenly she wants to cry.

Maria looks right into her eyes. 'Do you want to talk about it?'

Julia nods. Her throat is too tight to say anything.

'Will we go to the newspaper office?'

Again, a nod. Then, 'Give me a couple of minutes. I want to ask . . .' Julia indicates the boy with the too-neat hair behind the camera. 'It's nearly lunch, he'll be finished.'

Maria thinks, he'd drop the camera even if he wasn't, if Julia asked, but she nods anyway.

Gavin's aware of her before she approaches. His free hand – the one not holding the camera – slips into hers like it's the only possible place for it to be.

Do not shake him off, Julia. Julia! Do you hear me?

She looks at his hand, and hers, and she stays there, standing next to him, as their fingers clasp together. And even though I know how much it aches to not have that capacity for physical contact, the comfort of human touch, it's still sort of sickening, actually.

Chapter Eighty-Five

Some things about lunchtime in the newspaper office, the door locked from the inside to prevent anyone else from entering:

1. Julia sits between them, perched on the desk, bolstered by two people who don't quite know what's going on but are worried about her. She starts with the one day she was over at Deb's house, at the start of fifth year, talking to Dermot about journalism. About being super-impressed and delighted at being taken seriously. The thrill of being asked if she had that year's work experience sorted out and if she wanted to come into the paper with him. She keeps her eyes fixed on the opposite wall.

2. She thinks about the shredded red dress. She thinks it might be time to throw it away.

3. When she says, 'It was the first time I was ever – that I ever did that with anyone,' her voice isn't shaking,

but Gavin is, and he stretches his hand out to hers again and holds on.

4. She manages not to cry, even as she tells them about I'm-sorry-you-feel-that-way, about hearing from Deb about what had happened with Sylvia. She manages not to cry until she's finished with her story and Gavin says, 'What a dick.' Then she nods a little, and half laughs, and then suddenly there are tears.

5. Gavin's immediate instinct is: how do I make the crying stop? all panicky, and Maria pulls Julia into a tight hug and eye-signals Gavin to join in, until they have her surrounded. Maria's on the verge of tears herself.

6. Gavin's next thought is: she's not running away. And alongside everything else – the way he wants to go punch something, the way he wishes his hand moving over her shoulder blades could magically fix everything – he's grateful for that.

7. 'We need to report him,' Gavin says, once the tears stop. Julia shakes her head. 'Julia, come on. You need to –'

8. Maria interrupts him. 'Gav. Stop it. She was legal. And it was after she'd finished work experience; he wasn't her boss, he didn't have any duty of care

307

towards her, it's not – it's fucking *gross*, but it's not a crime.'

9. Julia steps in then. 'It wasn't gross.' But even as she says it, the memory of avoiding that hotel receptionist flits through her brain. 'I wanted it. Everything that happened, I wanted it, at the time. Except getting my heart smashed.' She spits out the last sentence.

10. 'I still think you should –' Gavin begins, but Maria glares at him and he drops it. Julia wonders if he's disappointed in her or something. But she doesn't want to report it, and even if she did – there's no law about ensuring that you don't use people as sorbet girls.

11. They sit in silence for a while, all three of them, and then Julia feels it, settling over her like a gorgeous mist. Because telling them, as it turns out, is what's made her feel the lightest she's ever felt.

Chapter Eighty-Six

The video doesn't quite go viral. Dermot is not important enough for anything starring him to go viral. But it gets watched. The girl in the school uniform asking the older man about teenage girls – and then watch how the camera zooms in on his face. The awkwardness. The sound effects, and the soundtrack, of course, help.

A summary of reactions:

1. Julia: messages Gavin immediately. *I can't believe you did that.* Followed up quickly with, *Thank you x*

2. Deb: closes the screen two seconds in. Hates Julia for using her dad to make some kind of mad feminist point, like anything could have ever really happened without her knowing about it. Come *on.*

3. Helen's mother: sees it linked on Facebook, clicks, and doesn't quite get it, and then thinks it's ridiculous. Grown men don't go for teenagers, not that way. It's a stereotype, a dangerous one. They might fantasise,

309

in the same way she thinks about movie stars, but
they'd never – actually – *would they?* She doesn't
realise yet that she's twisting her wedding ring on
her finger as she thinks about this. But she will.

4. Sylvia, after Dermot ranted about it. He doesn't
   want to show it to her, because it's so ridiculous, so
   immature, so naturally she goes looking for it. She
   stares at the screen for a long time.

5. Dermot's solicitor. Advises him to complain to the
   site but cautions against taking it any further. Thinks
   it'll blow over. (And it does. Eventually.) This is
   not a life-ruining thing. Just one of those things life
   throws at you sometimes. Grit your teeth and move
   on. He doesn't ask his client if there's any merit to
   the implications. He says, 'You don't even want to
   go there. That's the last thing you need.'

6. Mrs Kearney: calls Gavin into her office to ask
   if he knows anything about the video, as he was
   filming on the day. Gavin says, 'Not at all.' Notes
   that the username that uploaded the video isn't
   his own – why would he create a new username
   when he already has one? He explains patiently
   that recording apps on phones are so sophisticated
   these days that the quality is really good, and then
   of course you can clear things up when you're
   editing . . . The more technical information he

throws at her, the more confused she gets, until eventually she just sighs and says, 'How's the video for the school website going? Can you leave Mr Keenan's interview out of it, please?'

7. Julia's dad, who has the video shown to him by a colleague, eyes it up. Is it something they need to pursue, he wonders? He sits down with Julia for what is the most awkward conversation of both their lives. She says, 'Look, Dad, he was just kinda flirty. It was gross, you know?' She can't tell them. Won't tell them. Maybe someday, but not today. Her dad, who sees cases of abuse and incest and rape every day, looks closely at his daughter. Maybe if he'd looked at her this way a year ago, things would have been different. But now she stares right back at him, and then laughs a little, and says, 'Oh come on, Dad. I didn't make the video. It makes it look so much worse than it is. I just wanted to make a point, you know.' And when he tells her that it's maybe not the best way to make a point, she reminds him that Mrs Kearney thinks she's probably a bit stressed with upcoming exams and everything else and should be seeing a counsellor. He is relieved. Even so. He tells his wife she should take a look at the video, too. Just in case.

8. Julia's mum: 'I'm going to ring up Dermot Keenan right now and find out exactly what he said to Julia

when she was working with him.' Julia grabs her mobile before she has a chance to dial. Stands tall. 'Mum,' she says firmly, 'it's been sorted. It's over.' She says it several times, until her mother believes her. Until her mother puts her arms tight around her, because she should have known at the time, because her daughter is technically a grown-up but still her little girl just as much as Grace is, and she forgets that sometimes, and she thanks God (they're all at it, it's infuriating) that Julia is okay.

9. Julia, watching it again: she thinks, maybe someday I will tell Mum and Dad. Maybe. But she knows that definitely, definitely, she will tell Grace someday. There are certain things we owe our little sisters.

MAY

Chapter Eighty-Seven

'Julia's talking to one of you lot, you know,' I tell the Boss.

'What, a spirit mentor?' Oh, now she develops a sense of humour.

'A psychologist.' Julia being Julia, she went in the first day with a checklist of all the things she wanted to talk about. Food. Sex. Feelings.

'Do you think that's useful for her?'

If I could shrug . . . 'Maybe. Yeah, okay, probably. She's . . .'

She's doing the waiting game. 'Go on, Annabel. What is it?'

'She's getting better,' I say.

Which means. Which means she was sick.

'I made it worse,' I add.

'Maybe.'

I almost want to laugh. 'Thanks for the reassurance.'

'Maybe you did. I'm not going to lie to you, Annabel. I don't understand entirely how it all works, either. She was troubled before you reached her. She wasn't letting anyone in. And now – she seems happy.'

Happy. It surprises me that she's talking about this, not weight. It shouldn't, at this stage, should it?

'No, Annabel, it really shouldn't,' she says, and I realise my thoughts are pulsing out towards her.

I made her worse. I am trying to undo it, but it's so hard. So hard to say the things that people told me I wouldn't believe.

We are responsible for our own bodies, but sometimes the darkness crawls in and it lies, it lies, it lies.

'She got sick,' I say again.

I want so much to be able to cry right now.

I want my body.

I want my fucking body.

'I hate this,' I say.

'I know.'

'Do you know what I really hate?'

'Tell me.'

'Susan and her poem actually had it right. All the things I could have been. Do you know how galling it is to have such a terrible poem turn out to have such essential life truths in it?'

The Boss laughs, and it makes things just a little bit better.

'I was sick,' I say.

And I didn't ever really think this would happen. I didn't ever really believe them when they tried to scare me. I didn't want to let it sink in: the idea that they might be right. That I might be risking, well, you know. My life.

316

Chapter Eighty-Eight

'This is brilliant,' Gavin says, holding up Julia's latest article. They're back to their Thursday afternoons together, music in the background, chatting away. He knows she's seeing a counsellor. He knows she's got some stuff to deal with. He knows not to be too delighted when her face lights up.

'Seriously,' he adds. It's the first in a series of articles she's doing about girls and competitiveness and how aggression manifests itself, and it's good – smart and provocative, but with actual scientific research in there, too, so that Mrs Kearney won't despair over how Julia clearly has *an agenda*. At this point in the year, Julia doesn't really care – there are only a few weeks of school left, and then exams, and then she never has to see anyone from the Richmond School again if she doesn't want to.

'Thanks, Gav,' she says.

'Did you and Lorraine –' he starts, and then stops.

'Did we what?'

He taps the desk. 'Did you guys feel like you were competing?'

'Over you?' Julia asks.

Gavin reddens. 'No, I mean over the paper.'

'Oh,' she says. And laughs. And she thinks before answering. 'I felt it. Over both.'

'You don't need to,' he says.

'I know.' Then, another laugh. 'About the paper, obviously.'

He looks at her.

She looks at him.

Time stops for a moment.

'Oh for God's sake, Gav,' she says, and leans in to kiss him.

'Get a room, guys,' Maria calls a few minutes later as she passes by, on her way to the library to catch up on homework.

Julia detaches from the kiss just long enough to call back, 'We have one!'

Gavin looks at her. The smile, the joy. He thinks: she's beautiful.

And she is. She really is.

Chapter Eighty-Nine

'You're doing well,' the Boss says.

Her approval is unsettling. I can't quite tell Julia to eat and not worry about it, not just yet. She has a therapist for that. I ask questions, instead. *Julia, how are you feeling? Are you eating because you're really hungry, or are you just trying to deal with something else?*

She writes her articles. She keeps a journal (an actual journal for her thoughts, not just the number of calories consumed). She doesn't write terrible poetry, though. Her therapist suggests it as an option and Julia dismisses it immediately, nudged along by her spirit-helper girl.

Often, when it is late at night and she's finishing off her homework and staring goofily at the latest cute text message from Gavin, she will realise that she's starving, remember that she hasn't eaten anything since dinner. Here we are again tonight, the same old routine.

I shouldn't, she thinks.

Julia, are you really hungry or are you just trying to block out something else?

I don't deserve –

Are you really hungry?

I –

Are you –

Yes. Yes. Yes. She is. Real, true body-hunger.

And I am thinking about the Boss telling me I'm doing well. I am thinking about how much I wish I had arms to hug Julia, and Helen, and Imogen. I am thinking: *then, for fuck's sake, Julia, just eat something, please. It's okay.*

And she does. She does.

There you go. It's okay.

It really is okay.

If I had a body I would be trembling. It takes me a moment to realise I am no longer with her, that the Boss has called me to her.

'It looks like you've reached her,' she says. 'She's on a better path now.'

This sounds airy-fairy. 'What does that even mean?'

'It means you can get your message through,' she says.

Oh. Oh.

I've been waiting for this for so long and suddenly I'm not ready for it. 'Now?'

'Now. Well, soon,' she amends.

'What happens – after?' Do I sleep? Are there fluffy clouds? Where do I go?

'It's up to you. What do you want?'

You know what I want, I think.

'I can't give you back your life. I wish I could, Annabel. Believe me.'

'What can you give me?'

'We've got another soul in need of help,' she says.

'You've got a lot of those lying around, haven't you?' Getting out the words is hard, even though I don't have to really speak them aloud. Can't.

'Tons,' she says, and there is the faintest sense of a smile.

'I don't want to just be some – cautionary tale,' I say, which I suppose is my roundabout way of saying that she might as well count me in.

Chapter Ninety

The final article in Julia's series about young women and the challenges they face today is due to appear in the last issue of *The Richmond Report* to be compiled by this year's staff. It is about food. And it is about body image. And it is about a girl who died.

I found the photo on Facebook, Julia writes. *I'd forgotten she was even in school with us. Annabel McCormack wasn't at the Richmond School for that long, and no one told us what was happening to her. If it was cancer, we'd have known. There would have been a prayer service, or at the very least an announcement of some kind – but we don't talk about the silly things that teenage girls do to themselves. We stay quiet. We hope that it'll go away.*

This went away. Annabel didn't come back to school. She was in hospital – she'd been in and out of hospital for years. No one told us what happened. No one told us when she died, of heart failure, just before her eighteenth birthday. When I asked the school about contact information, I was told it wasn't appropriate – and that was it. A classmate of ours had died and it wasn't appropriate for us to know about it.

Annabel McCormack was anorexic and it killed her. This was a shameful secret, something embarrassing that she should have grown out of, instead of a disorder with the highest mortality rate of any mental illness. This was seen as a diet gone a bit too far, instead of a girl suffering.

I'd love to say that I'm outside this problem. That as a smart and ambitious young woman on her way to college, I don't care about how I look or how much I weigh. That I have never had an unhealthy relationship with food of any kind, never used it as a way of trying to control my life. But that would be a lie.

I am working towards a healthy relationship with food, one that's linked to what I physically need to keep my body working instead of what I think I deserve or what my feelings are demanding. I eat more healthily these days than I have in years. I am lighter, too, but I don't think I'll ever be as skinny as the girls on TV or in magazines. And I don't want to be. The truth is that most of the time I'd rather be someone who spends her energy trying to fix the world instead of obsessing over my thighs or my belly. But there are those moments when, like everyone else, I live in this world that glorifies skinny regardless of the cost, that sees it as the most admirable and worthwhile thing a woman can be . . .

It goes on like this – feminism and body image and blah blah blah. There are some details from the hospital notebooks, the material Helen gave her – Julia emailed my parents to ask if it was okay to use it. She's going to return those notebooks to the family soon. She doesn't need them, doesn't want them any more.

She is sad for Annabel. I can't tell if she'd feel that way even if it wasn't my own feelings creeping in, but I think she would.

She's angry, too. And I'm pretty sure that's mostly my anger. But it gives her strength, and makes her determined to sort out her food issues and everything else, and that's maybe not the worst gift a spirit helper can offer.

The night after the newspaper goes to print, that Thursday evening, that's when it happens. I get to step inside her body just once, just for this. Heavier than mine was but oh how it moves, how it breathes, how it feels. I press my – no, Julia's – hand up to her heart, and stay like that for a while.

Be grateful for this body, Julia, I tell her, and I mean it. Because this is a healthy body that won't get breathless going up a flight of stairs, that won't be always freezing even in the hottest summer, and I want to dance around in it.

My time is limited. I know this. I pull away from that gorgeous beat, that song of blood. I write the letter, and then slide it into one of the notebooks.

After all this time, it's strange to think we're almost finished. I wonder if I can check in on her, after the message goes through. I'd like to know how Julia gets on. What she does with her life.

What an incredible woman she'll become.

Chapter Ninety-One

This is the meeting I am allowed to witness. This is Julia sitting at the table in the same cafe they met in, anxious, clutching a copy of the newspaper in her hands.

In she comes.

My little sister, my beautiful, funny, talented little sister, is tired. She is sad and tired and no longer full of softness. All hard, sharp edges. Her thoughts are about big girls not getting hungry. About all the tricks her big sister used to use.

'Imogen,' Julia calls over to her. She has a hot chocolate waiting for her. I realise this is what Imogen must have ordered the last time. It makes me hope that Imogen meets Helen again someday. Talks to her.

'Hi,' Imogen says quietly. A little sulky.

'I have the paper for you, if you or your parents want a copy,' Julia says, suddenly awkward. Suddenly aware of exactly how screwed-up it feels to be meeting a twelve-year-old kid in a cafe like this.

Imogen accepts it, sits down and goes through it until she finds the piece. Reads in silence. 'It's good,' she finally says. 'It's – sad.'

Julia nods, her throat aching. 'I wish I'd known her better.'

Me too.

Julia opens up her handbag. 'I have these, too.' She hands over the notebooks, and like magic, it falls out. Imogen stares at her own name on the fold of the paper. My handwriting, through Julia's capable hands, is less messy than normal, on account of how not shaking with the cold and hunger does wonders for penmanship.

'This is for me,' she says.

'I didn't know that was in there,' Julia says honestly.

'You didn't read it?'

Julia shakes her head.

Imogen unfolds.

'Do you want me to leave you alone?' Julia half whispers.

Don't leave her alone, I urge, and am grateful when Imogen shakes her head. My baby sister might need a hug. Someone to hold her. And I can't.

Imogen. Hey, baby sis. I love you. I don't tell you that enough, but I do. You're my favouritest person in the whole world and I know you're going to grow up to be an amazing woman.

I'm sorry. I'm so sorry I can't be there to see that happen and to tell you every day how kind and smart and talented you are. I'm sorry I wasn't smart enough to see how sick I am. You were always right. You were right to tell, and you were right to worry, but this is a stupid illness and it makes people think crazy things. It's no way to live. It makes people keep secrets and it stops them from asking for help or even thinking that they need it.

You were nine years old the first time you knew I needed help and I hated you for it. I'm so sorry about that. Because I see now what an incredible gift that was. (I'm an idiot. Have I mentioned that?) Keep being the girl who sees that in people, and make sure to see it in yourself, too. Go tell people you care about them. Go have fun. Go find things that you love and that make you happy. You're amazing, Im. I want you to know that and believe in it.

Love, so much love, so much love I can't even tell you, always always always,

Annabel

Julia reaches out to put a hand on Imogen's shaking shoulder. But through her tears, my little sister's smiling. It lights up her whole face. It's the most beautiful thing I've ever seen.

Acknowledgements

Some quick thank-yous, because no woman is an island.

The first draft of this book was written mostly in the Tyrone Guthrie centre in Annaghmakerrig, and I am grateful for their hospitality and gorgeous food (Annabel would not approve). Thank you to Pete Galey, Di Howley (née Black) and Stefan Baguette for their notes on that initial draft.

Huge thanks to Deirdre Sullivan for her insights and cheering this book on right from the start, to Laura Cassidy for her thoughts and her determination that a tiny snippet of flash fiction was indeed a book idea, and to Eimear Ryan for her always-brilliant notes.

Thanks to the SCBWI Ireland Scribblers critique group 2013–14 and the TCD Creative Writing MPhil 2014 crowd for their notes on the opening chapters.

Many thanks to Sallyanne Sweeney for her insights and comments and getting this book into the right hands. Thank you to Naomi Colthurst for being those brilliant hands. Thanks to Georgia Murray, Jenny Jacoby, Rosi Crawley and the rest of the immensely shiny Hot Key team.

For general cheering-on and writerly/bookish wisdom, my

thanks to Regina de Burca, Declan Hughes, the TCD/Duke regulars, Nicole Rourke and everyone at Big Smoke, and the magnificent humans of the YA Bookclub. For 'helping' me write this acknowledgements page, along with endless procrastination and joy, thank you to the Twitterverse. A big thank-you to my family for putting up with A Writer – you poor creatures, you.

And finally: thank you, lovely reader, for picking up this book. You are clearly a delightful human altogether.

Claire Hennessy

Claire Hennessy is a writer, editor and creative writing teacher based in Dublin, Ireland. Born in 1986, she has written several books for teenagers and regularly does author visits and writing workshops for schools, libraries and festivals.

Claire is also a co-director and co-founder of the Big Smoke Writing Factory creative writing school in Dublin, teaches regularly for CTYI, and is the Puffin Ireland editor at Penguin. She is also the co-editor and co-founder of the literary journal Banshee. Follow Claire at www.clairehennessy.com or on Twitter: @clairehennessy

Thank you for choosing a Hot Key book.

If you want to know more about our authors and what we publish, you can find us online.

You can start at our website

www.hotkeybooks.com

And you can also find us on:

We hope to see you soon!